CW00548064

Mick Cummins was born in Tasmania, where he wrote his first full-length play, *Window Without a View*. It was elected for a reading at the Australian National Playwrights Conference and produced at Hobart's Theatre Royal Backspace.

In 1994 he moved to Melbourne with his partner and two children, where his second play, *Perfect Madness*, was developed with the Melbourne Writers' Theatre and produced at the Carlton Courthouse. In 2001 he won the NSW Premier's History Award for the documentary *Thomson of Arnhem Land* before co-writing the ABC docu-dramas *Monash: The Forgotten Anzac* and *Menzies and Churchill at War*. He wrote and directed the ABC documentaries *The Woodcutter's Son* and *Portrait of a Distant Land* and has written two unproduced feature-film scripts developed with Screen Tasmania, Film Victoria and Screen Australia. His latest screenplay, *The Hut*, is in pre-production.

So Close to Home is his first novel.

SO CLOSE TO HOME

MICK CUMMINS

affirm press

affirm
press

First published by Affirm Press in 2023
Boon Wurrung Country
28 Thistlethwaite Street
South Melbourne VIC 3205
affirmpress.com.au

10 9 8 7 6 5 4 3 2 1

Text copyright © Miok Cummins, 2023
All rights reserved. No part of this publication may be reproduced without
prior written permission from the publisher.

A catalogue record for this
book is available from the
National Library of Australia

ISBN: 9781922992239 (paperback)

Cover design by Luke Causby/Blue Cork © Affirm Press
Front-cover image courtesy of Dimi Katsavaris via Unsplash
Back-cover image courtesy of Iliya Jokic via Unsplash
Page 272 lyrics from 'Head Back' by Dick Diver printed courtesy of the artists
Typeset in Garamond Premier Pro 12.5/20 pt by J&M Typesetting
Proudly printed and bound in Australia by McPherson's Printing Group

MIX
Paper from
responsible sources
FSC® C001695
FSC
www.fsc.org

Content note:

This book explores themes of drug addiction, homelessness, suicide and trauma. It includes depictions of drug use, sexual abuse and violence.

For Mum

PROLOGUE

'Can we go in?' Aaron asks softly as he looks out at the house with his hand poised to open the car door.

'Of course. You have a nice warm shower to freshen up while I heat up our dinner. Sausages and chips. How does that sound?'

Play the game, Aaron. Just play the game and get it over with.

'Sounds good.'

He hears the click of the central door lock and then he is standing on the gravel driveway with the smell of blood and bone rising from the flowerbed under the bay window.

1

The waiting room is full and warm, with the soothing voice of the television cooking show host lulling Aaron toward sleep. Only the astringent smell of urine wafting across him is keeping him awake. He lifts his heavy eyelids and looks directly at a bearded middle-aged man chuckling to himself nearby, his legs shaking constantly in pants stiff with grime. Aaron scans the parts of the room further from the odour. He sees a spare seat at the reading table, but the familiar body language and furtive conversation between the men who occupy the other three chairs make it very clear that this is their private space.

On the black vinyl couch opposite Aaron, a young couple are completely entwined and fast asleep. Lucky them, Aaron thinks.

They must be in love, or stoned, or both. Next to them, on one of the two black vinyl armchairs, sits a man in his fifties; in the other is a weathered older man in a stained brown business suit clutching a leather satchel tightly at his chest. Aaron follows their blank stares to the excited cooking show host carving through the crisp, golden pastry of a beef Wellington to reveal the just-pink meat it encases. The cook's upbeat demeanour annoys Aaron intensely. It is a robust reminder of his own deteriorating mood. He turns away from the screen, back to the source of the urine smell and the woman directly opposite wearing a hijab. She smiles back spontaneously, and he receives it as her understanding of his predicament. He smiles back at her in an exchange that unexpectedly soothes him.

As the clock ticks on, Aaron feels his anxiety rising sharply. It has been five hours now, although he doesn't need the clock to tell him what his cramping stomach and legs are already saying. He stares at the automatic glass doors and the possibilities on the streets outside. He could steal something and score then find relief in a laneway or a park. But then what? He can't return to the gardener's shed in the grounds of St Peter and Paul's Church. Father Brian had let him stay there after his mother kicked him out, until some nosy parishioners had lodged a complaint with the Archbishop. The priest had no choice but to ask Aaron to leave. 'Do what your mother asked you to do in the first place,' Father Brian said. 'Go to one of the housing organisations. That's what they're there for.'

He wipes the sweat from his face and looks impatiently for any sign of movement from the two workers at the reception desk. One lifts her eyes to meet his briefly before returning quickly back to her screen. It's as if someone has pushed the pause button on the room. He reaches down to drag his large plastic storage bag of possessions closer to his feet, just to give himself something to do. Short-lived. He glances again at the hijab-wearing woman, hoping for another smile. But she is completely occupied with the five children gathering around her, speaking an unfamiliar language, obviously bored and impatient to go. He wonders about them. Where are they from? Africa, he thinks. But then he doesn't really know. Do they have Muslims in Africa? Are they homeless too? Surely not. How hard would that be? He forces himself to stay with these thoughts until they are broken by a voice calling his name.

'Aaron ... Aaron Peters?'

A young woman leans over the reception desk scanning the waiting room for a response. He stands to look back at her.

'Room 2,' she says pointing to the door closest to her.

He crosses the waiting room carrying his bag of possessions without a sideways glance at the envious eyes fixed on him. Opening the numbered door, he enters the sterile interview room in unison with the same young woman appearing through the door opposite. A desk spanning the width of the room creates a physical barrier between them.

'Hi Aaron,' she says, 'I'm Kate. Take a seat.'

He puts the bag on the floor and sits down to watch her click the mouse and scan the computer screen in front of her.

'Bear with me for a moment,' she says.

As she types, he fidgets with a biro attached to a long chain anchored to the desk. Who would want to steal a plastic biro? he ponders. You'd have to be desperate. He peers through the venetian blinds of the small window providing a shuttered view to the reception area where the two workers are now answering constantly ringing telephones while dealing with another needy person appearing from the street before them. He turns back to Kate, who is still focusing on her screen intently, occasionally twisting her mouth with uncertainty. He wonders how old she is. No more than twenty-five. He likes her orange cardigan and her matching lipstick. The ring in her right nostril intrigues him. He touches his nose. Perhaps he could get one too. Finally, she turns back to him.

'Okay,' she says, 'sorry about that but I've only just started here and there's all sorts of software and passwords and instructions. It's complicated. Anyway, you don't need to know all that. Let's try and get you sorted, eh?'

She tells him that she needs to complete an assessment so that they can get a clear idea of his circumstances. 'Is that okay?'

He nods.

She smiles and returns to the computer screen.

'Okay. Let's start with your date of birth.'

'April fifth, nineteen ninety-four.'

'So you've just turned eighteen?' she says, looking across at him.

'Yep.'

'Did you get a chance to celebrate?'

He shakes his head.

'That's a shame.'

A loud and agitated voice is heard from the adjoining reception area, and Kate and Aaron simultaneously peer through the slots in the venetian blinds. A thickset and angry middle-aged man is waving his arms and making demands in a thick European accent. He wants to see his caseworker; he knows the caseworker is here and he wants to see him now! Not tomorrow! Now! The softer, calming voice of the older of the two workers on reception patiently persists against the man's tirade. Kate turns back to Aaron. She shakes her head and smiles.

'I'm glad it's not me out there. That man scares me.'

'He's all mouth,' says Aaron confidently.

'I think you're right. But it's not very nice.'

This sharing of her feelings with him makes him smile inside. She must trust me or even like me to do that, he thinks. His anxiety melts further as he watches her return to her screen and the assessment.

'Phone number?'

He shakes his head while trying to think of a good story. 'I fell asleep on the tram and when I woke up my phone was gone.'

'It certainly helps to have one, doesn't it? I don't think I could live without mine.'

'I know. But I don't have the money to buy another one.'

For a brief moment he allows himself to think that she will offer him one of her old models, one that has been put away in her desk drawer and forgotten. But it doesn't happen.

'How long have you been homeless?' she continues.

'A couple of weeks.'

'Where were you living?'

'With Mum.'

'Why did you leave?'

His legs twist together tightly under the chair and the lie rolls out easily. 'I don't get on with her boyfriend.'

She asks why and he answers quickly to get it over with, hoping that it will be enough.

'He doesn't like me and I don't like him.'

'And your mum?'

'We're good, yeah.' Another lie, wanting it to be true.

'Only the boyfriend then?'

'Yeah.'

'What about your father?'

Now his stomach tightens several notches more. This question is leading somewhere else. Even the tone of her voice has changed. He hates this feeling. Perpetually there, lurking.

'I don't see him.'

Kate waits for more, but there is only silence. She looks at the assessment template on her screen and the many blank spaces still to be filled with words. She turns back to Aaron to tell him that she understands how difficult this must be for him but unless she gets more information she can't help.

He says, 'Okay,' without meaning it.

'Is there any chance you can fix things at home with your mum's boyfriend? Because that's going to make life so much easier for you.'

He shakes his head. 'Nah.'

She looks back at him for a moment, giving him the opportunity to change his mind. He gives her nothing. His imagination has already filled with a picture of him living with Kate. Just the two of them. Sharing breakfast together. Everything warm and fun.

'Drugs and alcohol?'

Reality returns like a door slamming in his face. Everything cold and hard again. 'What do you mean?'

'Do you drink alcohol? Take any drugs?'

The truth hovers on his lips for a microsecond only. 'No,' he says.

'Nothing?'

'I've tried a few things. Weed. Ice once or twice. I haven't got the money, even if I wanted it.'

She types into the space below the appropriate heading on the assessment and turns back to him.

'Any mental health issues?'

He looks down at his clenched fists, fighting the desire to stand and leave. She sees him struggling.

'You must feel anxious at times. I know I would in your situation.'

'Sometimes, yeah.'

She keeps digging. 'It must be depressing too?'

He shrugs his shoulders. Please stop. No more questions. Just tell me you've got a spare room at your place and I can stay with you for as long as I like.

'You know that if you are feeling overwhelmed at any time you could see a doctor about it. There are some medications that can help. In the short term, at least.'

'I'm good.'

Obviously unconvinced, she returns to the assessment and more typing. He watches her, wanting to tell her everything, but not here, not now. One day maybe, parked in her comfortable car above a beach, looking out over a vast ocean sparkling with promise, the horizon within touching distance, a warming sun.

'Okay, last one,' she says, looking directly at him. 'Violence?'

Black clouds eclipse the sun. 'What d'you mean?'

'Well, I have a sense you're not a violent person.'

'I'm not.'

'Have you experienced any violence aimed at you?'

'Some threats maybe.'

'From?'

Aaron sighs. This is definitely not where he wants to be. He looks back at her open, enquiring face. She is so pretty. She must know that. If only he could tell her it all, he thinks. But he simply can't go there. Not here, not now.

'You know what it's like out there.'

'I can only imagine, Aaron.'

He shrugs his shoulders and his story continues on the same path. 'It's not that bad. I can ignore it most of the time.'

She nods empathically, glances at her screen then back to him.

'I'll finish that off later. You've been here long enough.'

No, I haven't, he thinks, nowhere near long enough. She sighs as she thinks, tapping her fingers lightly on the edge of the desk.

'I have to be honest with you, Aaron, there are not many options for you.'

He watches as she returns to scan her computer screen, the words he wants to say to her locked tightly away in his brain. What about your place, Kate? I won't cause you any problems, I promise. I could do all the housework while you're at work. When you get home, it'll all be done. Washing up, vacuuming, everything.

'None of the rooming houses have a vacancy. Except for this one.' She looks across the desk at him, almost sheepishly. 'It's in Moe.'

'That's hours away. No. I can't go there.'

He sees the muscles in her jaw tighten, her brain ticking over.

'Actually, I don't blame you.'

She picks up the phone. 'Let me try this before we give up.' She glances back and forth from the accommodation list on the wall to the phone as she dials the number.

Aaron's thoughts are drawn back to the same beach, but this time he is standing on the hard sand under a heavy sky swallowing the horizon. Turning away from the dark ocean, he looks up the steep bank for her parked car. It's gone, replaced by a large black Mercedes-Benz, and his grandfather in the driver's seat with his wavy, silver hair and eager eyes.

'Well, that's better news,' Kate says.

Aaron doesn't register her words, but the sound of her voice brings him back to the room and her faint smile on the other side of the desk.

'Hostel Plus have a vacancy in their eight-bed dorm. It's for tonight only, though. They like to make sure whoever we send them is okay. You are, so there won't be a problem extending it. It just means you'll have to come back here tomorrow so we can book you in until your next payday. When's that again?' She looks at the screen and answers her own question. 'Um ... seven, yes, so you'll have seven days there on us.'

'Will I see you tomorrow?'

'I don't have a shift tomorrow. Even if I did, it could be any one of us that sees you.'

He can't hide his disappointment. She smiles encouragingly.

'Everyone's nice here. More experienced than me, that's for sure.'

She stands. 'I'll get you the cheque for tonight and you can get going.' She opens the door behind her. 'You can wait outside at reception. I won't be long.' She is half out the door before she turns back to him with a big, warm smile. 'We have some large backpacks in the storeroom – would you like one? That plastic bag's not a good look.' Then she's gone.

He stares at the closed door thinking that he couldn't care less how nice the other workers are or if he has a backpack. Instead all he has is an overwhelming desire to be alone with her again in their white-walled room so he can tell her the truth. He stands, picks up his bag and takes two mechanical steps to the door. He hesitates and looks back at the room as if he has left something behind, something of himself. He sees only two empty chairs.

In the waiting room, Kate passes a cheque and a large backpack across the reception desk to him.

'Good luck, Aaron.'

He takes it wanting to return her smile, but the muscles in his mouth and cheeks refuse to respond. He moves away from the desk to the space furthest from the eyes in the waiting room, where he transfers his meagre belongings to the backpack: a pair of jeans, shorts, a couple of T-shirts – all crumpled and soiled – some socks and jocks, a school pencil case and a blanket wrapped tightly in a thin, blue tarpaulin. He stuffs the plastic bag into the nearby bin and goes down the steps. The automatic glass doors slide open to the footpath and the chase.

2

Outside on the busy inner-city footpath, Aaron settles the backpack onto his shoulders and sees the dodgy looking trio from the table in the waiting room are now lingering on the street: reversed baseball caps, homemade tattoos and tracksuits. He goes to them without a second thought.

'Any chance of a smoke?'

They check him over briefly before one reaches into his pocket. 'Sure, mate' – taking a cigarette from a full packet and handing it to him – 'there you go.'

'Thanks heaps,' Aaron replies. As he leans in to accept the offer of a light, his greatest need propels two discreetly delivered words to his lips. 'Got anything?'

The skinniest of the trio nods back at him even more discreetly.

'I'll fix you up tomorrow.'

'Fuck off.'

'Tonight then?'

His potential supplier turns back to his mates shaking his head disdainfully. Aaron steps away from them. Pricks. He draws on the cigarette, looking across the street at the long row of renovated factory apartments. Melbourne's autumn sun throws leafy shadows across the late nineteenth-century red-brick facades, where a middle-aged woman in polka-dotted jeans grabs his attention. She is carrying a Uniqlo bag in one hand and a leash leading to a curly-haired dog in the other. She reaches one of the tall, black gates spaced between the various apartment blocks, clumsily swipes her card on the keypad then pushes the gate open just enough to squeeze through with her dog and recent purchase. The gate clicks shut, rapidly cutting off any thoughts Aaron's racing brain might have of a profitable entry.

He's driven on by his cramping legs and stomach, checking out the interiors of parked cars as he goes. Two young men in tight suits step out in front of him from an architect's office, forcing him to give way to them. Not a sideways glance. He must be invisible. That would be handy right now, he thinks. He could go anywhere. Do anything. An expensive-looking road bike captures his interest before he sees the heavy chain mooring it to the U-bar. He walks on to a cafe populated inside and out with heads over laptops and the sound of grinding coffee beans and steaming milk. He slows down slightly to scan for unattended handbags or briefcases, only to be met by wary eyes. Cursing silently, he turns the corner to continue his battle with the incoming tide of pain.

~

Aaron walks toward Hostel Plus, a double-storeyed ex-hotel situated in the not-so-trendy end of Collingwood. Opposite are a car repair shop, a kebab shop, a tattoo parlour and an abandoned house secured with corrugated iron sheets. Along with other brightly coloured graffiti, a giant mural of a bearded hipster is painted across an exterior wall of the backpackers in an obvious attempt to produce the right vibe. Aaron stops at the front door and reaches into his coat pocket to pull out the thirty-dollar cheque Kate gave him for his night's accommodation: one last look to verify its non-negotiability. He folds it in his hand and looks up at three residents, not much older than him, bursting through the door laughing and acting as if they are ready to take on the world. They acknowledge him with a collective 'Hey man,' before bouncing their way up the street.

The reception area is a large, open-plan room with walls covered in brightly coloured murals of the cityscape. It is at once welcoming and intimidating. He walks across the polished stone floor toward the reservation desk where a young, long-haired woman seems to deliberately be taking her time to acknowledge him. While Aaron waits, he listens to the music being piped through the room, tapping his foot and nodding to the driving rock beat of Sleater-Kinney in an attempt to ease his anxiety.

'Triple R,' he says in an attempt to gather the receptionist's attention. She looks up at him, thin-lipped and hollow-cheeked.

'What's that?' she asks flatly.

Ah, he thinks. Pretending to be something she isn't. It helps him. 'Triple R,' he repeats. 'The best.'

She wants the upper hand back. 'Reservation?'

He passes her the cheque. She glances at it then back at him. 'ID?'

He reaches in his jeans pocket, pulls out his creased Health Care Card and places it down in front of her. She shakes her head. 'Photo ID.'

'She didn't tell me I needed it.'

The receptionist glances at the phone ringing next to her and at the growing line of backpackers behind Aaron.

'Well, she should've. They know our policy.'

'She said she was new.'

The phone stops ringing and immediately starts up again. Her irritation grows. He needs to smile, and he does. She sighs and slaps a sheet of typed paper down in front of him.

'You're in the eight-bed dorm.' She points behind him. 'Down the corridor, second on the left.' The same nail-bitten finger lands on the sheet of paper. 'These are the house rules. Do I have to read them to you?'

He knew he didn't like her. His whole body is sweating now. He picks up the house rules – 'Nah' – and starts walking away.

'Any trouble and it'll be one night only. I hope she told you that!'

He raises his hand without looking back as he heads down the corridor and past a rowdy table tennis game, focused only on the next door to the left. Four metal double bunks are spaced along two walls. Two young men playing backgammon on a bottom bunk check him over as he enters. He nods at them and surveys the other bunks. Only one is obviously free; the others are unmade and strewn with bits of clothing, street maps or dog-eared novels – nothing of any value. The free bunk is on the bottom. He likes that. But he doesn't like the large mural of a wolf on the adjacent wall, its long, white fangs bared around a rainbow-coloured tongue, its fierce eyes intent on violence. No choice. He puts his backpack on the floor and sits down on the bunk.

What now? There's a sleeping form on the top bunk opposite, bulky under the sheet. Sleep would be nice, he thinks, but not possible now. He wipes his runny nose on the shoulder of his T-shirt and lies down anyway, shutting his eyes to avoid the stare of the wolf. The incessant sound of the clicking backgammon discs is now annoying him. It shouldn't, but he knows why it is. The same reason he is shivering in a warm room. He forces his brain to take him somewhere peaceful, a technique suggested to him by a child psychiatrist that has never worked, never more than a few seconds anyway. Right now, when it feels like a poison is creeping into every cell in his body, there is no escape. A vaguely familiar sound penetrates the bars of his cage. He opens his eyes to look across at a young man holding a nylon string guitar.

'Sorry, it knocked itself against the bed,' the young man says with a thick accent. 'You were asleep, no?'

Aaron shakes his head. Nice clothes, he thinks, must have some money. Nice haircut too. An outstretched hand reaches toward him.

'I am Philippe.'

'Aaron.'

They shake hands, and Philippe returns to his bunk to sit down and take off his wristwatch. He places it on the bed and rubs his wrist vigorously, as if the band has been annoying him. He looks at Aaron, who has already filed the watch's potential.

'You are Australian?'

'Yeah. You?'

'French.'

'You brought the guitar with you from France?'

'No, no, no! Today I saw it in the, what do you say? Pawnshop? It is not the best guitar, but I have something to learn with. Do you play?'

'A bit.'

Picking up the guitar and holding it out to Aaron: 'Here, you can try it for me.'

Yes please, a chance for some respite from his one-track brain. The wristwatch. He accepts the guitar and runs his eyes over it.

'What did you pay for it?'

'A hundred.'

'Ripped off.'

As Aaron is tuning it, he watches Philippe remove his shirt and throw it casually down on the bed over the watch. Aaron starts to play, random chords at first, just to get a feel for it while he surveys the room. He looks over at the backgammon players engrossed entirely in their game, up at the still-sleeping form above Philippe and then at his new-found friend removing a fresh set of neatly folded clothes from his bag.

What to play? His fingers respond as though they have a mind of their own with an up-tempo version of Nick Cave's 'Into My Arms'. The verse is almost unrecognisable, but the way his fingers pick every note precisely catches the ear of everyone except for Sleeping Beauty above Philippe. The backgammon boys return to their game. Philippe puts the change of clothes to one side and sits on the bed to watch Aaron play into the distinctive melody of the chorus.

'Ah, "Into My Arms"!' Philippe says, smiling.

Aaron nods as he continues, ready to follow this welcome detour for as long as he can.

'I went to the Nick Cave concert in Paris just last year. It was super.'

Sure, Aaron thinks. You've been everywhere and you've seen everything with your trendy clothes and nice haircut and please stop talking. He plays on, his fingers warm, his body light. Snapping open cans of beer, the backgammon boys stop their game to focus their attention on the music. Sleeping Beauty rolls over, angry eyes open.

'Shut the fuck up, will ya!'

Aaron stops playing, the backgammon continues, *click, click, click.* Back on the same aching one-way road, Aaron tries to smile at Philippe. The Frenchman glances up at the top bunk and the turning, groaning body. He lowers his voice.

'You are very good, Aaron. I wish I can play like that one day.'

Aaron holds the guitar out to him, but Philippe shakes his head.

'I must take a shower now, so keep it. Perhaps you can teach me something when I come back. In the lounge this time, I think.'

'Yeah, sure.'

The watch. Don't take the watch with you. Such thoughts return too quickly. It is the lack of control that scares him. He's on automatic pilot and he wonders how far it will take him. Philippe has been kind to him. They could be friends one day, perhaps. He could even visit him in France. No. Philippe turns to him with fresh clothes in hand, his dirty shirt still covering the watch on the bed.

'I think Nick Cave is too difficult for me. I can start with something more simple. Three chords only. Yes?'

'Okay. You have a shower and I'll think of something.'

Philippe exits the dorm and Aaron glances up at Sleeping Beauty who is now facing the wall, snoring. The backgammon boys play on, beers in hand, intent only on winning. Aaron feels the guitar in his arms, thinking for a moment he'll take it too. No. Keep your eye on the ball, Aaron. Don't draw any attention to yourself. He imagines the steps Philippe is taking in the shower room. Clothes off, water running, soaping up. Time to move. Without looking up at Sleeping Beauty, Aaron steps casually across to Philippe's bed below him. He places the guitar down while artfully sliding a hand under the shirt to grasp the watch. It disappears quickly into a front pocket and he returns to his own bunk to pick up his backpack, the open, snarling mouth and frenzied eyes of the wolf mural glaring at him.

He avoids eye contact with the woman at the reservation desk and walks casually out through the front doors. As soon as he steps onto the footpath, he sprints away from the hostel toward the city end of the street, where the giant metal arms of a crane reach across the blue sky above a construction site. He weaves his way through the late-afternoon footpath traffic, his swinging backpack almost knocking over a little girl wandering freely from her mother. He glances back to check she is okay before ignoring the red pedestrian light and blasting car horns to cross the busy intersection. Still running, past the Tote Hotel advertising the week's gigs and up the incline, expelling from his hard-working lungs the last remnants of guilt he feels at betraying

22

Philippe. The hard edge of the watch in his front pocket rubs against his leg and fuels anticipation.

He reaches Smith Street at the top of the hill – a plain name for a bustling, eclectic strip that Tripadvisor might say has *something for everyone*. Stopping to get his breath, he is thinking that same thing. All he needs to do now is find it. He pulls the watch from his pocket. It looks and feels expensive. A Citizen Eco-Drive with a band made of heavy metal. That's why Philippe took it off, Aaron thinks. It must've been irritating his wrist. The number 86 tram rattles up to the intersection in front of the Birmingham Hotel as two likely types emerging from the side door grab his attention. Their focus is intense and their movements are in unison. They are on a mission too. The tram stops and they get on to march purposely to the rear seats. Perhaps they have already got what they came for. He checks the time. Almost five o'clock: he's in the red zone now, with panic creeping in.

Last-minute shoppers, workers heading home or to the pub, impatient drivers trapped in traffic jealously watching cyclists weaving through it. The pungent smell of Thai food reminds Aaron that he hasn't eaten since breakfast. He repositions his backpack and quickens his pace past a beggar sitting outside a 7-Eleven with the ubiquitous cardboard sign asking for money to pay for a night's accommodation. Aaron knows it's not for a bed. Good on the guy for trying, but it's not something Aaron would do. He's not that desperate.

Feeling for the watch in his pocket, he continues on past the automated toilet block. He wants to go but decides he can hold on. Two policemen stroll toward him and his pulse quickens. Avoid their eyes, avoid their eyes. They walk on, as does he. A businessman tosses a half-smoked cigarette into the gutter and it's swooped on by a seagull-eyed gentleman pulling a cart loaded with his worldly possessions under a frayed plastic sheet.

Not far to go now, if Aaron remembers correctly, and he starts to rehearse his lines for his watch-inspired fiction. At the next intersection, a group of First Nations people occupy a square defined by boulders and pavers painted in cultural designs. They seem comfortably ensconced in conversations, immune to anything outside their own space. There isn't a sign, but you need their permission to enter. Aaron tries not to be seen looking, but he holds his gaze long enough for one of the women, certainly older than his mother, to catch his eye. She is smiling at him and he can't help but smile back at her. Just like the smile of the woman in the waiting room, it soothes him, if only momentarily.

He walks on, wondering why it is that only women smile at him. He tries to remember a man's smile, but his memory doesn't bring one immediately to mind. He has to go back to his childhood: playing with his friends at school, walking home slowly with them afterwards, going to their birthday parties. He remembers his own seventh birthday because of a photo in his mother's album – nine happy, smiling boys all in a bunch. Aaron in the middle at the front, the smallest kid with the broadest smile. So happy in his freshly unwrapped North Melbourne football jumper. A reminder of how much fun it was then, before that night when everything changed.

He stands outside Cash Converters surveying the interior of the shop through the glass frontage. He would prefer not to have an audience, and luckily there are only a few customers searching the merchandise for a bargain. In he goes. The automatic doors slide open, and he heads toward an employee at the counter rearranging goods in a glass cabinet. Aaron holds the watch in his fist as he stares down at the top of the employee's shaved head and watches a fat, heavily tattooed hand moving a mobile phone two inches to the left and then back to its original position. Aaron coughs.

'Yes mate, I know you're there.'

Aaron's right foot makes up its own mind to start tapping on the floor. No music, just the anxiety boring into him.

Finally, the bald head rises to address him. 'What're you after?'

Aaron places the watch down on the glass cabinet. The employee picks it up to inspect it closely. Aaron starts his story.

'It was my old man's. He died a couple of weeks ago and left it to me. I don't wear watches so I'd rather put the money to something else.'

'Is that right?'

'Dad wouldn't mind. He'd just want me to get as much for it as I can.'

The employee looks back at him, nodding his head knowingly. 'I bet.'

'So, what d'ya reckon?'

He opens the laptop next to him and types into Google. Aaron watches his wide-spaced eyes scanning the screen for a few moments.

'I'll give you a hundred.'

'One fifty?'

The employee recognises the sweat on Aaron's face, the jagged movements of his body. Perhaps he's been there himself. 'Give me the hundred points of ID and we've got a deal.'

Aaron pulls his Health Care Card from his pocket. 'This'll do, won't it?'

'Nah. Driver's licence, passport?'

Aaron drops his head, his eyes on the threadbare toes of his runners. He tries to take a deep breath, something to calm the anger coursing through him, but his lungs refuse to expand.

'Come on, mate!' Aaron's raised voice attracts the attention of the bargain shoppers.

The employee moves quickly to non-engagement mode. He closes the laptop and gives Aaron a wordless stare. Then, with a flick of the head clearly indicating the exit: 'Piss off.'

~

The peak-hour tram is crammed body-to-body. Aaron has positioned himself close to the middle door, a well-practised strategy to escape the clutches of the ticket inspectors. He knows it is unlikely they'll board the tram, given the volume of passengers, but it's an ingrained habit. Besides, it means he's closer to jumping off if he sees something that will satisfy his all-consuming need. He knows exactly what he is looking for. The last option he has. His eyes dart between the heads around him to any gathering of likely types conducting their business against office walls or deep in narrow laneways. Basically, anyone not moving is a focus.

The metal wheels of the tram screech against the tracks as it approaches Stop 6 on the busiest street in the city. Aaron feels the weight of bodies leaning into him as passengers position themselves to get off as quickly as possible. He reaches for the backpack between his legs. He's ready to go. The tram stops and an eager hand brushes past him to press the button to open the doors. They slide open and he forces his way through the chaotic exchange between those getting off and those getting on to find himself staring into his image in Vodafone's gleaming shopfront window. He pushes his long blond fringe away from his eyes, thinking the style is caught between fashions, neither modern nor retro. His mother could fix it for him. He doesn't like his jeans either; they have completely lost their shape, but they were all he could afford.

He crosses at the lights at the top of the Bourke Street Mall where a busker is playing and singing a note-perfect version of Dire Straits's 'Sultans of Swing'. Aaron stops momentarily to listen and watch the coins and notes piling up in the guitar case. A tinge of regret for not taking Philippe's guitar is rapidly overridden by his body screaming at him to keep moving.

He swings south toward the Yarra River, the footpath as packed as the tram. Passing an overflowing rubbish bin, he scoops out an empty Coke can and slides it into the side pocket of the backpack as he skirts the oncoming foot traffic by stepping into the bike lane. A bad idea. Bells ring and abuse flies from a swarm of lycra-clad commuters. Back among the throng on the footpath, he spots a prostrate form in a small alcove next to the KFC. All that is visible is a mess of grey hair poking out from a grubby blanket. He hesitates momentarily before moving on, trying to erase the image from his mind. Is he the busker or is he the rough sleeper? Somewhere in between, he thinks, as his keen eye falls on a half-full bottle of spring water abandoned on a metal seat. He swoops on it and forces it into the backpack pocket with the Coke can. All good. Now for the main item.

Waiting amongst the pressing crowd for the lights to change opposite Flinders Street Station, Aaron's memory rolls back to his seven-year-old self, holding tight to his father's hand as they jostle with a myriad of supporters queuing to get into the Melbourne Cricket Ground. He has his new football jumper on, and his father is smiling reassuringly down at him. The loud *click, click, click* of the pedestrian crossing signal snaps him back and he weaves his way through the tidal wave of pedestrians to stop at the steps below the gaping entrance to the train station. His eyes dart across groups of high school students, some holding hands, some flirting, others sharing cigarettes. Panic fuels the anxiety again. No, no, no? Where is he? Where are they?

He glances up at the horizontal rays of orange sunlight sliding through the narrow gaps in the silhouetted office towers and apartment blocks before his distressed body drags him back with no choice but to keep moving. Further down Flinders Street, through the wall of foot traffic, he spies two sets of legs protruding from a recess in the line of shopfronts. It looks promising and his pulse quickens as he approaches. He stops in front of the seated man and woman attached to the legs and looks directly at the man, probably forty years old, displaying huge muscles under a super-tight T-shirt. Aaron raises his eyebrows and the man leans his head toward the skinny-legged woman next to him. They exchange knowing nods before she stands and heads off down Flinders Street with Aaron following closely behind her.

They pass by the busy side entrance to the train station where there is a mangled intersection of rushing commuters. Aaron stays close behind her short but fast-paced stride, his eyes glued to the back of her denim jacket. They reach the dormant section just beyond the train station where the deserted Liberated X Bookshop is boarded up and plastered with concert posters. She leads him on to the vacant block next door and up the bare dirt embankment to a private space behind the old bookshop. Aaron pulls the watch from his pocket.

'You'll get two fifty for it.'

'No way.'

'I just got it valued. Twenty minutes ago.'

She shakes her head. 'You're wasting my time.'

'Two hundred.'

She starts to walk away and he puts his arm out to stop her.

She snaps at him. 'Don't fucking touch me.'

'One fifty then! Please.'

She stops and reaches out for the watch with a bony hand bright red with eczema. With one eye closed she very quickly comes to an opinion.

'A point of brown and no more talking.'

'Come on, it's got to be worth two at least.'

She bends down to roll up the bottom of her jeans where she removes a tiny zip-lock bag containing a thin brown line of powder from a false hem. She holds it out to him in one hand, the watch in the other. He doesn't hesitate to take the drugs. She pockets the watch before offering him a thin smile revealing a row of gapped teeth.

'How old are you, by the way?'

'Eighteen.'

'I would've said sixteen.'

He wants to say what he thinks she looks like, but bites his tongue. 'Whatever.'

She disappears around the corner of the building and back onto the streets. He removes his pack and sits down to lean against the brick wall. Through the bricks, he can feel a train rumbling into the station. The sun continues to leave the day, but the closest street lamp is at exactly the right angle to light up the dirt in front of him. He riffles around in the pack to remove his pencil case, then the Coke can and the half-empty bottle of mineral water from the side pocket. It's all laid out in front of him now and his whole being is in a state of high anticipation. A bomb exploding on the street wouldn't stop him going through his well-practised ritual to what is always an unpredictable outcome.

First, he places the Coke can between his knees with the concave bottom facing up. Inspecting the line of heroin in the zip-lock bag, he decides to try half. If it's good, he'll be okay for another hit tomorrow. If it's crap, he'll be pissed off. Next, he mixes the brown powder with the water in his makeshift mixing bowl. It dissolves into a murky, grainy solution. He should really heat it up, but a cigarette filter does a good enough job. Pressing carefully on the can with his knees, he unzips the pencil case and takes out a syringe and the butt of a cigarette. His heart rate increases as he tears a filter from the cigarette and fits it to the end of the needle, draws up the mix, flicks out the air bubbles, pumps his fist and vigorously taps the skin on the bend of his arm until the blue line of a vein stands out. The needle goes through the skin, and blood is withdrawn into the syringe. Aaron stops breathing, pushes down on the plunger and closes his eyes to feel the rush of the heroin through his body. He is disappointed that it only lasts for a few seconds – a telltale sign that it isn't as strong as it should be – but still a beautiful warmth spreads through his body, smothering the embedded tension and anxiety. He opens his eyes, feeling safely cocooned in this narrow space between the building and the brick wall. Two palm trees close to him add to his feeling of security. Why hadn't he noticed them before? Their tall, branchless trunks rise in layers of matching segments to an open umbrella of fronds. He decides in an instant that this is where he will sleep.

~

The first rays of a pink-purple dawn fall softly across the top levels of the city's tallest buildings. In the half-light of the street lamp, Aaron rolls up his blanket in the tarpaulin and jams it into his backpack. He stands and slings the pack onto his back to stare out at the day with a cramping stomach and creeping anxiety demanding his attention. It's an expected but always unwelcome reminder of who he is and what lies ahead of him.

The circular brushes of a street sweeper spin along the gutter on a deserted Flinders Street. Aaron pushes the green button on the automated public toilet outside the train station and enters the stainless-steel interior. After relieving his bladder, he pulls down the baby change shelf, removes his drug-taking paraphernalia and lines it up in front of him like a priest preparing for Holy Communion: a ritual promising a pathway to heaven, but with no guarantee.

The job complete, he leans closer to the scratched stainless-steel mirror to check the pupils of his bright blue eyes. They are pinned but who'll notice? Or even care? He runs his fingers through his matted and greasy hair and thinks of his mother. She'll fix it for him. His soft, patchy beard shows no indication of growing. Still, he likes it. Kurt Cobain, perhaps? The automated voice reminds him that his ten minutes are almost up and the doors will soon open. He squeezes a fresh pimple on his cheek and is ready to face the world feeling contented and ready to smile. This is normal. He knows that because he used to feel like this when he was a child, believing then that it would be forever.

3

It is just after 8am and Aaron watches the passing traffic from his bench seat outside Naomi's Hair Salon, near the entrance to Woolworths and Spotlight in the gentrified suburb of South Melbourne. The morning sun warms the other side of the street, and he briefly considers moving out of the shade until he catches sight of a familiar figure crossing at the roundabout. It is his mother. She has changed the colour of her hair – blonde now, and much shorter. He watches her approach with nervous anticipation, uncertain how she will react. She is talking on her phone as she reaches the door to the hair salon. He watches her fumbling around in her bag for her keys and he stands and walks toward her. As she inserts a key into the lock, she sees his reflection looming in the glass door. She turns to him, offering a wary smile.

'You need a haircut.'

'Yours looks good.'

He follows her inside onto the glossy black-and-white tiles and watches her hang her handbag on the coat rack outside the kitchenette. As she covers it with her jacket, he knows exactly what she is thinking. There is money in that bag and he wants some of it. It doesn't make him feel good. She moves quickly with no words, taking his backpack and putting it against the wall before indicating a chair in front of a washbasin. She opens the tap and feels for the right temperature, wraps a towel around his shoulders and leans him gently back into the spraying water with one hand while the other lathers in the shampoo. He feels good, and her hands gently massaging his scalp add to his feeling of contentment. But then a question abruptly emerges through the cascading water.

'So, where did they find you to stay? I hope it's nice.'

He feels the heavy weight of maternal expectation with the water rushing over the smooth walls of the basin and down the plughole. She turns off the water, wraps a towel around his hair and lifts his head up. Their eyes meet in the mirror. What to say?

'I tried, Mum. But they had nothing for me. Not yet anyway.'

'Don't tell me you're sleeping rough.'

He nods and he feels her agitation through the vigorous rubbing of his hair with the towel.

The door of the salon opens and he hears a female voice. 'Morning, Vicky. You've started early.'

Aaron's mother removes the towel and he turns his head to Naomi, a woman in her fifties with coiffed hair wearing a tight red two-piece tracksuit.

'Ah, it's you, Aaron. Good to see you.'

'Same,' he says, thankful for the interruption.

He follows his mother to a cutting chair where she places a black cape over him. He glances across at Naomi hanging her bag on the coat stand. Their eyes meet briefly, enough for him to imagine exactly what she is thinking. He can't be trusted. He looks at his mother holding a comb and scissors in the mirror.

'You're stoned.'

There is no point in denying it.

'Just tell me what I'm doing with this,' she says, flicking his hair impatiently.

He wants it just like Philippe's, so he explains as best he can. The back and sides cut short, but not too short, and the fringe kept long, but parted at the side. She nods and gets to work. He drifts away with the *click, click* of the scissors and the smell of hair products infused in the walls.

Vicky and Naomi's heads turn to the door as it opens. Their first client is greeted and shown to a chair by Naomi with the conversation flowing easily into a familiar rhythm. Aaron drifts back to the time he came into the salon with his father to pick Vicky up after work. He'd been at his grandparents all day, behaving himself, and his energy levels were high. He took off his shoes to skate across the shiny black-and-white tiles in his socks, through the cut hair Vicky was trying to sweep up. She growled at him, and when he didn't stop, she growled at his father. It started a big argument between them, and Naomi intervened, putting her arm around Aaron and leading him into the kitchenette where she gave him a Tim Tam, a glass of blackcurrant cordial and a kiss that left lipstick lips on his cheek. On the way home, he sat in the back seat thinking it was his fault that his parents were still arguing. He cried and they stopped.

The whir of the hairdryer brings him back to Vicky fluffing up his hair with her fingers, checking it out in the mirror, turning her head to one side, then the other like a painter examining a canvas. Finally, she stands behind him, placing her hands on his shoulders and meeting his gaze in the mirror.

'Happy?'

He nods. His hair is much straighter than Philippe's, and the clothes are all wrong but it's a start. One day, he'll travel to the other side of the world too. He'll buy a guitar, a really good one though, and busk on the busiest city street. The phone rings and the door opens. Again, Vicky and Naomi's heads turn in unison. The working day is gathering speed. Vicky goes to the phone while telling the next client to take a seat, she won't be long. Aaron plays briefly with his fringe and then looks across at Naomi, who is putting foils in her client's hair. She smiles at him.

'It looks really good, Aaron. Are you pleased?'

'Yep.'

'Very handsome.'

Vicky returns from the phone, removes the cape and shakes the cut strands of hair to the floor.

'Are you hungry?'

He nods with a half-second thought that she will offer him some money. Of course she won't.

'There's some chicken curry and rice in the fridge.'

He sees an opportunity. 'But that's your lunch, Mum.'

She cuts him off at the pass. 'I'll get myself something from next door.'

Damn. She knows what he's thinking. He knows what she's thinking. It's all become so obvious.

'Come on. I'll pop it in the microwave for you.' She looks over at her waiting client. 'I'll be right with you, Mrs Russo.'

They both go into the kitchenette where Vicky puts the container of food into the microwave. She turns to her son.

'Nothing's changed, has it?'

'It will, Mum.'

For a long moment there is only the loud hum of the microwave. It has all been said before, loudly, softly, with anger, with tears. Now, in this tiny space, there is just shared sadness. The microwave *dings*. She opens it and places the hot food down on the bench.

'I've got to get back to work. Come by tomorrow and I'll wash those clothes for you.'

A sliver of light, he feels it.

'Okay.'

He sits on the stool at the bench eating the curry and rice, looking out into the salon at Vicky and Naomi working and chatting on autopilot like true professionals, encouraging the recitation of another chapter in the life of their client. As he scrapes the last of the food from the bowl, his eyes focus on the coat rack and the two bags. He can just see a corner of Vicky's under her jacket. He takes the bowl to the sink and runs it under the water, forcing his thoughts from the money dangling between him and his mother and a woman who has always been kind to him.

He walks back out into the salon, picks up his backpack and looks at his mother.

'Tomorrow then?' she asks.

He nods, knowing that her offer to wash his clothes is code for *a talk*. He continues to the door with the phone ringing again. It's Naomi's turn to answer it.

'Bye, Aaron,' she says as they cross paths. 'Where's my kiss?'

He bends down to offer his cheek, then goes to the door, pausing for a moment with the same feeling he had leaving Kate at the housing office. Again, he has glimpsed the life that he craves, but then it's gone.

4

Aaron stands on the footpath rubbing the lipstick off his cheek with a sleeve of his shirt as an Armaguard truck pulls into the car space in front of him. Two uniformed guards jump out with guns holstered at their hips. One marches off with authority toward the entrance to Woolworths and Spotlight, while the other saunters to the rear of the truck to lean lazily against it. Aaron doesn't waste any time on cunning contemplation. A nasty outcome would be assured. Instead he walks past the reclining guard and crosses to the sunny side of the street, then turns into a narrow, bluestone-paved laneway providing rear access to modern apartment blocks and commercial enterprises housed in Victorian brick buildings.

Walking across the uneven surface, his brain is ticking over the limited options he has. He scans the bright green mould growing in the spaces between the bluestone pavers, the overflowing rubbish bins and the graffiti-tagged brick walls, searching for an opportunity. Fifty metres in, he sees a sign saying *Private Property No Unauthorised Access* at the open entrance to a car park. No people, just a dozen or so cars taking up half the allocated spaces on the perimeter of a cracked concrete rectangle. A five-storey apartment block is at the far end with a series of industrial roller doors spaced evenly along one side and a concrete wall on the other.

He walks in and begins a circuit of the car park with alternating glances between the interiors of the cars and the surrounding buildings and doors. No people, and nothing in the cars. It is strangely quiet, with only the low sound of traffic in the nearby street. As he turns back toward the alley, under the tiny balconies of the apartment block, he sees it. On the back seat of a two-door Honda Civic is a laptop in a thin, yellow case. He slows his pace but not his wits. Early model car so it shouldn't have an alarm. He scans the surface of the car park, his heart racing, spots a loose chunk of concrete among the spider web of cracks. He takes off his backpack and kneels down to remove his hoodie. He double-checks for any movement around him before prising out the lump of concrete and wrapping it up in the hoodie.

Leaving the backpack on the ground, he walks rapidly back to the car and without hesitating smashes the cushioned chunk of concrete into a rear-side window. Instantly, an alarm screams out (wrong about

41

that!) across the enclosed rectangle, setting off simultaneous reactions from three different directions.

A man's voice from a balcony just above him screams, 'Hey, you!'

A metal roller door screeches open just behind him.

A car pulls into the car park.

Flight mode. Shaking the concrete free of his hoodie, he scoops up his backpack and sprints toward the exit. The driver of the incoming car slams on his brakes, but as he opens his door, Aaron disappears.

Sprinting onto the busy street at the end of the laneway, Aaron is almost skittled by a four-wheel drive reversing from one of the diagonal parking spaces. He stops, out of breath, when he reaches the footpath, which is heavy with foot traffic on the other side. It is just past midday, and the coffee shops dotted between the clothing boutiques, bookshops and graphic designers are already buzzing. This is close to the heart of the new South Melbourne and it almost smells of money: the cars, the clothes, the architect-designed town houses where once stood a workers' cottage or a shoe factory. But this is home to Aaron, where he roamed the streets as a ten-year-old after his parents split up, where he first tasted heroin as a sixteen-year-old; the place he returns to like a homing pigeon.

Another bluestone-paved lane leads him to the next street, where he allows himself to slow down. No one's behind him; he's the only one doing the chasing now. He stops in front of the Persian Carpet Warehouse, panting and contemplating his next move. He knows exactly what it will be, the only question is how he goes about it. He's distracted by a young couple who brush past him, holding hands and laughing. As he watches them go into the warehouse, under the archways and through the wood-panelled double doors of what was once a church, he wonders why seeing happy people annoys him so much. It comes on him so quickly and with such force it scares him.

He wanders through the passing traffic and turns the corner into a tree-lined street, walking with jagged urgency up the short, gentle incline toward the rear of the South Melbourne Town Hall, an imposing late nineteenth-century building sitting squarely on top of the mound known as Emerald Hill. He has been inside only once, to shoot up. It felt more like a palace than a council building, intimidating with its high ceilings, polished timber and ornate tiling, even in the toilets. Everything had an echo.

He reaches the narrow one-way street running along one side of the Town Hall and pauses for a moment to look across at a grubby-looking two-storey Victorian building: a men's rooming house that everyone refers to as 'Layfield Street'. Dave will be there, in his ground-floor room with a large window giving him a clear view to passing traffic. Aaron crosses his fingers that Dave will be nice to him, again.

Aaron pushes open the unlocked front door and walks into the stale air. Rooms are numbered along both sides of the ground floor, separated by a staircase to the first. He knocks on Number 6.

'Yep.'

'It's Aaron, Dave.'

'Okay.'

Inside he is looking through a plume of cigarette smoke amplified by the sun's rays streaming through the window. Dave is sitting on the end of his single bed, painting on a thin piece of plywood propped on a makeshift easel.

Someone else speaks. 'Hey, Aaron. How's it going, bro?'

Aaron turns toward the voice and the source of the smoke: a young Filipino man with a goatee and a big, happy smile is sitting at a card table in the corner, smoking and drinking white wine from a cask.

'Yeah good, Timmy.'

'Drink?'

'No thanks, mate.'

Aaron immediately turns his focus back to Dave.

'How's things, Dave?' he asks the thin man with grey hair and glasses. Dave reminds Aaron of his high school principal, but not as intimidating.

Dave turns his painting toward Aaron. 'Who's this, then?'

Aaron looks at a man's head composed of bright colours and thick brushstrokes, with eyes that bore into the viewer in a very familiar way. He thinks he knows who it is, but he doesn't want to make a mistake.

'I'll give ya a hint,' says Timmy from the corner.

'No you fucken won't,' says Dave, staring at Aaron waiting for an answer.

44

'It's you,' Aaron says with hopeful confidence. 'Without the glasses.'

'Good boy,' Dave says as he dabs his paintbrush into a mound of red paint. Aaron looks across again at a grinning Timmy.

'Good to see you, bro.'

'Same,' Aaron replies. Timmy was three years ahead of him at school and they bonded over stolen cigarettes and how much they disliked their respective fathers. Timmy's was violent, very violent. Aaron divulged very little about his, and eventually Timmy stopped asking him. He liked going to Timmy's house because his mother fed him spaghetti with very sweet tomato sauce and sliced hotdogs on top. Timmy was expelled in Year 10 for coming to school drunk. It didn't stop him drinking then, and nothing has since.

Aaron glances at Dave painting but decides not to interrupt him just yet. He looks back at Timmy squeezing another cup of wine from the bladder of the cask.

'I thought you got chucked out.'

'Nah, they let me stay. I just have to pay 'em an extra twenty bucks a fortnight till I clear the debt. You should get your name down on the waiting list now you're eighteen. That'd be cool, eh?'

No it wouldn't, Aaron thinks. Then, as if on cue, a man's voice screams expletives above them before a door slams violently shut. Aaron is getting edgy now; he wants a private conversation with Dave. Timmy knows exactly why Aaron's there, but it will be a tricky negotiation and Timmy will want to have his say – he can't help himself.

As if to prove Aaron's point, Timmy babbles on. 'Come up and play some guitar when you've finished here. The guy next door's got one you can borrow. A Maton Black. Real nice, it is. He's let me play it a few times. Nice guy. Got a bit of a temper, but.'

'Go back up to your room, Timmy. You're giving me a fucking headache,' Dave says firmly as he wipes his brush clean with a paint-splattered rag.

'Yeah, sure, Dave. No worries.' Timmy collects his wine cask and cigarettes, addressing Aaron on his way out. 'See you later then, eh?'

Aaron nods with his brain already rehearsing his lines for Dave. He turns to him nervously, ready to speak, but Dave is holding up his self-portrait – now complete with oversized red glasses – for approval. Before Aaron can give him his inflated praise, a woman appears at the door.

'That's brilliant, Dave.'

Dave looks admiringly at it. 'It is, isn't it?'

'Hello, darlin',' she says as she makes herself comfortable at the card table.

It's Samantha, another of Dave's hangers-on. As far as Aaron can tell, it's a quid pro quo arrangement. She gets her drugs and he gets what he wants when he wants it. She is in her early thirties, he thinks. Not unattractive but slightly mad in a nice way. Every time he sees her, she rails about the depot injections she is forced to have once a month for her schizophrenia. She's always saying she's going to challenge her community treatment order but never does.

She offers Aaron a tailor-made. He feels like he needs it now and accepts it readily.

'Don't let me interrupt your business,' she says, lighting it for him.

He draws the smoke into his lungs, and as he exhales it he can see Dave looking back at him through the sunlit plume. This is his moment, but Dave beats him to it.

'No more credit, mate.'

'I'll definitely fix you up this time, Dave, I promise ya.'

'Nah.'

Aaron sucks again on the cigarette and looks over at Samantha, his desperation evident. She smiles back sympathetically.

'You could always give it up,' she says from her position of security.

Aaron looks back at Dave, who simply shrugs as if to say, there you go, you do have a choice. No one in the room believes that to be true, especially Aaron. His stomach tightens even more, and the nicotine is making his head spin.

Samantha has a solution. 'Look at you. You're a good-looking boy. I'd say you'd be very popular. Especially with that new haircut. Eh, Dave? If you were that way inclined, I mean.'

Aaron feels anger gripping him now. He wants to scream at her. What's my life got to do with you?! Instead he looks back at Dave, not wanting to plead with him, but he can't help it.

'Please, Dave. It'll be the last time. Absolutely.'

'There are ways and means, Aaron. Always. Shut the door on your way out.'

The voice in Aaron's head is very loud. So you want me to shut your door, do you, Dave? Why's that? So you get what you want and she gets what she wants? What about me? He almost slams it shut, but he doesn't.

Aaron stands in the hallway with the smell of sausages cooking in sour oil emanating from the communal kitchen, his thoughts a scramble of anger and rising anxiety. It is now six hours since he last hit up and he badly wants to run into the afternoon and night without the weight of the chase bearing down on him. He chastises himself for expecting too much. A voice calls out to him from the landing at the top of the stairs. He looks up at a grinning Timmy holding up a strip of pharmaceutical pills.

~

Timmy's room is one of nine on the first floor, each one numbered around the perimeter of the U-shaped stairwell. The walls and ceiling are painted grey-green with blue office carpet covering the squeaky floorboards. The whole building smells of sausages, BO and stale tobacco smoke. There is the low hum of a television coming from one room, otherwise all is quiet.

Aaron follows Timmy into his room and shuts the door behind him. It is half the size of Dave's room, and with only one tiny corner window facing south, it is dark and dingy. Clothes are spread out across the floor, and the first thing Aaron sees is a plastic juice bottle under the single bed half-filled with a pale yellow liquid.

'There you go, bro,' says Timmy, passing him the strip of pills. 'Don't take 'em all though, eh?'

Diazepam, 25mg. That'll help, Aaron thinks. Four should do the trick. He looks for something to wash them down with but there is only the offer of white wine in a dirty cup. Unlike Timmy, he doesn't love alcohol; it depresses him, and if he has too much, he loses control of his anger. He chews the pills to make them digest quicker, takes a mouthful of wine and puts the cup back down on the school desk with the ghetto blaster, the cask of wine and the ashtray. Okay, he decides, he'll hang out here for a while, play some guitar, avoid Timmy's bullshit and when the pills kick in, he'll make a plan.

'Guitar?'

'I checked before,' says Timmy. 'He's not home.'

Aaron is not surprised, but he's unhappy. He really feels like playing something heavy, some Metallica riffs maybe – anything to channel the agitation taking hold of him.

'Where's yours, then?' he asks, already knowing the answer.

'Cash Converters. I'm getting it back out soon.'

No you won't, Aaron thinks with his head ready to explode. Shit. What now? Go? Stay?

Timmy fumbles through a pile of CDs scattered on the floor.

'I'll put some music on, eh? What do you want to hear?'

Aaron doesn't respond; he knows that whatever he says will be ignored. In any case, he knows he'll like what Timmy chooses to play. Their shared taste in music will not have changed. Aaron sits down on the edge of the bed and lies back staring at the patches of paint peeling off the ceiling, Timmy's slurred words boring into his ears before colliding with his jagged nerves. Through it all, he hears the opening track of Radiohead's album *Hail to the Thief*: '2+2=5'. He forces himself to concentrate on the song's hypnotic build-up to help fight off his attention-demanding demons. First, there is the driving drumbeat, then the melodic guitar, joined by the high-pitched vocals releasing the tension.

He can hear Timmy talking under the music. He doesn't need to listen to his words because he has heard them all before, delivered in an alcohol-driven rave about their friendship and how much it means to him – well-intentioned, but in the end meaning very little. They were genuinely close once, drawn together in the school grounds because they recognised each other's wounds; they could have been two boys with matching prosthetic legs. They played stolen CDs in Aaron's tiny bedroom, pausing every track as they pretended to be DJs on their own FM station, complete with made-up ads about anything that popped into their heads. They played guitar together – although Timmy never ventured beyond three chords – and Aaron talked him into barracking for North Melbourne. That common ground has almost all gone now, stolen by alcohol.

The first song ends, and in the silence between tracks Aaron hears the end of Timmy's soliloquy.

'It's all true, bro.'

Aaron waits for him to say, 'I love you,' but it doesn't come this time. Perhaps Timmy doesn't believe it anymore either. The next track starts.

'A bit more volume.'

Timmy doesn't hesitate to do as he's asked. Neither of them cares that it is the middle of the afternoon in a rooming house full of men with walls that are not that thick. Aaron decides he will drink some wine after all; it will add to the effect of the pills. He skols a full cup, lies back on the bed and closes his eyes to drown in the music, wishing it was heroin taking him away in a blissful rush. Instead he finds himself thinking about another time at Timmy's house watching North play Collingwood on a Friday night. North were winning a close game and they were cheering and high-fiving every goal. He can remember Timmy's mother, Lita, barracking with them even though she knew nothing about the game. It all changed when Timmy's father walked in the door. Roger barracks for Collingwood and he was drunk as usual. Lita got up immediately and went to the kitchen to get him his dinner. He went straight to the television and turned it off before telling Aaron to fuck off home.

Aaron opens his eyes to see Timmy right next to him pissing in the fruit juice bottle and looking like an exact replica of his father, until his habitual grin spreads across his face.

'Let's dance, bro.'

Before Aaron can respond, Timmy is already on the floor, scratching through the CDs and putting on an album from the American electronic rock band, LCD Soundsystem. The first track is 'Dance Yrself Clean' and Timmy is moving with the almost primal drumbeat, sparse synthesiser and teasing vocals. Aaron can't help but tap his feet and nod his head as the tension in the song builds slowly but inevitably to an explosion of instruments and voice, compelling him to his feet to abandon everything to the exhilaration of the moment. The song seems to be permeating every cell, blending with the pills and the alcohol to carry him to a place of joy.

Suddenly the spell on Aaron is broken by a loud and persistent knocking noise. He opens his eyes and looks at Timmy, who is still dancing, totally oblivious to it. Aaron shakes him and points to the door. Timmy shrugs – nothing to worry about – and goes back to dancing. The door flies open to reveal a man in his fifties with a bloated red face. He's wearing a stained blue singlet and has a large belly hanging over loose tracksuit bottoms. He marches straight toward the ghetto blaster, shoving Timmy to one side before ripping the cord from the power point. In the silence, he turns and walks back out through the door. Timmy goes straight to the power point and plugs the cord back in, selects the second track and turns the volume up even louder.

Within seconds, the angry neighbour is marching back through the door to pin Timmy by the throat against the wall. Aaron grabs his backpack and quickly exits the room, knowing there is nothing he can do to change the course of the narrative; Timmy will get badly hurt.

The steps on the stairs squeak loudly all the way down to Dave's closed door, through which Aaron can hear Samantha laughing. Immediately, her unsolicited advice comes rushing at him: *You're a good-looking boy, Aaron. You'd be very popular. Especially with that new haircut.* A seed of dread has been planted, and as he walks along the narrow footpath away from the rooming house, he can feel it growing.

He crosses the street to sit down on the grass in front of the Town Hall's muscular pillars and sky-reaching spire to consider his next move. A police car pulls up outside the police station opposite. The building's Spanish-style arched windows and red-tiled roof make it seem less intimidating – more like a station in a small village somewhere in the country. Two policemen get out of the car, laughing as they go inside. On the other side of the T-junction is the co-joined Victorian workers' cottage where he lived with his mother until she recently threw him out.

The remnants of Timmy's pills, the warm sun and the soft grass, and perhaps the proximity to what was once his home, combine to conjure an image of himself as a happy six-year-old, kicking a football with his father outside on the street. Every now and again, his father calls, 'Car!' and they have to step back onto the footpath until it passes.

His father compliments Aaron on his kicking, and then on the next kick, the ball slides off the side of his shoe, smashing the side mirror of a parked car. The owner gets out of his car and makes Aaron cry. His father puts a consoling arm around him, making him feel safe and protected.

The clock in the tower above Aaron strikes loudly and he is snapped back to the present. What next? The house is still there in front of him, but his father is long gone. Just his mother now. She'll still be at work, and for half a moment he thinks about the possibility of looking inside for something he can sell. No. She has changed the locks.

5

Leaving South Melbourne, Aaron turns down the road leading to Albert Park Lake. He first needs to find somewhere safe to sleep and hide his backpack before starting the serious search to put something in his arm. The tarmac on the road he walks is even and smooth, as you would expect of a Grand Prix racetrack. On one side of the five-kilometre circuit is the lake; on the other are sports fields, sailing clubs, golf clubs and swimming pools spread out across the surrounding green and tree-spotted acreage. Ahead of him are the southern suburbs bordering Port Phillip Bay; behind him city skyscrapers rise like Lego blocks toward dappled clouds.

He dismisses a few shelter options among the trees before deciding to check out a double-storey training shed sitting between a rugby field and a soccer ground about fifty metres from the road. A man is exercising his dog, but he is too busy throwing a ball to take much notice. Aaron walks quickly to the back of the building where a set of iron stairs run up to the first floor, creating a sheltered alcove. But where to hide his backpack? He scouts around while keeping an eye on the man and his dog. A small rubbish skip is nearby, and when he lifts the lid he has his answer. It's empty except for a punctured soccer ball and a pile of used strapping tape.

First item ticked off, he leaves the lake and the parklands to enter the wide, tree-lined streets of the suburb of Albert Park itself. He quickly dismisses any idea of breaking into one of the diagonally parked late-model cars, or jumping a fence to enter one of the large brick houses. The flat and open terrain upon which most of them were built in the nineteenth century makes it all seem too risky. Video cameras and alarms will be everywhere, and where would he run to, where would he hide? Again, Samantha's words niggle away at him. And now Dave's too: *There are ways and means, Aaron. Always.* The foggy calm of the pills is wearing off and the growing inevitability of what they are suggesting scares him. He needs something to distract him, for the moment at least, and he knows exactly what it is.

One more block and he walks through an open front gate leading to a building that always reminds him of his old primary school, with its two-storey red-brick facade. Written in gold letters on the central column are the words, *International Society for Krishna Consciousness.*

56

He turns the corner at the rear of the building toward the expansive vegetable garden, with its rows of staked tomatoes, eggplants, beans and capsicums, ripe and ready to be picked and cooked. And there she is, just as he'd hoped, sitting with her older woman friend on a bench beside the circular water feature. He has seen her and her friend here once before. They exchanged knowing looks, recognising each other as the same species. She has spiky blonde hair, wears a faux-leather jacket and has hyperactive hands. She turns to him with a lovely smile that he's sure is just for him. His heart rate quickens and he smiles back with an awkward motion of his hand that makes him feel slightly silly. She must be at least five years older than him. He walks self-consciously toward the rear door of the building, wanting to hide until he can regain his composure.

He has eaten at the Hare Krishna's several times. He likes the food, and it's free for him and people like him who don't have the money to donate. At first it was intimidating, but he found that no one bothered him. A young man with a shaved head in an orange robe acknowledges Aaron gently as he climbs the wide wooden staircase to the dining room. Most of the tables are taken, and there is only a short line to the self-serve vegetable curries and rice kept warm in several bain-maries. Behind them, two other orange-robed men silently stir large aluminium pots on a gas stovetop. It is so quiet Aaron is almost afraid to think, fearing that his thoughts will echo through this large room with its high ceiling, polished floor tiles and ornate window frames, where everyone seems to move and sit and eat in silent contemplation. His brain is in another gear, racing, as always, in pursuit of a pathway to score.

He plates up his curry and rice – not too much, and quickly – hoping madly that she will still be there with her friend when he goes back outside. He'll walk toward them and she'll offer him a seat next to her in the sun. She'll tell him how much she likes his haircut and then invite him back to her nice-smelling bedsit where they will shoot up together and lie on her single bed talking until they fall asleep in each other's arms. He descends the stairs with his plate of food and his heart beating a little bit faster. Just as he steps outside, the sun disappears behind a cloud and he sees two aging hippies on the bench seat where once there was promise.

He eats only because he knows he must. His aching body doesn't want it, and he is angry that he has once again allowed himself to get excited by his wishful thinking. It brings him momentary lightness but he always feels worse when it leaves him. If only it was the other way around and the darkness was fleeting. Isn't that normal? Not for him and not now. He stares at the red-brick building and sees his eight-year-old self in the classroom the day after the night it first happened. As he sits at his desk with trauma and confusion bottled up inside him, warm piss soaks through his shorts and pools on the wooden floor under his chair.

Aaron stares through the headlights of cars flashing past him on the busy double-lane road separating the suburb from the foreshore of Port Phillip Bay. He feels more miserable than he has in a long time. Not bothering to cross at the lights, he steps out onto the road to dodge speeding cars and angry drivers blasting horns. He makes it to the palm tree–lined walkway bordering the water, where he just avoids being cleaned up by a lycra-clad cyclist. He turns east toward St Kilda with an intense need for heroin and a heightened anxiety jumbling his brain. He's like a starving hunter at nightfall, eyes flicking here and there in search of a bicycle left unlocked while the owner chats nearby with a friend, or a handbag on a seat next to an unsuspecting tourist – anything that he can sell to get what he must have, anything to postpone what he now feels to be inevitable.

Empty-handed, he stops at the next set of traffic lights to look up through the steady stream of foot traffic toward the Gatwick, a last-resort rooming house where chaos is the norm and anything and everything illegal can be bought and sold, often with violent consequences. Desperation pushes him up Fitzroy Street, with its reputation for all-night eating and action. Ahead of him, the gentle light from an old-fashioned street lamp shows off the yellow letters on the portico above the footpath: *Gatwick Private Hotel.*

At the entrance to the tired-looking two-storey building, he is greeted by a very skinny man marching back and forth with stiff arms and legs, his head shaved dramatically on two sides, muttering loudly to someone only he can see. Aaron steps warily to one side as he quickly scans the faces of the others, recognising only a baseball-capped guy in his early twenties sprawled out on the marble steps, tracksuit pants rolled up to his calves, shirt open to a bare chest, cigarette burning between raised fingers. Mr Big in his own mind. Aaron raises his eyebrows questioningly. He gets back a subtle nod, so he sits down next to Mr Big, trying hard to stay casual and cool.

A big bearded man sitting against the lamppost is smiling at him. 'It's my birthday today.'

'How old are you?' Aaron asks.

'I don't know,' the bearded man says, laughing.

Still, the skinny man marches back and forth. Aaron wants to run away now with something in his pocket. The front door swings open and he can hear a man playing a guitar and singing 'Knockin' on Heaven's Door' almost tunefully. A middle-aged woman appears on the steps next to Aaron wearing a short red skirt and matching tube top. She hitches up the top and walks off down the street as though she owns it.

Mr Big sucks on his cigarette and whispers to Aaron, 'Nothin' now, but it's comin'.'

'When?'

'Can't say exactly.'

'Tonight?'

Nodding and looking Aaron over. 'Cash.'

Aaron almost says he will have it in four days when he gets his Centrelink payment but very quickly decides to keep it vague. 'Sure.'

Mr Big turns away and drags again on his cigarette, blowing smoke rings into the air in a perfect imitation of the character he is playing. Aaron walks back down Fitzroy Street on the restaurant side, where diners at outdoor tables are drinking and eating and laughing with a watchful eye on their phones and bags. They know exactly where they are. He treads on toward the dark expanse of Port Phillip Bay knowing that he is about to come face to face with the horror of the past.

6

The continuous hum of three lanes of traffic and flashing headlights accompanies Aaron as he makes his way along the foreshore to reach the St Kilda Sea Baths, a grand building sprawling from twin-domed Moorish-style structures at one end to an outdoor dining area at the other. He pauses to look across the expansive car park to the long row of arched entrances dominating the facade. As well as hanging out badly for pain relief, he is now racked with nerves and uncertainty. He watches two men emerge from the building carrying sports bags and laughing. They get into a car and he decides to move further into the car park where he will be more comfortable watching in the half-light. As the car drives off, he realises he has to be bolder if something is to happen. But this is a new game entirely and he doesn't know the rules. He can't sit, he can't stand, he can only pace a circuit of the car park with his sparking brain ready to explode.

On his third lap of summing up and dismissing unlikely looking types arriving and departing, he sees him emerge from the main entrance to stand on the steps and light a cigarette. Instinctively Aaron recognises something about him, and he quickens his pace to get to him before he moves. He is wearing a black dinner suit and bow tie – maybe sixty, Aaron thinks – with a paunch above his long legs. Aaron throws him a glance, like a fisherman casting a fly to kiss the surface of the water just long enough to capture interest. The Man's eyes meet Aaron's in a way that fills him with dread. He turns away and keeps walking with a voice in his head screaming at him to stick with the plan: the reward will come, you've got no choice, just do it.

He waits at a bollard close to the exit feeling as if every muscle in his body is trying to strangle him. Relief is all he can think about as he stares into the headlights of the black late-model Lexus gliding toward him. It stops, and the Man leans across to open the passenger-side door. Aaron gets in to the strong smell of aftershave and classical music playing softly through the stereo speakers. 'Seatbelt,' the Man says without looking at him. Aaron obeys and they accelerate into the thick traffic on Jacka Boulevard.

'Where're we going?' Aaron blurts out.

'Somewhere close. I haven't got a lot of time.'

Aaron thinks quickly; he wants some control of this. Once it's over, he needs to be close to the Gatwick and to his camp.

'Lakeside Drive.'

The Man nods and indicates to turn right, and at the first intersection they stop at a red light outside the Gatwick. Aaron watches Mr Big stroll into the laneway beside the hotel with an eager customer following closely behind. As the car takes off, Aaron sinks into the leather seat holding onto an image of himself following Mr Big into the laneway to reach that same blissful end. But in the confines of the car, with a strange man and orchestral violins playing through the speakers, the image evaporates quickly to him feeling like he's in a fast-flowing river with his head barely above water. Unconsciously, he draws in a deep breath.

'You okay?' the Man asks with a hint of concern.

'Yep,' Aaron lies.

They continue on and Aaron steals a glance at the Man in the driver's seat. He is older than he first appeared. More like seventy than sixty. His hair is oddly jet-black against the sagging skin and lines on his face. They drive past the St Kilda Bowls Club with the green of the grass and the white of the players' uniforms heightened under the bright lights. With the violins building dramatically to a crescendo, he could be in the middle of a bad dream.

They turn into Lakeside Drive, which carries traffic away from the busy streets of St Kilda and into the southern end of Albert Park Lake – the opposite end to Aaron's camp and the racetrack.

'Just up here on the left,' Aaron says softly, almost to himself.

On cue, the Man swings the car left and then left again a few metres further on, into an empty, unlit car park at the back of a sports pavilion. He turns off the music, the motor and the headlights, and as the interior lights fade to black, the Man shuffles in his seat to look directly at Aaron.

'How old are you?'

Aaron turns away to look out through the window into the dark and the first drops of falling rain.

'Eighteen.'

'I thought you might be younger than that.'

'What d'ya want?'

'To suck your cock.'

'Hundred bucks.'

'Okay.'

He reaches across to touch Aaron's face and he pulls away. 'Money first and just do what you said. Nothing else.'

The Man reacts to Aaron's feistiness with a self-satisfied smile. He removes his wallet from his jacket pocket and hands over a hundred-dollar note. Aaron tucks it quickly into one of his socks and turns back to the rain and the dark. He feels the Man's hand on his crotch.

'What's your name?'

'Timmy,' Aaron says spontaneously. It's the first name that comes to replace his own.

'It suits you.'

He can feel the Man's eyes on him, and then his hand reaching across to unbutton his jeans and unzip his fly. He can hear him breathing short, sharp, excited breaths before he takes Aaron's penis in his mouth and brings it quickly to an erection. Aaron is bombarded with a confluence of pleasure and pain, with what he feels in his groin and what he sees through the mist building on the inside of the window: his eight-year-old self sitting on a couch with his silver-haired grandfather, watching the cricket. His immaculately dressed grandmother walks into the room to say she is off to play bridge. She kisses them both goodbye and then disappears. His grandfather's hand slowly moves across to rest on young Aaron's bare knee.

Aaron comes. He looks down to where black hair dye has leaked a line onto the skin of the Man's neck. All he wants to do is to smash his fists into that head, over and over. The Man sits up straight, wiping his mouth with a perfectly folded handkerchief. Aaron reaches for the doorhandle.

'Wait.'

The Man leans across and opens the glove box to take out a notebook and pen. He scribbles down a number, tears out the page and hands it to Aaron.

'Ring me whenever you like.'

Aaron opens the door and quickly gets out to sprint into the dark, through the rain toward the Gatwick Private Hotel.

7

Aaron's eyes open to three teenagers in red-and-white rugby jumpers jogging the perimeter of the adjacent rugby ground. He doesn't think they can see him lying here, in the alcove under the stairway to the first floor of the sports shed where he has woken up shivering in still-damp clothes. His second thought goes immediately to the heroin he has left in his pocket. He wants a piss too, but that can wait. He'd best shoot up and get moving.

The drug surges through his veins and he sighs, euphoria banishing the cold, the guilt, the ache in his stomach, the pain in his legs and his arms – in a glorious instant, all gone. Basking in the wonderful feeling of contentment that follows the rush, he packs up his camp slowly, throws his backpack across his shoulders and sets off across the green grass to the smooth tarmac of the road. Ahead of him is South Melbourne and the day he has planned with his mother. He will have a shower, she will wash his clothes, and while they are drying, he'll spend time with her trying not to argue.

A car horn blasts at him when he wanders too far onto the road. He crosses another patch of green grass to the gravel pathway running alongside the lake. The morning sun is warm on his face, and he allows himself to think about the night before, with the Man. He feels for the slip of paper in his pocket, pondering if he will ring him. Is the reward worth the ugliness, the distress and the pain? Right now, with his emotions as calm as the water he looks out across, it is a question easily answered. Pain is his constant companion anyway; he will be just adding another layer to it, but without the desperate and grinding daily chase to relieve it.

He takes the back streets through South Melbourne, wanting to avoid the busy main thoroughfares just as he did when he was a kid on a skateboard. Around a corner he has turned into a thousand times and he is heading up the gentle slope toward the Town Hall imposing itself on the hilltop. The clock in the tower tells him it's just after eleven o'clock, and for half a second, he thinks about dropping in on Dave or Timmy at the rooming house – his mother will still be at work for another couple of hours. But no, not while he's feeling this good. Lurking chaos could ruin it. Instead, he pushes open the creaky gate to the tiny front garden of his mother's co-joined brick Victorian.

Sitting on the cracked concrete front steps in a warm late-morning sun, he can see a half a dozen police cars lined up outside the station directly opposite the Town Hall. Dave has been dealing from his room for a long time and has never been busted. It's curious, and Aaron wonders again if the rumour that Dave's in league with one of them, or some of them, is true. It could just be that his circle of customers is confined to the twenty-nine blokes in the rooming house and some others he trusts. Whatever. It's convenient and Aaron hopes it lasts.

His thoughts wander to last night and him using the name Timmy. Why did he do that? Perhaps it was just because in that moment he didn't want to use his own name, he didn't want to be Aaron. He's not sure. It was completely spontaneous. The whir of an electric motor approaching easily shifts his attention to the front gate, where a forty-something man in a motorised wheelchair stops to say hello, his pronunciation slurred by brain injury.

'Hey, Charlie. How you going?'

'Good. You?'

'Yeah, good.'

'Okay, see ya.'

Aaron raises his hand as the wheelchair continues on up the street. Charlie Doyle always says hello but never much more. The story is he'd been celebrating after Essendon defeated Melbourne in the 2000 Grand Final and got hit by a car while crossing Punt Road on his way home. He's still a big Bombers supporter – and a really good artist, according to Aaron's mother, Vicky. She says he paints with his fingers because he can't hold a brush. There you go, Aaron thinks. One minute it's all going good and the next it's not. A bit like your mother kicking you out of home. No, nothing like it at all, really.

Under the warm sun, with the comfort of the heroin still with him, Aaron lies back down on the faded hardwood boards of the porch, imagining Vicky begging him to come back home. But that's not going to happen. Not while he's still on the gear – she has made that very clear. The last straw was stealing from her. He wishes he hadn't, but he couldn't help himself. It was bad before that happened anyway. She had been badgering him to see a counsellor for months, but he kept refusing and she just got more and more angry with him. She believes it's the only way he can deal with what happened to him. He simply can't go there, not with a complete stranger. It's too hurtful, like probing for a splinter buried deep in flesh.

'How long have you been here?'

He opens his eyes and sits up to see Vicky silhouetted in front of him.

'A couple of hours.'

She moves past him to open the front door and he follows her into the dark hallway, past her bedroom before stopping outside his old room. He peers in to see that she has converted it to a sewing room with his single bed covered in fabric.

'Curtains for the front room. Now, jump in the shower and I'll chuck your clothes in the machine.'

A poster of the North Melbourne 1999 premiership team is still on the wall of his bedroom alongside pictures of his favourite musicians cut from magazines. She's kept those at least. His cupboard and drawers have been emptied of clothes and shoes, but he'd stopped wearing them anyway. It's funny about the curtains, he thinks as he empties his backpack. She's been talking about making them since his father left, or was told to leave – he's not sure which. He just remembers the ten-year-old boy blaming himself for the shouting and crying he could hear beyond his closed bedroom door. Vicky returns to toss him her pink tracksuit pants and top.

'I'm not wearing those.'

'Go naked then, I don't care.'

Aaron undresses in the bathroom and drops his clothes out into the hallway. The shower water feels luxurious on his skin, another reminder of the comforts of home. Suddenly, he remembers the piece of paper and phone number in the pocket of his jeans. He flies out of the shower leaving the water running, grabs a towel to wrap around his waist and hurtles through the lounge room to the laundry where Vicky is about to close the door to the front-loader washing machine. He scrambles a hand around inside it searching for his jeans while she complains about all the water he is dripping through the house. He takes the folded piece of paper from the pocket and puts the jeans back in.

'What's so important?' she asks.

'It's a job.'

He turns and heads back toward the shower, not wanting an interrogation. She calls after him.

'Why don't I believe you?'

Aaron walks into the open-plan kitchen–lounge area at the back of the house wearing the pink tracksuit. She looks up from whisking eggs at the bench with a big, spontaneous smile.

'Very cute.'

He shakes his head with a mix of annoyance and embarrassment. He picks up her guitar from the stand next to the television and plonks himself down on the couch.

'I'm making an omelette. Is that okay?'

He nods as he strums a few warm-up chords on the Fender steel string. It's only three-quarter size but it has a nice sound and he's pleased that he resisted the urge to hock it. That would've been one step too far. He starts adjusting the tuning, and Vicky immediately throws him a 'what are you doing' look.

'I'll change it back, don't worry.'

Tuning completed, he starts to play Nirvana's 'Something in the Way', with its haunting tone. The lyrics reflect Cobain's own experience of living underneath a bridge, with a leaking tarpaulin and making pets of the animals he traps.

Vicky listens as he continues through the first verse, pouring the beaten eggs into the frying pan before joining him on the chorus. She has a lovely voice and they blend beautifully together. Another verse and chorus, and the song ends with Aaron trying hard to hold tight to the sense of wellbeing their singing together has given him, but it evaporates with the gentle hiss of the gas flame under the frying pan.

They sit eating together at the small table next to the windows spanning almost the entire width of the rear of the house. The naked glass has been an issue since the renovations were done just after Aaron started school. Too hot in summer and too cold in winter. His father wanted venetian blinds but Vicki wanted to make her curtains, and it took them breaking up and Aaron getting chucked out for her to get what she wanted. Today the temperature seems just right, with an autumn sun leaking its warm rays onto the overgrown lawn and scattered pots of succulents. They finish their omelette in silence bar a few words here and there about the neighbours. Anya sold her house next door and has already gone back to Russia. Spiro, her much older Greek husband, died three years ago and left everything to her. Vicky never liked Anya. Called her a gold digger. She takes the plates to the sink and Aaron hears the short, sharp clearing of her throat, before a familiar uncomfortable silence. Instinct tells him something he won't like is coming, so he turns his attention through the glass to a blackbird flicking over a bare patch of dirt for a morsel of food. He doesn't want an argument; he wants Vicky to buy him a phone.

'One of my clients told me her cousin is on the methadone program.'

Aaron watches the blackbird fly off with a worm dangling from its yellow beak, dreading this conversation. He says nothing, hoping it will go away.

Vicky turns to face him with a heightened urgency in her voice. 'She said it's been really good for him: he's not chasing every day, he's not strung out, he's not stealing from his friends, from his family. He's even started working again.'

'Good for him.'

'I'll come with you. To the GP first, I think she said. Then whatever you need to do after that.'

'You had a good old conversation about me then?'

'Of course not.'

He doesn't believe her. Discretion is not part of her make-up. She returns to the table and sits down in front of him. He stares back at the determined look in her eyes; she's not going to let go of this.

'Mum, I know heaps of people who have been on it and none of them like it. It makes you constipated and rots your teeth.'

'It's not going to kill you, Aaron. Not like that stuff you put up your arm. For God's sake, can't you at least think about it?'

The temperature has risen sharply and he doesn't know what to say or do to bring it back down again. He just can't imagine living without heroin. But he can't tell her that. Her hand reaches out for his. It's warm and he lets her hold it.

'Every time there's a knock on the door, my stomach turns upside down. Can you imagine what that's like? How horrible it is?'

His eyes fall to the pink of the tracksuit screaming up at him. He pulls his hand from her, overcome with a feeling that his life is completely and utterly out of his control.

'How long before my clothes are ready?'

'I don't know, Aaron. Perhaps you could go and look,' she says with a heavy dose of sarcasm added to the disappointment.

Transferring his clothes from the washing machine to the dryer, his brain is calculating a pathway to the next hit. The need is growing in intensity and three ingredients for relief are dominating his brain waves: a number, a phone and the Man. He shuts the dryer door, selects the fastest dry option and *ninety minutes* blinks red on the tiny screen. Way too long but he has no choice. The clothes clunk around and around and around and he stays squatted in front of them thinking everything depends on the tactics. Oh, the tactics. Is working on them part of the attraction? Is it the sense of purpose it gives him? The hunter again, stalking his prey before returning proudly to his hungry tribe with a dead animal across his shoulders.

He goes back to the kitchen ready to launch his strategy.

'Have you got any weed?'

'You know I have.'

'Let's chill out then. Play some guitar.'

She cocks her head sceptically at him before draining the water from the sink. He wonders if he's overplayed it, made it too obvious. She knows him too well.

'Okay, I'd like that.'

They sit on the couch with Aaron playing riffs on the guitar and Vicky rolling the joint. He keeps an eye on it, hoping that it's not going to be too strong. For him, weed equals anxiety. It's never been his drug of choice. Unlike Vicky, who doesn't use anything else – doesn't drink, nothing, just likes to get stoned every now and then. It's her stress relief, and he knows that when he wants something, the best time to ask for it is when she's smoking. She blows a thick plume of smoke toward the open sliding glass doors into the backyard and smiles at him.

'I did a great job on your hair, didn't I?'

Taking the joint – 'You did' – he draws on it lightly and hands it back. 'What do you feel like singing?'

'"Drunken Angel",' she says without hesitating.

Okay, this has to be Vicky's way of telling him something. A Lucinda Williams song taking to task a friend for letting his demons get the better of his art. His name was Blaze Foley, a binge-drinking musician who wore duct-taped shoes and slept on pool tables and friends' couches. Foley was shot dead by the son of his friend after Foley accused him of stealing his friend's pension and welfare cheques. The friend chose to testify against his own son but was proved an unreliable witness because he liked a drink too. The son was acquitted on the grounds of self-defence. Aaron fits a capo to the second fret, rejects the offer of another toke on the joint and starts to play with Vicky. She is giving it all she has and sounding not unlike Lucinda, the country rock feel suiting her voice: strong and clear.

The joint is butted out in the ashtray and she turns to him with her best smile. This is his moment. But before he can open his mouth, she reaches across and squeezes his knee with her smile fading to a serious, almost nervous expression.

'I think you should go and see your father.'

Instantly, he feels like she has pushed him nose-first into a brick wall.

'Jesus, Mum, you've thrown that one in out of fucking nowhere.'

'Now his father's dead he might finally own up to abandoning you, for being the gutless fucking wonder he is!'

He feels her anger and it disturbs him. It's too close to the truth. He doesn't want to go there – certainly not now, and he can't even imagine a time when he would. He retreats to his search for comfort.

'I need a phone, Mum.'

She says nothing, giving him only the look of a mother whose last thread of hope for her child has been torn from her grasp. He gets up and walks to the rear windows to look out at another day turning relentlessly toward night. The blackbird returns to the dry dirt and cocks its head at him briefly before two spotted doves drop in unannounced and bully it back into the air. Seconds pass as he formulates his final pitch.

'We could walk down to 7-Eleven together. They're selling them for thirty-nine bucks.'

Her answer comes quickly and firmly. 'No.'

The pink tracksuit, his mother's rejection, the unrelenting need for relief, all driving him to his pleading voice. 'Come on, Mum. Please, please.'

'What have you ever done for me, Aaron?' she asks in a flat, sad tone that worries him even more. How to respond? What *has* he ever done for her? He takes a couple of steps toward her with the deliberate intention of adding weight to his delivery.

'I'm your son. And I love you.'

'I love you too, Aaron. But it's not enough anymore, is it?'

His eyes fall on her phone. 'Can I at least use your phone then?' The question delivered in a child's whining tone – *if you don't let me I'm going to be really, really upset!*

She says nothing. Her expression is blank, spent. She swings her feet up onto the couch, pushes a button on the television's remote control and waves him away dismissively.

He wastes no time reaching for her phone, his one-track mind already anticipating the call he is about to make. But something in his brain connects with the voice of the sports reporter emanating from the television. Enough to tell him that North Melbourne have had a mixed start to the season. There was a time when this would have interested him. After his father left, Spiro insisted Aaron go next

78

door to watch all the North games with him. He was a big soccer fan, but he eventually learned the rules and barracked as loudly as Aaron. Spiro and Anya had no children of their own and they always made him feel welcome. She had a habit of winking at Aaron behind Spiro's back. Was she flirting with him? He was never really sure. Her Russian accent was intoxicating, and her image was always with him when he first started masturbating.

The glass door slides open, interrupting the spotted doves' lovemaking antics, and Aaron steps onto their patch of dirt, punching in the numbers on the crumpled piece of paper he rescued from the wash. His restless legs keep him pacing in random lines as he waits for a voice to replace what seems like an interminable dial tone. He presses the mobile harder against his ear to stop his hand shaking, not breathing until he hears his voice, clear and authoritative.

'Donald Richmond.'

He takes a deep breath, trying hard to hide his desperation. 'It's me. Can we meet?'

'No. Not tonight.'

Defaulting automatically again to the child. 'But I really, really want to.'

There is a long pause through which he is a six-year-old boy looking up at his father, waiting for him to say yes, you can go, but only if you promise to be a good boy.

'I'll pick you up at eight.'

Aaron glances at the time on the phone. It is three-thirty.

'That's too long.'

The Man's tone leaves absolutely no room for negotiation. 'Outside Southern Cross. You know my car.'

The Man hangs up. Aaron turns to look through the glass at his mother staring blankly at the television and is overcome with a profound feeling of sadness. It is the same couch where they once sat together as a family every weeknight with meals on laps, watching *Neighbours*. Afterwards, his father, Max, would slide onto the floor to help Aaron follow the instructions on his latest box of Lego, until Vicky finally got her way and packed him off to bed. The happy house that was.

8

Aaron paces back and forth at the entrance to Southern Cross railway station. Above him, a web of metal tubes supports a rollercoaster roof with alternating clear panels through which a galaxy of stars shines in the jet-black sky. At street level, a myriad of lights from passing cars, street corners and empty office blocks add to his feeling of utter detachment from the world. He can see it and hear it, even smell it, but he feels terribly and utterly alone.

With his legs and feet aching badly, he sits down on one of the cube-shaped concrete bollards that prevent cars from accessing the large, open approach to the trains. Across its smooth surface commuters come and go, many with eyes on phones, some biting hungrily into snacks purchased from the food court, others knowing exactly where they're going, walking into the night with big, happy smiles.

A cold southerly wind blows directly up Spencer Street, and Aaron takes his clean hoodie from the backpack. Pulling it over his head, he smells his mother through the remnants of her favourite laundry liquid and it loads him up again with the guilt he carries for the way he treats her. She is the one person in the world he should be kind to always. Vicky believed him when he told her through sobs why he didn't want to go to Grandpa and Nanna's anymore. She told him she had sensed a sadness in him for a long time and now she understood exactly why. Max, his father, refused to believe that his own father would touch anyone inappropriately, let alone his own grandson. His anger was intense and Aaron felt every stroke of it. His parents argued furiously for days until Max did as Vicky demanded and confronted his father with what Aaron had told them he'd done. Grandpa, a religious ex-army man, said he was just teaching the boy simple anatomy, what it meant to be a man, the sort of thing every boy needed to know. He may have discussed a few things that might have appeared to some to be beyond the boy's years, but it was all innocent, completely innocent. Max chose to believe his father and not his son, so Vicky threw him out.

Somewhere in Aaron's mud-filled brain, a female voice registers. 'Hello, handsome.'

In front of him is the young woman from the Hare Krishna's in Albert Park. She looks different in clothes better suited for a night's clubbing and a face heavy with make-up – more beautiful than he imagined.

He stands up to face her with a shy smile creasing his cheeks. 'Hi.'

'What're you up to?'

He feels the same warm longing filling his chest as he did when he last saw her, but stronger and more urgent. The words tumble from his lips.

'Nothin' much. Just hangin'.'

A car horn sounds loudly beside them and they both look down at the front passenger window of a black Lexus as it slides silently open. The Man's head leans into the frame, making it very clear that he wants Aaron to get into the car, and quickly. In a millisecond, the lovely warm swelling in Aaron's chest is sucked out of him. He turns back to the young woman, who is still smiling at him.

'It's my grandfather.' It comes out easily, the lie. As if there could be no other explanation. He opens the car door, driven by an automatic pilot set on default.

'Hey!'

His head swings back to her.

'123 Stokes Street. Room 11. Okay?'

Oh God, he thinks, I love her. Then he is in the car next to the Man and the nauseating smell of his aftershave. Aaron sinks back into the soft leather seat, wired and incredibly angry as they accelerate up Spencer Street past a packed tram. From a dream to a nightmare, and he wants it over as quickly as possible.

'Where're we going?'

The Man brakes at the red light and turns to look at him. 'My place.'

'Where's that?'

'Little River.'

'No, that's too far.'

He smiles, as might an assassin before a kill. 'You can stay the night and catch the train back in the morning.'

A rat trapped. Neurons firing with the sound of the car's indicator – *click, click; click, click; click, click; click, click* – Aaron reaches for the doorhandle. Too late. The light turns green and the car is U-turning back down Spencer Street. The road is thick with cars.

'How much?'

'Two hundred.'

'Three.'

Their eyes meet briefly before the Man nods. It's a deal. Aaron allows himself to breathe with the thought of all that cash and what he can do with it while he searches through the bodies clogging the footpath for a glimpse of the long legs under the short skirt of his girlfriend, something to reassure him that their brief encounter was real ...

Nothing. Gone, somewhere into the night.

The car stops in the banked-up traffic.

'I've got to score first.'

The Man shakes his head firmly, and Aaron quickly decides he'll have more power negotiating from outside the car. He pulls on the doorhandle. The door stays shut. He tries again with more urgency before accepting that the Man has engaged the child safety lock and he's not getting out. The car moves slowly forward, and Aaron looks across at his captor. Another strategy.

'If I'm happy, you'll be happy.'

The Man is thinking, his very long fingers drumming away on the steering wheel. For the first time, Aaron notices that he is wearing a suit and tie again – not the dinner suit and bow tie from the night before, but an expensive suit, certainly, with a crisp white shirt and shiny gold cufflinks and highly polished black shoes. Everything about him says money, real money and opportunity. He sighs and looks at Aaron warily.

'Where?'

Aaron indicates for him to go left at the lights, toward the heart of the city. The Man turns on the radio to Classic FM but the piano concerto only vaguely registers at the back of Aaron's brain, now locked firmly in hunting mode. They stop on a red light at the busy intersection with King Street, infamous for its nightclubs, adult entertainment and late-night violence. It is still early. Aaron knows that around here, many will be looking to buy the drug that will keep them going through a long night. It won't be heroin; the main purveyors of that particular trade will be further in, closer to the laneways and customers looking to escape the night, not prolong it.

The lights change to green and they continue on up the street where the foot traffic is dominated by clusters of young men with bulging biceps, tight pants and pointy-toed shoes talking loudly and confidently as they strut into the night. The well-lit empty laneways hold no promise for Aaron: too shiny and too modern, just like the tall glass-fronted buildings reflecting a melange of taxis and trams and people back at him. As they approach the next intersection, the music shifts to a stringed quartet piece building tension like the score in a 1950s black-and-white gangster film with Aaron playing the highly agitated passenger turning to the driver:

'I need to get to Cuba, South America, anyplace where I can get lost.'

'You sound like you're in big trouble.'

'Yes I am.'

The Man smiles back at Aaron, the driver with all the control. The lights change to green and Aaron breathes slightly easier as they cruise slowly downhill with the dramatic music fading to the soothing voice of the announcer:

'That was Puccini's "Crisantemi" performed for you by the London Symphony Orchestra. You're listening to Classic FM.'

At Hardware Lane, Aaron finally sees them. A giant Maori man in a wheelchair with a petite Vietnamese woman outside the McDonald's store. He is eating a hamburger and she is smoking a cigarette: to Aaron's eyes, open for business. He asks the Man to pull into the car park next to them.

'Give me fifty.'

The Man holds his eyes on the giant. 'The fellow in the wheelchair?'

Aaron nods. The Man barely hesitates before pulling out his wallet and handing over a fifty-dollar note. This is a whole new world for him, Aaron thinks, and the bastard looks like he's enjoying it. Aaron gets out of the car, and as he walks toward his suppliers he is wondering where he'll shoot up. The laneway's too open and populated with people coming and going from McDonald's and the cafe opposite. Why not in the car? That'll show him something he hasn't seen before.

The dealers welcome Aaron as a regular customer, and one they obviously like. Aaron fist-bumps James, whose wheelchair story tells of a drunken late-night dive into a shallow river. Ping has been his companion since the accident. Aaron has met her son, who is about his own age, so he thinks she must be around forty years old; she's a smart operator who took control of the business after her husband was stabbed to death by a rival dealer. She likes telling people the wheelchair is a ruse to put the cops off. It also makes her customers think twice about ripping her off. James plays the role perfectly.

Ping butts out her cigarette and walks into Hardware Lane. Aaron follows behind, leaving James on lookout. The deal is done imperceptibly as Aaron and Ping walk side by side. In less than a minute, they are back beside the wheelchair.

'Who's the old dude, bro?'

All three look toward the Man in the car clearly watching their every move. The grandfather lie won't go down with these two, Aaron thinks, but an explanation is not needed. A knowing Ping touches him on the arm.

'Have a good night, sweetheart. You take care, eh?'

Then he is back in the passenger seat, U-turning away from them.

9

On the West Gate Bridge, the lights of the western suburbs shine through the high transparent railing installed after a father threw his young child into the river sixty metres below. The injected cap of heroin is flowing through Aaron's bloodstream and he would like the music changed – Triple R, please – but the words slip away before reaching his lips. He doesn't see or hear the semitrailer brushing past them, nor the 1967 Volkswagen Beetle struggling to get out of second gear directly in front of them. Aaron only sees the girl, the beautiful girl. Is she real? She must be. She told him where she lives. 123 Stokes Street. Room 11.

'Do you like music, Timmy?'

In his semi-conscious, blissful state, Aaron sees the suit, smells the aftershave, feels the leather: stabbing reminders of where he is and who he's with. The drug soothes him, protects him. He nods – or thinks he does – yes, he likes music very much.

'What sort of music are they teaching you at school?'

School? Did he really ask that? Or is it a question from the past echoing in his head, a question he doesn't want to hear, or answer, so he doesn't? The semitrailer veers left under a well-lit exit sign and the Man steers straight ahead on the M1, a four-lane highway lined with giant power poles, light industry and warehouses before the lights of new housing estates appear in clusters across the dark landscape. A voice in Aaron's foggy brain is pressing questions at him. *Who is he? Where is he taking you? Don't you think you should get to know something about him, be better prepared for what's to come?* He gazes at the man behind the wheel as if he is a specimen in a scientific study.

'What's with the suit?'

The Man turns to him, smiling, superior. 'Why do I like to wear suits, you mean?'

'Whatever.'

'That's a good question,' he says while pondering his answer. 'I've always worn suits. I have several. And I have a dinner suit for Lodge. You saw me in it last night.'

Aaron doesn't want to remember last night. He tries to drift completely back into the soft, safe clouds in his head, but there is that voice again telling him to pay more attention. Stay alert, Aaron.

The Man checks the rear-view mirror before crossing to the left lane.

'We wore suits at school,' he goes on. 'Well, a blazer and trousers. And I wore a suit to church. Not everyone did, but I did. Still do.'

'Do you wear a suit to bed?'

'No, Timmy, I don't.'

He wants to say his name's not Timmy but very quickly decides against it. The pseudonym shelters him. He stares out through the passenger window into the pitch-black landscape with a niggling wariness poking again at his consciousness. What is waiting for him at the end of this road? He hears the *click click click* of the indicators, and the car slides left into the exit lane to Little River before looping back across the M1 to head directly toward a gathering of granite ridges lying across the western horizon under a dark, starlit sky. Aaron wants to keep his captor talking because it offers reassurance, real or imagined. He searches his slow brain for the right questions, but all inspiration is carried away with the dream-like piano and cello piece playing through the car stereo. In the gaps between the gentle notes, he hears him speak.

'It's beautiful, don't you think?'

Even though the cello touches a deep sadness in him, he has to agree: it is beautiful.

'Gymnopédies One, Two and Three. Composed by the Frenchman Eric Satie in 1888. He named it after an Ancient Greek rite performed by naked youths.'

He is smiling at Aaron again. A familiar, hungry smile. So many reminders. Too many. Aaron turns away from him to the headlights on the straight road and the granite outcrop looming larger beyond. Something about the way the peaks roll across the horizon triggers a memory in him – but it seems impossible. He has never been this far from the city, so he dismisses the thought quickly. Instead the distilled, unrushed notes of the piano and cello help him find an image of a three-year-old boy clinging tightly to a woman's legs. It's his mother, Vicky. He no longer hears the voice of the Man at the wheel, just the music and his mother telling him everything is going to be okay. He sinks peacefully into sleep.

The *thud, thud, thud* of tyres on a metal cattle grid and Aaron's eyes slit open to a narrow gravel driveway enclosed on both sides with dark pine trees that seem to go on forever, eventually opening out into a stately courtyard illuminated by an automatic security light. The Man steers the car past several rows of perfectly pruned rose bushes and around a large tiered water fountain. He parks close to the front door of the modest light-green 1940s Californian bungalow. Its only nod to the faux regal entrance is a gold plate fixed beside the front door bearing the name *Enfield House*.

The interior of the house is a mirror reflection of the Man: the covers on the lounge-room furniture pulled tight like a newly pressed suit; the matching cushions arranged with precision, the paintings and photos on the wall thoughtfully hung and perfectly level; the blackwood dining table as shiny as his shoes. Aaron watches him putting on an apron in the kitchen. What is he doing?

'I made some gnocchi earlier. It won't take me long to heat it up.'

Ah, he is being nice. Don't do that please. It's too confusing, too recognisable and too painful.

'I'm not hungry.'

'It will be ready in twenty minutes.'

'Can't we just do whatever it is you want right now?'

'But I have exactly what I want already, Timmy. You with me, here, in my home for the whole night.'

All Aaron sees is the Man walking toward him, a slightly comical old man with his chef's apron over his suit and tie. His thinking feels slow, but it isn't. In an instant he reassures himself that he is sufficiently out of it to cope with whatever this man throws at him. His eyes find the digital clock with large white numbers showing it is precisely 10pm. Time is still on his side. The Man places his hands on Aaron's shoulders and leans into him. Oh, the aftershave.

'Why don't you have a shower while I get our dinner ready.'

'I had one already. This morning. At Mum's.' He mentions his mother because he wants him to know that someone will notice and care if he goes missing.

'Well, today you're having two showers. Off you go.'

~

Aaron steps, dripping wet, out of the glass-panelled shower and reaches for a towel from the carefully folded stack on the shelf, all the same lilac colour that matches the flowers on the wall tiles. Seeing a blurred image of his skinny body behind the fog on the mirror, he doesn't wipe it clear. He prefers the pretence that it is someone else, someone he doesn't know.

They sit opposite each other at the blackwood dining table, now covered in a white lace tablecloth. Classical music led by a violin is playing softly, a piece Aaron vaguely recognises, which surprises him. Something from a television show perhaps? He pushes his silver fork into a piece of gnocchi and places it in his mouth as Donald tops up their glasses with red wine.

'It's a new recipe. I've cooked gnocchi many times before, of course, but never with a burnt butter, sage and walnut sauce.'

Aaron is not hungry, but it tastes nice so he tells the Man so and they sit together eating and sipping wine with the music playing and no conversation. Despite the drug in his system, the prolonged silence between them is making Aaron anxious, and it's not helped by the self-satisfied smile he sees across the table every time he looks up. Once again, Aaron looks for reassurance in conversation.

'I've heard this before somewhere.'

'Then you must have seen *There Will be Blood*?'

'Yeah,' he says, remembering he watched it with his mother not long before she kicked him out.

'It's Johannes Brahms's concerto in D Major. We hear it at the climax, after the Daniel Day-Lewis character says, "I'm finished!" It has to be one of the most perfect uses of classical music in a movie. Don't you think?'

Aaron nods, not because he knows, only because he feels the need to agree. It makes him feel safer. Returning to pick at his food, his gaze is drawn for the first time to a series of framed photographs on the wall behind his dinner companion. The largest shows the Man beaming proudly in his dinner suit with white gloves and white bow tie. At his waist is a dark blue apron with gold frill and gold symbols matching those on his elaborate gauntlets and chain collar. Behind him is an Australian flag next to a row of smiling men, also in dinner suits but with light-blue aprons and significantly less decoration. The Man is obviously of higher ranking. Aaron's curious eyes scan further up to the top photo showing an enlarged replica of the decorative apron with an image of an eye in the centre of a triangle and rays of light emanating from it. Now that he has seen it, it doesn't matter where he looks, the eye follows him, boring into his brain and unnerving him. Once again, he needs a distraction – anything to ground him before his imagination runs too far away. The question leaps out of him.

'What the fuck is that?'

The Man's head turns to follow his pointing finger. When he looks back, his smile has disappeared behind hard lips and his words are stained with irritation.

'That? That is the apron of a Master Mason. My apron, in fact.'

It's all going in the wrong direction now for Aaron. Somehow he needs to pull it back, and quickly. In the fog of the moment, he is instinctively honest.

'It's the eye.'

The Man appears to grasp it immediately. He is smiling again, filling his lungs with air before standing, then pausing as if he is about to make a statement of great importance, one in which he has a great deal of personal pride. He steps to the wall as if it is a blackboard and he is the teacher.

'This, my boy,' he says, pointing at the eye, 'is the Eye of Providence. It symbolises the omnipresence of the Great Architect of the Universe, a reminder that our thoughts and actions are being observed by a force greater than us.'

As the Man talks, Aaron allows himself to sink back into his soft, drug-induced cocoon. Perhaps it will stay like this, he thinks. This man will just keep on talking and then the morning will come and Aaron will go back to Melbourne stoned on what he has left in his pocket and cashed up to keep it going. Life is sweet and his question rolls gently across the table from his lips.

'It's a religion then?'

'No. It's Freemasonry.'

Aaron's head falls to one side. Explain please. Keep talking so I can think about something else. The Stokes Street Girl. Donald needs no prodding.

'Freemasonry is an organisation of men connecting us with the stonemasons of the Middle Ages. When they were building the cathedrals, they wore leather aprons to protect them from the stone chippings. This one is purely symbolic, of course. Instead of cathedrals, we're building ourselves into better people. That's really what Freemasonry is all about.'

Aaron can see the Man's lips moving, but the words float like balloons, going nowhere. Aaron is with the Stokes Street Girl in one of the glass cabins on Melbourne's Observation Wheel, one hundred and twenty metres in the air. She is scared of heights and he is holding her tight with the sweet smell of her shampoo in his nostrils. A heavy tapping sound brings him reluctantly from his reverie to the Man's finger on the symbol below the eye.

'Here we have the Square and Compasses. Probably one of the oldest and arguably one of the most recognisable symbols in the world.'

Aaron sees what looks like the steel compass set his father gave him when he started school, telling him it would come in handy one day. It never did. He lost it somewhere and told his father another boy must have stolen it. It wasn't the first lie he had told but it was the first time he realised he was quite good at it.

'The circumscribed circle drawn with a pair of compasses defines the boundaries we set between ourselves and others. The self-restraint and moderation circle is our foundation of wisdom and morality.'

There's that word again, thinks Aaron. Morality. His grandfather, being a religious man, often described others as lacking any sense of it. Then Aaron would be left alone with him for several hours and the word seemed as though it must have another meaning. All very confusing for an eight-year-old boy.

He watches the Man sip from his wineglass then return to his blackboard and his pride-filled lecture. His long, thin index finger traces the right angle depicted below the compasses. 'You can see the square here on this apron – an apron worn only by a Master Mason, as I told you, if you were paying attention.' He points at the photograph below the apron. 'Here I am following my election as the Master of the Little River Lodge.'

Aaron nods his acknowledgement like an attentive schoolboy. The Man barely takes breath, pushed on by a large dose of self-importance.

'The square was used by stonemasons to make sure the stones were perfectly aligned. Today, for us Freemasons, it symbolises our ability to determine how right our actions are.'

He pauses to peer down at Aaron with a look that says he is very pleased with his presentation.

'Now, my boy, do you have any questions?'

Aaron looks at the gold letter *G* between the compasses and the square. The voice of experience is telling him that it is safest to be compliant, to fake interest.

'What's with the *G*?'

'Ah. A bright little boy like you should be able to tell me that.'

I am not a little boy! The words rise with force in Aaron's brain but he keeps them locked away. 'It's God,' he says with disinterest.

'Yes, it could be God, but as I said, Freemasonry is not a religious organisation. However,' he says, raising high his index finger, 'to become a Freemason one must believe in the existence of a Supreme Being.'

The Man is holding his wineglass as he glances up at the ceiling like a priest before a kneeling parishioner receiving Holy Communion. All that is missing is the bread. Aaron seizes the moment to swing his eyes to the digital clock and back again without the Man noticing his inattention. It is almost 11pm. Time is doing what it always does and he needs the inevitable to happen soon, while the drug is still fully protecting him. The Man puts his glass down on the table and steps closer. Aaron instinctively feels for the small insurance package in his pocket and forces himself to breathe.

'There is another possible meaning for our *G*. What do you think that might be?'

Aaron's got no idea, but this is good, he thinks. He can play the submissive role he knows so well to hurry things along. No words are required; his body language does it better. The hungry man steps even closer, almost standing on Aaron's toes.

'In the past, geometry helped the masons achieve perfection with their buildings, and it is the same for us Freemasons today. We are striving to make ourselves as perfect as possible. So, you could argue, as I do, that the letter *G* represents both geometry *and* a belief in a Supreme Being.'

Aaron watches the Man's hand reach across the aftershave-filled air between them. Then he feels long fingers running through his hair.

'You really are quite beautiful.'

Instantly, Aaron is taken to a place from which he must escape. It is there within, a bruise upon his soul. Entering the Man's bedroom, his brain scrambles for a distraction, unexpectedly projecting an image of his father, Max. Aaron allows it to stay with him. His mother's words have given him a glimmer of hope. Maybe Max will be more receptive to seeing Aaron now that his own father is dead. Aaron imagines standing with Max on the showroom floor of his dealership, among his new range of Mercedes-Benzes and the smell of polished duco, listening to him apologise for abandoning him. The Man's voice abruptly smothers the fantasy, and instead of standing in the showroom with his father, he is looking at his own image in a full-length mirror with an eager man in a suit hovering behind him.

'We'll undress now.'

Aaron undresses thinking only of the point of heroin in his jeans pocket and that moment in about four hours when he will mix it with water and inject it into a vein in his arm. He avoids looking at the naked seventy-something man to focus instead on the king-size bed where he will be able to find some physical separation if this is where he is forced to sleep.

A symphony of wind and stringed instruments turns his attention toward the Man standing by a digital radio, a bottle of massage oil in his hand and delight pulsing from his eyes. The dramatic music makes Aaron feel like he's in a horror film, and for his own sake he needs to get to the end as soon as possible. He takes the bottle of oil, squirts some onto his right hand then reaches for the man's limp cock.

The Man slaps Aaron's hand away, his voice hard-edged. 'Don't do that.'

The orchestra's violin section is now forcefully demanding questions of the wind instruments, and their gentle, submissive answers only increase Aaron's sense of dread. The Man steps up to him and kisses his forehead.

'Sweet, sweet boy.'

Aaron keeps his eyes firmly closed. He doesn't want to smell him either, but that's impossible. His nose is full of his aftershave and his body odour. He hears oil being squirted from the bottle and then he feels the Man's oil-smeared hands slide across his shoulders and down his arms. Aaron knows this moment too well, the mounting tension between deep pain and ugly pleasure that always resolves in overwhelming guilt. There's no avoiding the guilt, he knows that, so he tries again to go to another time and place. The music from the radio shifting gear to a lighter clarinet-led piece helps him to conjure a time with his father at the Melbourne Cricket Ground watching North play Fremantle. It is half-time in a close match, and the Little League games are being played across the arena. He is watching on keenly because he will be eligible to play himself after his ninth birthday. Max goes off to buy them both a pie and chips, and almost immediately Aaron feels a hand touching his thigh under the blue and white picnic blanket that has been keeping him warm. He turns and looks up into the smiling face of his grandfather. Always there, waiting.

~

It is 5am and still dark. Aaron is lying fully dressed on a banana lounge in the Man's manicured backyard, his veins streaming half a point of brown heroin through his body. As the night departs slowly for the dawn he nods on and off, on and off, until his eyes open fully to a great carpet of bright yellow canola flowers rolling out from the Man's back boundary to the foot of the waking granite peaks known as the You Yangs. He feels the urge to walk through those yellow flowers, to climb the ridges undulating across the horizon, and to yell abuse at the world below. But he hasn't the energy to do that.

The faintly familiar shape of the ridgeline teases him again until his attention is diverted to an axe leaning against neatly stacked firewood under sheets of corrugated iron. Nearby is a small pile of wood waiting to be split. He has seen it done on television but has never held an axe, let alone wielded one, so he walks across to pick it up. The handle is smooth in his grip, and he wonders why red electrical tape has been wound halfway along its length. To protect the Man's soft hands, he thinks as he positions a block of wood in front of him ready to be split in two. He raises the axe awkwardly above his head, and when he brings it down the head glances off the edge of the hard wood and slices through the lawn into the clayey soil below it. That's exactly where he leaves it.

He walks into the kitchen quietly, enjoying his time without the Man wanting him. It is six o'clock and he hears only his snoring. He goes to the fridge and opens the container of leftover gnocchi, grabs a fork from the drawer and goes out through the front door to the morning sun warming the courtyard. The driver's door of the Lexus is open and he slides in behind the wheel to finish off the gnocchi. Nicely stoned with a full stomach – if only he had the keys. If only he could drive.

A fist bangs hard on the window and Aaron looks into the angry eyes of the suited Man. The car door swings open.

'Move over.'

Too abruptly, the world is rushing at him, aggravating him. He badly wants to return to his warm cocoon but does as he's told and slides uncomfortably across to the passenger seat. The Man shoves his backpack at him before handing over two hundred dollars.

'Three. You agreed.'

'I agreed to you being with me all night. That includes being there next to me in the fucking morning.'

He's angry and Aaron knows it's better not to react to it. Two hundred is a bonus whichever way he looks at it.

'Will you teach me to drive?'

The Man shakes his head and sighs, and Aaron senses his anger dissolving. 'I might,' he says as he starts the car.

With the gravel crunching under the tyres, they drive around the fountain at the centre of the courtyard, past the roses and the green lawn and down the pine tree-lined driveway to the cattle grid, where they meet a white Toyota ute turning in off the main road. The Man brakes to a stop and opens his window to greet the driver warmly. His name is Geoff. He has his elbow propped casually on the doorframe, a rolled cigarette burning between his fingers and a wide smile on his lean face.

'Thought I'd have a look at those rotten weatherboards for you, Mr Richmond. Not a good time?'

Aaron decides to look at Geoff. Their eyes meet and the Man is forced to explain the young man sitting beside him. He makes up a story, delivered spontaneously – and, Aaron suspects, partly true. He probably did work for Community Corrections and may well still be in contact with former colleagues, but he's definitely not providing a probationer with extra support to get him back on his feet. Aaron is sure he sees a flicker of doubt in Geoff's eyes, but very quickly the two men are conversing freely as brother Freemasons. Of course, his story fits: the Man is the Worshipful Master of the Little River Lodge engaged in helping out the less fortunate, as every true Freemason does. Geoff offers to come back another time, but the Man tells him to go on ahead. He won't be long, just dropping the young man at the station.

Neither of them says a word on the short drive to the Little River train station. The Man's secret sailed close to being revealed, and Aaron feels like the scales might have shifted in his favour. The exchange with Geoff showed him that there is some power in their secret, something he can take advantage of one day, maybe. But as he glances across at the Man behind the wheel, he senses that he is thinking the same thing. He's going to end it, to nip any advantage Aaron's thinks he's gained swiftly in the bud. They turn into the train station car park and stop in front of an 1860s bluestone building with a red iron pitched roof and every window and door boarded up. The Man turns off the motor and turns to Aaron, self-assured, cocky even. He is driving this car, in control and infused with desire.

'Our arrangement has a future, Timmy. But only if you do exactly as I want. Is that clear enough for you?'

10

Aaron sinks back into the comfort of his V/Line train seat and closes his eyes to concentrate on what lies ahead of him. He feels good with the Man's money in his pocket, which is enough to give him a sense of freedom he hasn't felt in a very long time. It has been five hours since he last used and anxiety would normally be growing in partnership with the stomach cramps and the restless legs. Not today. Relief is guaranteed: he doesn't have to chase it, to scam anyone, to rip anyone off. The gentle rocking rhythm of the train is helping him to relax and avoid the dark reminder of what he had to do for the money.

Through the window he gazes at the flashing parade of brand-new houses in brand-new suburbs spreading across the flat volcanic plains. On the grassed fringes, wooden frames are being erected on ground where a great network of Aboriginal clans lived for thousands of years before invading Europeans claimed it as their own, fencing it off for their farms, and now subdividing it. Aaron sees only the identical brick houses with their double garages, grey roofs and colour-matched roller doors.

Suburbia eventually gives way to the city's high-rises dominating both sides of the train tracks. Aaron is concentrating on what lies ahead, a short-term plan starting with a rendezvous with Dave, quick and sweet, and then to the Stokes Street Girl and the promise of love. Behind him a woman starts talking loudly on her mobile phone, and without warning his contented thoughts are invaded – *You need to talk to your father, Aaron.*

No! Why did she say that? No. He can't do it. He won't do it. It would be too hard. Nothing would change. He knows that. Or does he? Agitation forces him to his feet and he waits impatiently by the carriage door, shifting his backpack back and forth on his shoulders as the train rolls slowly into Southern Cross Station.

Striding up the stairs from the platform, he fixes his mind on what is waiting for him at Dave's. He needs a well-timed tram directly to the source. First things first though, he needs to get through the closely guarded station barriers without a ticket. But he's not expecting it to be a big problem; it never has been, even if it's meant copping a fine and then ignoring it. The only issue is the time it takes to deal with the officious guards. Today he's in luck: a family of tourists are getting advice from a V/Line employee at an open double gate reserved for wheelchairs and prams. He gets through it without being noticed and within minutes is on a crowded tram crossing the Yarra River with anticipation consuming him.

It is a short walk from the tram stop to the northern slope of Emerald Hill and the Town Hall, where a catering truck is delivering trays of food through the rear door. Aaron crosses to Layfield Street and walks straight into Dave's room to find him sketching on a large sheet of white paper sticky-taped to his easel. Aaron peers over his shoulder to look at a charcoal drawing of what is obviously a teacher – no, a headmaster – propped up on a desk, his oversized legs crossed and a whip held menacingly across his lap.

'That's real good, Dave.'

'You heard about Timmy?'

'No.'

'Overdosed.'

'Fuck, not again. Where is he now?'

'In the morgue.'

Like being hit in the stomach with a wet football. He can't breathe. He wishes Samantha was there to comfort him. But she's not. There is only Dave. Aaron chokes back tears but he can't stop the snot running from his nose. He wipes it away with the sleeve of his dirty hoodie. Dave leans back from his easel, cocking his head from one side to the other, inspecting his work.

'I take it this's not a social visit.'

'I've got money.'

'Good for you.' He puts down his charcoal, goes to the drug drawer next to his unmade bed and opens it with a questioning glance back at Aaron, who has been considering doubling his usual order. Why not? He has the money. But in this moment, with Dave's eyes on him, he dismisses it. He likes the social aspect of doing the deal when he has money in his pocket.

'Just the fifty.'

Dave walks back to pass over a neatly wrapped foil in exchange for the cash. They face each other with the spectre of Timmy filling the space between them. Dave extends his right hand toward Aaron, making him think he's about to touch him in some consoling way. It doesn't happen.

'You'll be right,' Dave says, and goes back to his easel.

Aaron steps out into the hallway on autopilot, his eyes glancing up to the stairway landing wanting to see Timmy's gap-toothed grin, but there is only pain laid upon pain. He walks into the urine-smelling communal bathroom and works quickly at a sink to prepare the hit, thinking he could easily double the dose. Is that what Timmy did? Or did he just underestimate the purity? He's not here to report back this time. A resident walks in, sleepy-eyed, three-quarter polyester pants, bare-topped. He goes into a cubicle and locks the door. Aaron squeezes the plunger on the syringe to the sound of him shitting.

Men in tuxedos and women in evening dresses gather on the steps and around the pillars of the Town Hall while police motorcycles escort a white limousine to park directly in front of the building. Aaron skirts by, seeing only a blur of colour, and crosses the street. Two doors down, he stops at the front gate to his mother's house, wanting to go in and tell her Timmy is dead, wanting her to hold him close and make everything better. But he knows she will ask how he died and then they'll argue. Of course they will. She will make it all about the heroin and not his friend. He won't cope. Not now, especially not now.

He adjusts the weight of the backpack across his shoulders and walks away, wishful thinking filling his head with an address and no idea where it is. He throws his arm out to hail a taxi crawling along Park Street and jumps into the front seat with the driver looking him over warily. He feels an unexpected surge of anger.

'I've got the money, mate, don't worry.'

The driver turns away and indicates to pull out into the traffic. 'Where to?'

'Stokes Street.'

'Port Melbourne?'

'Yep,' he says, remembering Samantha was evicted from a women's rooming house there for not paying the rent. It has to be the same one. But as the taxi accelerates away he starts to doubt himself. Was that really the same young woman he saw at the station? Did she really give him her address? As the two-storey co-joined Victorian houses, workers' cottages and leafy parks flash by, he becomes more and more uncertain about her. He sees the Square and Compasses symbol on the South Melbourne Masonic building – that's real. Further on, the dominating structure of the St Peter and Paul's Church where he was sheltered in the gardener's hut by Father Brian – that's real too. But is she? The questioning won't stop. By the time they turn into Bay Street, where expensive cars jostle for parking spots and shoppers search for a spare cafe seat, he has worked himself into a mild panic. The heroin he put in his veins in the bathroom at Layfield Street stopped the cramping and the nausea, but there is no contentment this time. There is only self-doubt, confusion and anger. Fuck you, Timmy.

'What number?'

'What?'

'Stokes Street's coming up, mate. Am I turning left or right?'

Aaron looks up to see that they are approaching a roundabout on a wide tree-lined suburban street.

'Let me out here.'

He pays for the fare and steps out onto the footpath where a line of workers sit on milk crates eating their lunch in front of the Swallow & Ariell Biscuit Factory, an 1840s building being converted to luxury apartments. Turning away from the high-visibility vests, Aaron takes a punt and goes right, away from the bay and toward the freeway end of Stokes Street. Past St Joseph's Church, next to it a modern town house, then a long row of wooden single-fronted cottages with numbers confirming he's made the right choice: 111, 113, 115 ... He slows down, wrestling with opposing voices in his head. One saying 'stop', the other saying 'go'. When he is almost at 123, he compromises and crosses to the other side of the street. He needs time to breathe and to think.

Stokes Street is a no-through road ending at its landscaped junction with a modern freeway. Aaron stands in front of an old stone hotel, now a private residence. Directly opposite is an almost identical old stone hotel that has been converted to a two-storey rooming house. The front door is propped open in the shade of a London plane tree growing strongly from the footpath. He can see a portion of the dark-red hallway carpet in the dappled light, but beyond that there is only the scary unknown. He fights the urge to walk away, to find a park nearby with a toilet block where he'll fill a syringe for Timmy, and for himself, to escape the ugly, blunt-edged emotions creeping through him.

'Hello, darling.'

His head turns slowly but with anticipation. Standing beside him is a woman he only vaguely recognises. She is older than his mother, with a round, soft face and thinning hair through which he can see her pink scalp. Tucked under one arm are two bottles of something in a brown paper bag.

'You're not here to see me, are you?'

Aaron shakes his head without even trying to find the words. She reaches out for his hand.

'Come on. I'm sure Zoe will be happy to see you.'

They cross the road hand in hand, and he remembers seeing her with Zoe (he even loves her name) at the Hare Krishna's. Her hand is warm and soft like her face, and he doesn't want to let it go. They stand together on the dark-red hallway carpet with sunlight streaming promise through a window above the stairway. A woman laughs in one of the ground-floor rooms as Aaron follows his new friend up the stairs, through the sunlight to the first floor and along the corridor to where they stop in front of Room 11. The woman smiles and starts to move away. He wants her to stay. Just until the ice is broken, that's all.

'What's your name?'

'Julie.'

She flicks her head toward the door as if to say, go on, you're a big boy, you don't need me to hold your hand. He watches her walk to the next room and disappear inside, leaving him to ponder the closed door in front of him. This is it, his big moment, his *Moment Critique* as his Under 12s coach was very fond of saying. He used it to describe those moments when a player did something to change the course of a game, like backing into a pack to take a mark. He was an old-fashioned guts-and-determination coach and loved acts of courage. Aaron was the smallest player in the team but he was runner-up in the best and fairest. The trophy was inscribed with the words *Courage Plus*. His father said he would come to the presentation, but he didn't. Not even a phone call to congratulate him. Aaron didn't play football again.

A deep breath and he knocks lightly on the door. Seconds pass, too many, with only the distant hum of freeway traffic. Then suddenly aggressive guitar chords and a drumbeat explode directly under him. He recognises Eddy Current Suppression Ring's 'Which Way to Go'. Stay or leave, he doesn't know. A verse, then a screaming voice somewhere else in the building. 'Turn that fucking music off!'

Another few seconds and the music stops abruptly mid-chorus. A distant car horn, a closed door, a park calling to him. He is at the top of the stairway when he hears her voice.

'You found me then?'

She is wearing green pyjamas and yawning, her hair now dyed pink. He wants to run toward her and hug her but his feet stay glued to the top of the stairs.

'Coming in or not?'

Of course he is. The blind on the only window snaps up to light up a small, narrow room with just enough floor space to accommodate a single bed, a white laminated wardrobe, a TV balanced on a wooden stool and a bar fridge under shelves constructed of milk crates and timber planks. Zoe jumps into bed, and once again he is frozen with indecision, needing her next instruction.

'Make me a coffee. There should be enough water in the jug. White, four sugars.'

Good, he can make himself useful, a distraction from overthinking. He puts the jug on, picks out two mugs and spoons the instant coffee in. Four sugars for her and the same for him. He needs the energy. While he waits for the water to boil, he scans the crayon drawings sticky-taped to the wall in front of him: bright-coloured stick figures of a woman and a little girl together with various pieces of playground equipment and the words *Mummy* and *Ella* written across them. She has a child. That's not part of the script.

'What's your name?' she asks.

'Aaron,' he says as he pours the hot water into the cups. Then, feeling a burst of confidence, he turns to her and smiles. 'And you're Zoe.'

'You've done your homework.'

He nods, pleased with himself as he adds the milk and hands her the mug. She tucks her legs up under the doona and pats an empty spot on the bed for him to sit. This is it now; he can't stop his imagination racing forward. He's in heaven, on a bed with her, filling a giant hole in him. It's the heroin too; he knows that as he sips his coffee and looks across at his backpack near the door. It spills out of him without a second thought.

'I've got some Harry.'

'No thanks.'

He feels her feet move back from him.

'But you go for it, if that's what you want.'

He's fallen off the wave now, paddling hard but going nowhere.

'No, it's okay.'

No, it isn't.

'Later maybe.'

No, later definitely.

They sip their coffees.

'Did you have a late night?' He's getting better at asking questions, at avoiding the anxiety-building silences.

'Yeah, I'm working at a club. In King Street.'

'Okay.' Wow, he thinks. She's a pole dancer, she must be. All those pissed old men drooling over her. He doesn't want her to be a pole dancer.

'I'm a hostess.'

She pulls her knees further up under her chin. All he wants is to get into bed with her. Just the two of them wrapped up together just like he has imagined, laughing at funny stories, keeping out the doubt, answering the questions that are niggling away at him, the ones he's too scared to ask. Why did she tell him where she lives? Does she love him like he loves her? No, don't spoil it. Let it play out.

'How old's your little girl?'

She looks up at the drawings, a loving smile locked in place. She tells him that Ella has just turned three and lives with Zoe's ex's parents in Canterbury. Her ex is doing time, five years for attempted murder over a drug debt turned nasty. She was there when it happened, in possession and out of it on ice with Ella asleep in her cot. She's allowed supervised visits once a week only, in a playground. To get custody back, she has to show clean urine tests for twelve months and have a two-bedroom flat for them to live in. The smile fades to a look that tells him she is determined to do it.

'Okay,' she says as she bounces out of bed. 'We're going to the beach. I need some fresh air and vitamin D and you're going to tell me why you're so sad.'

~

He waits for her on the street below her room trying not to smile with too much anticipation, but it's proving difficult. She's let him leave his backpack in her room – she wouldn't do that unless she wanted him to go back up there with her. She comes out wearing denim shorts and a flannelette shirt, her feet bare, the April sun warm and bright. They walk side by side up the footpath toward a line of blue water spanning the gap between two tall buildings at the end of the street. He wants to hold her hand but resists the urge, content for it to be just more proof that he loves her. He knows this because of the two short but meaningful romances he's had. The first was with Katie in Year 9. He wanted to hold her hand and they did, constantly and comfortably for two months until she decided she wasn't ready for a serious relationship. He was devastated for a couple of weeks, then Katie's friend Monica invited him back to her parents' empty house where they had sex regularly for about a month. He tried holding her hand, but it didn't feel right at all. He liked her a lot but he couldn't pretend to love her.

At the roundabout they cross the street to avoid the workers and trucks and various pieces of building equipment at the worksite of the Swallow & Ariell Biscuit Factory. Aaron knows that the workers will have their eyes fixed on Zoe and it excites him. It's like he can believe that they really are a couple and he could yell back at them, 'She's my girlfriend and she doesn't like being fucking wolf-whistled, okay!'

The gap between the two tall buildings at the end of the street grows increasingly wider until they step onto the footpath running along Beaconsfield Parade with almost the whole width of Port Phillip Bay spread out in front of them. Zoe reaches out to take his hand and he breathes in, filling his lungs with sweet air and feeling deep within him the possibility of another way of being. Cars are rushing past in both directions and they run, stop and run again through four lanes of traffic, across the promenade then up the red-brick steps of a rotunda where they stand together laughing like teenagers who have just stolen a packet of cigarettes from the newsagent.

They watch a woman throwing a ball into the flat, calm water for her dog to retrieve. It returns to drop the ball at her feet before spraying her with droplets from its long black-and-white coat. A paddle boarder enters the water close to Station Pier where she is dwarfed beside the moored Spirit of Tasmania ferry. Cargo ships crisscross the bay's horizon, and closer in, small sailboats tack regularly to hold the breeze.

The long silence between them as they take in the panorama sparks Aaron's anxiety. He needs to talk before she begins her flagged questioning of his sadness, to hold on to the joy for as long as possible.

'What does a hostess do?'

He blurts the question out quickly, too quickly perhaps. She smiles at him in a way that makes him think she sees straight through the avoidance tactic. She turns away to look pensively at a father with a toddler filling a bucket with sand on the beach before explaining that a hostess is basically a waitress with more flirting and less clothes. The money isn't as good as the strippers but she's learned a few tricks pretty quickly, like taking the punters their drinks with most of their change in coins to encourage them to tip. She says you've got to put up with lots of creeps and weirdos and it certainly doesn't make you love men, but it's funny, she feels safer than walking on the street alone at night. There are lots of rules, the security guards are friendly and if a punter crosses the line then he's turfed out quick smart. She does feel safe, and there's the money she couldn't earn anywhere else that gives her the only chance she has to get Ella back.

They walk slowly along the beach past the father playing with his daughter and the woman with the bounding dog. Zoe wanders off into ankle-deep water, and Aaron sits down on the warm sand to watch her playfully kicking circles of spray into the air around her. He feels as content as he can imagine without heroin, just the two of them together in a world that is so intensely nourishing and joyful, but also so fragile. One false move, one false word. She walks toward him from the water with the towering red bow of the Spirit of Tasmania behind her. She is smiling, but not at him, and she sits beside him flicking wet sand from her pink toes, saying nothing. She is telling him it's his turn to speak. He feels it strongly.

'My friend died yesterday. Overdose.'

Still she says nothing, just a quick sideways glance at him then back to watch the paddle boarder sliding her board from the water up onto dry sand. He wants to show her strength. Yes, his friend has died but he's keeping it together. Her silence gives him an opportunity to take his time, to construct a story that will help stop the world he has created for them both from falling apart.

'I'm okay though. Better than I thought I'd be. Like, I haven't cried or anything.'

He picks up a handful of sand and lets it sift through his fingers wondering if he might have overplayed it, the false bravado. Should he have shown more vulnerability? Now he just wishes she would give him something, anything to drive away the doubt and the seeping anxiety.

'I've felt sad though,' he adds, perhaps too quick, too contrived. More doubt, more anxiety. He stabs his index finger into the sand, trying to free his thoughts.

'I can't help thinking he did it on purpose. He talked about it. Not heaps but, you know, every now and again. When he was pissed mainly.'

'What about you?' she asks, looking directly at him. 'Do you think about it, Aaron?'

He wants to say no, but her using his name disarms him, her eyes are so beautiful.

'Sometimes.'

A heavy cloud sweeps across the sun, the breeze blows cold and his stomach cramps. It's all heading in the wrong direction now. He feels it strongly. The paddle boarder quickly gathers her belongings. The man and his daughter and the woman and the dog are already scurrying toward the promenade and the line of parked cars. Zoe jumps up, brushes sand from her legs and shorts then reaches down for his hand. He doesn't want to leave, but he has lost all control now.

They cross Beaconsfield Parade slowly and separately. When they reach the other side, she turns and looks back at the dark weather now shadowing the entire bay.

'That changed quickly,' she says, but he doesn't respond. He can only look toward the other end of Stokes Street, the rooming house, her room, his backpack and the pencil case.

They walk in silence to the Swallow & Ariell Biscuit Factory conversion, where the workers are packing up their utes, their legs bare in khaki shorts, their muscled arms lifting and carrying. She smiles at them. He doesn't see it, but he's sure she does. They certainly smile at her. He looks down at his worn runners and his ragged-edged jeans reflecting his rapidly deteriorating mood straight back up at him.

'Why do you think about killing yourself?' she asks as they walk toward the immaculately mowed lawns of St Joseph's Church. A priest steps out from the red side door and stands with his hands folded, looking directly at Aaron as if imploring him to unburden himself. Tell her, my son. What troubles you?

'Can we talk about it later?'

'I'm going to work.'

'When you get back, I mean.'

'You won't be there when I get back.'

His heart sinks heavy to the bottom of his chest, sweating, nauseous, with a sharp-edged reality biting into his skin. He has one more card to play. The desperate card. He glances back at the priest, who nods at him. Tell her, my son.

'I love you, Zoe.'

She stops. So does he.

'It's not going to happen, Aaron.'

'You made me think that it was. Why did you do that?' He feels like a child stamping his feet.

'I gave you the wrong impression and I'm sorry about that. I'm on a mission to get my daughter back, Aaron, and that's where all my energy has to go. I can't let myself get too distracted. You're very sweet, but I just can't.'

The priest has gone now. There is just a bluestone building with a shiny slate roof and a cross at its peak reaching to the sky. Rejection. Aaron believes it is his fate, learned the hard way. There is no point in prolonging the pain. Accept the rejection and move on. And, of course, there is the heroin to help him.

Light rain is falling as they walk in silence to shelter under the leafy limbs of the plane tree at the front door to her rooming house. He says he is not going up to get his backpack and asks if she can drop it down to him from her window. She nods; yes, she will do that. Then she reaches out to hug him. He resists. It's not part of the 'escape quickly' plan. But she gives him no choice, and he melts into her sweet, salty skin and warm flannelette shirt. It is cruel bliss, and he is unable to hold back the tears this time.

'Be brave, Aaron,' she whispers, and then she is gone.

11

It's raining heavily, but he's dry enough. Zoe dropped his backpack down from her window with a thin plastic poncho tied to it. It is yellow, like the ones they hand out to the crowd at the MCG on a wet day. Umbrellas are not allowed, they block everyone's view. Water drips from his nose as he strides along Dorcas Street toward Emerald Hill where the stone clock tower high above the Town Hall looks proudly down over the gleaming wet rooftops around it, telling Aaron it is five o'clock. He feels good with his blood circulating the last of the heroin, injected in a park not far from Zoe's place. There's still an empty space in him where only a few hours ago there was something very nice, but the sadness and the anger have been diluted. Knowing there's enough of the man's money left to last him another two days adds to his sense of everything being okay, almost.

Aaron walks in through the front door of Layfield Street with his runners squelching water onto the stained carpet. He knocks on Dave's closed room door in wet socks and with a wet fringe stuck to the side of his head. The door opens and a big man, who Aaron instantly recognises as the resident who assaulted Timmy for playing loud music, brushes past him with a wink. Samantha is sitting on the bed eating a souvlaki, with Dave counting his money on the other side. She looks up at Aaron with an exaggerated look of sympathy.

'Oh, darlin,' she says, putting her half-eaten souvlaki down on the bed and standing. 'I'm so sorry.' She wraps her arms around him and hugs him tightly, unfussed by his wet clothes. He sinks into her warmth.

'Come, sit down next to me.'

He does as she says, expecting more comfort.

'I've got some news that'll cheer you right up.'

Okay, what could that possibly be?

'Me and Dave are getting married,' she says with a huge smile.

'Fair enough,' Aaron replies. What else can he say? He doesn't feel happy for them.

'I'm off the community treatment order now too. The lawyer sorted it for me. Dave wrote me an awesome reference, didn't ya, Dave?'

'I did,' he says as he slips the small stack of folded notes into his back pocket.

'He's gunna look after all my pharmaceutical needs from now on. And ... we might even have a baby. Eh, Dave?'

Aaron looks directly at Dave for confirmation, not believing it to be true. Dave gives Aaron an uncharacteristic sheepish look.

'Yeah well, I'm nearly fifty-five fucking years old so it's now or never, eh.'

Aaron looks across at a beaming Samantha wondering if she really believes it . He likes her, and he hopes it will turn out just as she hopes, but he doubts it.

'They're not cleaning Timmy's room until after the coroner's report,' says Dave, going to his drug drawer. 'Another fifty?'

Aaron nods and they do the deal with Dave talking all the way through it.

'One of the guys upstairs picked the lock so we could go in and pay him our respects. It means something, don't you reckon? That room. Him dead in it and all. Anyway, it's open, like I said.'

No, he doesn't want to do that. What would be the point? Samantha places a hand on his, smiling softly, empathically.

'Have a nice hot shower, dry your clothes and get yourself sorted. Stay the night, Aaron. Timmy would want you to do that.'

Her words are soothing and certainly practical. She holds out the half-eaten souvlaki to him.

'And here, take this. You need it more than me. Look at you. Like a drowned rat.'

'And I've got something else for you,' says Dave, going to the wardrobe to open the door hanging off one hinge. He picks through a dozen mobile phones before making a choice and tossing it across to Aaron with a charger wrapped around it. 'There you go.'

There you go indeed, thinks Aaron. He's not remotely hungry, but the phone is an unexpected and very welcome gift. He slides it into his pocket next to the heroin, aware for the first time how cold his skin is under his rain-soaked jeans and runners. Dave and Samantha are looking at him like parents sending their son off to his first school camp. It all seems very odd to him, as though he has entered another reality where one friend no longer exists and others are behaving in strange ways. Heavy rain pelts hard against the windowpane. The headlights of a passing car flash like lightning, its tyres spraying water from the saturated bitumen.

~

He opens the door to Timmy's room, takes a deep breath and feels for the light switch. *Click*. No one's at home, otherwise all is exactly as it was. The ghetto blaster next to the bladder of the wine cask, the clothes strewn across the floor, the yellow liquid in the juice bottle under the unmade bed, the overflowing ashtray and the pervasive smell of cigarette ash. Avoiding emotion is Aaron's well-practised strategy: concentrate on the practical. He feels the oil column heater against the wall. It's warm. Good. He takes his phone and charger and plugs it into the nearest socket, deciding that he'll turn it on only when he needs to make a call. The foil of heroin is hidden under the mattress and he pulls off his wet clothes and lays them over the heater, placing his wet runners on the floor directly in front of it. Completely naked, he searches through the pile of clothes to find a towel, smelly and stiff. He folds it around his skinny waist and goes back out through the door, closing it softly behind him.

He walks down the creaky set of stairs to the first-floor bathroom with the sound of three male voices rising up from the kitchen below. They are planning something, he can tell by the tone of their conversation.

The bathroom has four shower bays, all of them empty. He chooses the only one that is complete with two tap handles, a showerhead and a bar of soap. He locks the door, adjusts the temperature of the water and lets it fall over him, willing it to wash away the deep sense of detachment he feels, to connect him again to a familiar world. Through the fog, he hears a cistern flush, heavy footsteps and then a raw voice.

'Other blokes like hot fucking water with their shower too, mate!'

Aaron turns off the water and stands under the dripping showerhead until the heavy footsteps leave the bathroom and fade away up the creaky stairs. Drying his body quickly, he peers out from the bathroom door to check that he has a clear run back to Timmy's room. The bathroom visitor has reminded him it is better no one knows that he's staying the night. The clinking bottles and women laughing indicate a party is getting underway on the ground floor, but otherwise all is quiet. This time he doesn't switch the room light on – it would be seen under the door. The grey, rain-filtered light seeping through the small window from a nearby street lamp is enough for him to do what he has to do. He won't be reading any books. Music and heroin dominate his thoughts. Not yet the souvlaki, sitting cold and hard on the TV.

Dragging his backpack closer to the window, he searches through it to find his pencil case, a clean pair of jocks and a T-shirt. He tosses the pencil case onto the bed and pulls on the jocks and T-shirt with a persistent voice in his head telling him it is too early to shoot up. His response is to say he'll be careful, adjust the dose. Maybe. The irony of doing this in the same room where his friend died of an overdose two days earlier is not lost on him, but he has no fear and is desperate for complete comfort.

The ghetto blaster is tuned into Triple R, and Aaron immediately recognises the relentless synthesiser of the London-based post-industrial band, Factory Floor. The track is 'Lying', from their debut album, and Aaron almost smiles knowing that Timmy shared his enthusiasm for their music. He prepares the mix in the spoon to the driving, hypnotic beat of the synthesiser, heating up the murky brown liquid as the female voice joins in, her words oblique and sparse. His whole being is totally locked into the beat now: no thoughts, only heightened anticipation. The vein is pumped, the syringe loaded, and the plunger descends at the exact moment the drumsticks hit the floor tom and the violin bow smashes against the guitar strings. In a prolonged rush of euphoria, his eyes close and his head rolls back before he falls irresistibly asleep and descends into the world of a dream.

Timmy waves Aaron to an open door and leads him into a floating space that seems to have no ceiling or walls and is full of mute people either walking about aimlessly or simply standing. A very thin middle-aged man with a bass guitar in his arms turns to look directly at Aaron, who recognises him immediately as Dee Dee Ramone. Then it is Sid Vicious staring directly at him, young and angry with a heavy metal chain locked around his neck. Aaron hurries after a disappearing Timmy but is confronted by a bare-chested Jim Morrison with his long wavy hair framing his handsome face. Aaron thinks the young woman he sees is Janis Joplin, her face barely visible under a tangled mop of hair. He knows that it's Kurt Cobain beside her. Then there is only Timmy facing him.

'It was an accident, Aaron, waiting to happen. I drank too much and I used too much. I would rather be a live teetotaller than a dead addict.'

Then he is gone. Aaron searches desperately for him but finds only a woman, soft and grey, emerging from the fog. It is his grandmother.

'I couldn't bring myself to believe that the man I knew and loved could do the things he did to you. I turned my back on the truth and stayed silent. I'm so sorry for that, Aaron. Don't you stay silent too.'

Aaron steps toward her, his arms out, wanting to hug her, to tell her that he won't be afraid, but she vanishes before he reaches her. Materialising in her place is his grandfather, silver-haired, broad shouldered, imposing.

'How can a man be sorry for something that thrilled him so?'

Aaron squeezes the handle of the knife in his hand and, full of uncontrollable rage, he lunges at the old man, stabbing at him violently but meeting only air. Spinning around and around through the eternal dark space.

He is awake in a quiet room. Through the window he can see the moon in a clear black sky. The people in his dream are still with him, embedded in a mix of emotions soothed by the heroin. He longs to dance with Timmy again, for him to be here with him now, grinning and talking bullshit. He yearns to be comforted by the smell of his grandmother as she holds him against her flour-splattered apron. The anger he feels for his grandfather sits deep inside him, rock-hard and immovable.

He nods on and off until the dawn becomes the morning and the roads fill with traffic. A door slams shut across the landing and he swings his feet to the floor. The souvlaki still waits for him on the TV and he knows he should eat it, but he can't. His stomach is cramping and his anxiety is rising quickly. He only wants the dose of heroin he has left, and after that, his mother.

12

Aaron turns the corner into York Street and strolls to the entrance to the Spotlight and Woolworths shopping centre, where a grey-haired, bearded man is squatted on a blanket playing a didgeridoo with his beagle dog at his feet. Aaron looks down at the pile of coins in the busker's upturned hat and then into the contented eyes under the man's bushy eyebrows. He isn't alcohol- or drug-affected, Aaron is sure. Music and a dog – is that all it takes to be happy? Maybe he could try it one day. But not today. Two doors down, he stops and peers into his mum's workplace, where Naomi is preparing to wash a client's hair. She looks up to give him a broad, welcoming smile, and he pushes open the glass door to stand on the shiny black-and-white tiles, his eyes meeting his mother's as she looks up from taking a booking on the phone.

'Hello, darling,' Naomi says as she approaches him, drying her hands on a towel. He knows exactly what's coming. This time he doesn't automatically wipe her lipstick lips from his cheek; he wants to keep them there for a while, a reminder of the warmth and love she always shows him. The elderly client on the black vinyl couch peers up at him from her magazine. Her vacant look tells him that she is not in the salon waiting to have her hair done – she is somewhere else, far away. His mother puts down the phone.

'You look terrible,' she says as she walks toward him.

'Thanks.'

'It's not a good time, Aaron. I have a client waiting and ...'

'Take him next door for a coffee, Vicky,' Naomi interrupts as she massages warm water through the hair of her client. 'Shirley won't mind waiting, will you, Shirley?'

The elderly woman on the black vinyl couch shakes her head with a smile that says she couldn't be happier staying where she is for as long as it takes.

~

A young waitress carries two coffees and a chocolate muffin to Aaron and Vicky at a table in the corner of the tiny cafe. Vicky slides the muffin across to him, and despite the nerves rattling around in his gut, he breaks it in half and starts to eat it. She says nothing, and he

knows that she is waiting for him to speak first. He waits until the noise of the coffee grinder stops and he has swallowed the mouthful of dry muffin. Then he looks across at her just as the morning sun hits the shopfront for the first time, catching her face in its soft glare, highlighting a web of creases around her eyes that he notices for the first time. She shifts her chair slightly to avoid the light and gives him a look that says, come on then, get on with it. His hands are shaking, his voice uncertain. 'What you said about me going to see Dad ...'

'So, you're going?'

'If you come with me.'

She sips from her coffee then reaches for the sugar bowl. 'I just can't drink it without sugar. I've tried but it doesn't do it for me.'

He watches her stirring the sugar in, desperately wanting her to say, yes of course she'll go with him to hold his hand, to do all the talking. But she doesn't.

'It's between the two of you now, Aaron. Nothing to do with me, not anymore.'

Anger stabs at him, then when he sees the tears welling in her eyes it dissipates to a familiar sadness. He knows she has done everything she can to support him. It hasn't been enough, but it's not her fault. He knows that. It must only be his.

'I tried so hard to make him accept what his father did to you,' she says as she dabs at her tears with a tissue. 'But he chose to believe a cruel and despicable man instead of his little boy.' She reaches across to hold Aaron's hand. 'Ask him why he did that, Aaron. Will you do that? Please?'

Just the thought of asking his father that question terrifies Aaron. He turns away from her, and his eyes fall on a mobile phone left on a nearby table by a businessman paying for his coffee at the counter. When he looks back at her, she pulls her hand away from his. He can see she knows exactly what he's thinking and it makes him feel worse. This is who he is, completely exposed, an eighteen-year-old heroin addict too frightened to ask his father one question. They finish their coffees in silence, stuck in mud up to their knees.

They stand together on the footpath outside the cafe still without words, both knowing that it's all up to him now. She doesn't need to say it again, and he can't promise that he'll do what she asks. She wets a tissue on her tongue and rubs Naomi's lipstick lips from his cheek just like she did when he was a little boy. Then she is gone, leaving him standing in the steady flow of foot traffic feeling completely disconnected and utterly alone.

~

The bearded man is still playing his didgeridoo next to his sleeping dog, but Aaron takes no notice. His brain is too busy wrestling with the thought of visiting his father. He throws his backpack across his shoulder and walks away, head down, counting each step he takes up the street as a way of avoiding the anxiety and fear-provoking thoughts stabbing away at him.

He passes by a row of double-storey red-brick Victorian terraces, co-joined proudly, before stopping at the next corner. He has a clear view of Park Towers, a 1960s-built public housing estate twenty-nine stories high, with an expansive green space surrounding it. He sees himself walking with Timmy in their school uniforms and carrying their schoolbags along the concrete path to the lobby, then taking the blood-splattered lift to the rooftop where they'd drink stolen whisky and smoke stolen cigarettes until one or both of them vomited.

A passing truck brings him back to the street where he stands with sadness adding to the heavy weight of emotions he is already carrying. He turns away to walk the short distance to the grassed area in front of the Town Hall. There he picks a spot to lie down and allow the heroin he still has in his bloodstream to settle him before it's time to score again, and then maybe, only maybe, to visit his father.

'Hello, Aaron.'

Aaron doesn't want to open his eyes, but he does, already knowing by the slurred speech that it is Charlie Doyle in his wheelchair, his head tilted to one side, his long fingers clawed around the controls.

'What's up, Charlie?'

'I read in the local paper that there was an overdose at Layfield Street. Your mate, Timmy, wasn't it?'

Aaron nods. He doesn't want to have this conversation right now.

Even though it is Charlie.

'He seemed a nice young man to me. Always had a smile.'

Yes, he did.

'Not good. Shouldn't happen.'

No. Never.

'I'm really sorry for that.'

See you later, Charlie.

'I'm painting portraits at the market tomorrow. Small ones. Come down and I'll do yours.'

Definitely not, is his immediate thought. Posing for a portrait is for a time when the world is sweet and he is happy to expose himself to it. Certainly not now.

'I don't reckon, Charlie.'

'I got a grant from the council. There'll be an exhibition, and you get to keep yours when it's over.'

'I'll think about it, eh,' he says, knowing he won't.

The wheelchair whirs off leaving Aaron feeling pathetic in comparison to the man steering it around the corner. He hasn't been knocked over by a car and paralysed from the waist down. He can walk, he can run and he can speak without slurring his words. He lies back on the grass with a voice in his head echoing Zoe's words – *Be brave, Aaron!* And his mother's too – *You need to talk to your father!*

He glances up at the clock in the tower high above him. It is two-thirty on a Friday afternoon. His father, Max, will be in the showroom until at least six o'clock. Aaron has to control his nerves, he must stay calm. So he will visit Dave first. That's a no-brainer, really. If he doesn't, an hour from now he'll be fully wired: not good for staying calm and being reasonable. After scoring, he'll shoot up – not too much, because he needs to appear as normal as possible when his eyes meet Max's. He promises himself a reward when it's over.

~

As he turns the corner into Layfield Street, Aaron sees Dave putting his easel into the back of a rental ute parked directly outside the rooming house. Samantha follows him out to do the same with a bedside lamp. They're moving somewhere, Aaron thinks. The question is, why? He knows it won't be far away; Dave's a dealer who relies almost solely on his rooming-house clientele.

'Hey,' Aaron says as he joins them.

Samantha can't contain her excitement. 'We're moving to our own place, Aaron. We just decided, didn't we, Dave? You can't have a baby in a rooming house.'

'What sort of place?'

'Two-bedroom joint. On Moray. Right next to the milk bar on the corner,' says Dave, securing the load on the ute.

'Two bedrooms?' It wouldn't have to be a permanent thing, just somewhere to crash now and then.

Dave is on to him. 'Yep. Just me and her.'

Wishful thinking again; getting ahead of himself. 'You can afford that?' he asks, feeling the weight of disappointment.

'We've got both our Centrelinks. And Dave's business is going real good. Eh, Dave? He's expanding into new areas.'

'Tell the fuckin' world, why don't you,' Dave says under his breath as he disappears inside.

New areas. *What does that mean?* he almost asks a smiling Samantha, but doesn't. Right now, he doesn't care. He just wants to score and get going. He has an appointment he is dreading. He follows her into the room, where Dave is stacking up his collection of paintings and drawings.

'Can you fix me up?'

'He's on a mission, this boy,' Samantha says. 'Look at him. A bundle of nerves.'

'I'd better do as he asks, then,' Dave says as he goes to his supply.

Aaron asks him to double the order this time. He wants a break from them both. From the world at the moment.

'He's got something bothering him. I'm right, aren't I, darlin'?'

They exchange the money and drugs, and she is looking at him in a way that invites him to be honest with her. She has that 'tell me what's wrong and I will make you feel better' way about her. So he does.

'I'm going to see someone.'

'Who?'

'My father.'

She looks knowingly at Dave before turning back to Aaron. 'Well, you make him take some responsibility for what he did to you.'

'You know fuck all about his father, Sam. Jesus!'

'I've got one of my own, Dave. I know what they can do.'

Aaron picks up his backpack and slings it across his shoulder, thinking only of the route across the hallway to the communal bathroom.

Dave picks up his box of brushes and paints. 'Number two thirty-nine. Ring me before you come,' he says, leaving the room with his easel.

'It's our new policy,' Samantha says, sitting down on the solitary wooden chair, trying hard to look like the matriarch she isn't.

Whatever, Aaron says to himself as he shrugs his shoulders. If he has the money, he can score. That's all that matters.

'I can see things really clearly since I've been off the depot. Everything's going to be good, Aaron. It is.'

He wishes he could be so certain, but he is not convinced. Despite her kindness and current contagious enthusiasm for the future, he cannot ignore her history of losing touch with reality, especially when she goes off the depot injections. He genuinely likes her, and he can only hope that her faith in Dave as her doctor and pharmacist is not misplaced.

When he steps out into the hallway, Aaron immediately thinks of

Timmy. Out of the corner of his eye, through the open front door, he sees Dave rolling a smoke by the ute.

'When's the funeral, Dave?'

'Tomorrow some time.'

Aaron doesn't have to ask where. It'll be at St Peter and Paul's with Father Brian.

The rear fire door slams shut behind him, and he descends the metal staircase to the small concreted backyard. A cracked plastic chair is upturned on a patch of weeds in a sheltered corner, and he flips it over to sit down and prepare a hit. Music reaches him from the first floor of one of the Victorian buildings backing on to the laneway directly opposite the rooming house. Through the open window, Aaron sees a young man dancing to a song he has only heard once but recognises immediately as Dick Diver's 'New Start Again', the title track from their first album. The young man moves with the slow and distinctive rhythm of the bass guitar and drums overlayed with the jagged guitar melodies and catchy lyrics. The music and the dancing man offer Aaron some respite from the relentless tension overwhelming him. It helps too that Aaron is holding a syringe filled with the guarantee of relief. As the heroin enters his veins, a truck enters the laneway and its noisy diesel engine mutes the music completely. Aaron's moment of bliss is shared with a vision of himself as an eight-year-old, dancing to a silent soundtrack.

13

Aaron walks down the footpath, through the light industrial end of South Melbourne toward Kings Way, a major arterial road carrying multiple lanes of traffic to and from the city centre. He doesn't hear the cars or the sounds of industry because he is focused on his breathing – in and out, in and out – and on making sure his heavy feet move him in a forward direction. His nerves are calmer after the self-prescribed lower dose of heroin he injected in the backyard of Layfield Street. But still, he is filled with trepidation at the thought of meeting with the father he has seen only twice in eight years, on both occasions exchanging no more than half a dozen words. *Hello. How're you going? Not bad.*

The front glass door of an auto electrical workshop reflects his image like a mirror, and he pauses in front of it. He looks shit, to be honest. Samantha's right. He's got skinnier. He looks like a homeless kid. Running his fingers through his hair, he sees a stain he can do nothing about on the front of his hoodie. The door opens to a man in grease-covered overalls, and Aaron turns away to resume his trek. Too quickly, he reaches the intersection with Kings Way where, through eight lanes of Friday afternoon traffic, he glimpses the circular glass-panelled facade of Max Peters Mercedes-Benz a hundred metres away. The sight of his father's business name spread in large bold letters around the top of this ostentatious building anchors him to the footpath with fear. His immediate instinct is to retreat into the streets of South Melbourne, but a chorus of voices in his head are blocking him. He can hear his mother and Zoe and Timmy and his grandmother, and he can feel Charlie Doyle beside him, all of them urging him to keep going, to be brave.

He tells himself he can at least cross to the other side of the road and still be able to retreat. His hand reaches out to push the round metal button at the traffic lights, and while he waits for the lights to change, he feels his body rocking backward and forward like Samantha sometimes does on her antipsychotic medication. The rocking stops when the green pedestrian signal appears, and he steps out on to the road to feel the eyes of a dozen drivers on him, not happy that they've been forced to stop by a pedestrian. It gives him a welcome feeling of control, a reminder that he is not completely powerless. If only it was as simple as pushing a metal button.

Standing on the opposite side of the road with the traffic accelerating away from the lights, Aaron faces a cityscape dominated by clusters of very tall and shiny buildings, some still under construction, with cranes atop reaching for the clouds like disjointed metal fingers. A large, green sign spans the traffic, pointing the drivers north to the city or on to massive concrete ramps leading to the west and to the east. The silver circle and three-pointed star of the Mercedes-Benz logo seems to hover in the air above his father's business and what could be a source of great pain.

He feels his body rocking again, mimicking his scrambled thoughts. Forward or back, forward or back? Where are the voices telling him to be brave now, when he most needs them? Why isn't Charlie Doyle beside him in his wheelchair? Then he hears it under the sound of the roaring traffic – faint, but clear enough: the gruff voice of his Under 12s coach presenting him with his *Courage Plus*-engraved trophy. But this is not a game of football, with no time to think before backing into an oncoming pack and taking a game-saving mark. Somehow, he needs to channel that freedom from thought, otherwise he'll retreat to the streets to comfort himself with the contents of the foil parcel in his pocket. He closes his eyes to imagine himself running onto the frost-covered grass of a football ground with his Under 12 teammates. He sees himself jogging to his position on a wing and scanning the spectators scattered around the boundary fence, hoping to see his father among them. But he doesn't, and it makes him angry and even more determined to play well so that one of the other kids' fathers will tell Max what a great little player Aaron is, and how he should be very proud.

When he opens his eyes, that same anger and disappointment is still sitting solidly in him, driving him down the footpath toward his father with the help of his mother's voice returning to him at full volume: *Don't let him get away with it, Aaron!*

Before he realises it, he is walking through a ring of used cars in the display yard of Max Peters Mercedes-Benz and up to the tinted glass facade, feeling like he has just tackled a boy twice his size and been rewarded with a free kick directly in front of goal. All he needs to do is kick the ball through the two big sticks.

He takes a deep breath and peers through the tinted glass into the expansive showroom, where he sees his father with an expensively dressed woman inspecting an E500 Coupé . Max looks shorter than Aaron remembers him; perhaps it is because the woman is so tall. He has put on weight too, Aaron thinks, and lost more of his hair. His salesman's performance hasn't changed though. Still full of charm, with the perfectly timed smile and excessive hand gestures. It is something Aaron witnessed many times after school while waiting for his father to finish work. He went to his father, even though his mother's salon was closer to his primary school, because he was allowed to sit in the latest-model car, listening to music on the radio. He had just turned eight when he discovered Triple R while surfing the FM bandwidths and heard 'She Wears a Mask' from Machine Translations' album *Happy*. The catchy repetition of the one-line chorus stuck in his head. When he got home, he played around with his mother's guitar while she cooked dinner. He kept at it until he found the notes to accompany him singing the chorus. At first, she thought he was referring to *her* wearing the mask, but after he told her where he'd heard it, she was so impressed she booked him in for guitar lessons the next day.

Aaron watches his father open the door of the coupé for the woman to sit behind the steering wheel. He closes the door for her and his gaze wanders across the showroom floor to fall on his son looking directly back at him. Aaron sees the look of bored assuredness on his father's face replaced by shock and uncertainty, and it unexpectedly gives his confidence a boost. His Under 12 teammates are patting him on the back and telling him to go back and kick the goal.

Aaron stands just inside the showroom, smelling the duco from the various models of brand-new Mercedes-Benzes displayed across the highly polished concrete floor. Over the bonnets of a half-dozen cars, he can still see the agitation in his father's movements around the woman customer and the furtive glances coming back at him from both of them. Aaron unshoulders his backpack and places it down next to his ragged runners, through the thin soles of which he can feel the cold lacquered concrete.

One long and uncomfortable minute passes before Max leaves the customer and walks to the door of a younger salesman's glass-panelled office. Aaron watches them exchange a few quick words with their heads turning in the direction of the woman. The salesman puts the phone down and walks eagerly to attend to her at the E500 Coupé. Max hesitates briefly before he turns and begins his walk across the showroom floor toward his son. His hips roll with a slight limp, caused by a botched operation after breaking his leg in a car accident when he was seventeen. It was the end of a very promising football career, according to Max, but Aaron has never heard or seen any corroborating evidence.

Aaron tries hard to keep his body still as his father approaches, but his heart is beating too fast and his legs have a hyperactive mind of their own. It doesn't help that Max stops in front of Aaron with his eyes scrutinising him as if he is a used car.

'I wasn't expecting to see you.'

'Well, here I am.'

Aaron reads the embarrassment on Max's face as his eyes dart around the showroom, and he can almost hear the words bouncing about in his father's head – *Have they noticed me talking to this street kid? Do they realise I know him? Will they guess it's my son?*

'I'm really happy to see you too, Dad,' Aaron says, unable to hide the sarcasm.

'You've taken me by surprise, Aaron, that's all. Am I happy to see you? I don't know. It depends.'

'On what?'

148

'What you want.'

'To talk,' he replies with a confident tone that surprises him, and for an instant he feels like he's got Max on the back foot.

'What about?' Max asks suspiciously.

This is not a question he wants to answer now, so he lies. 'I dunno, Dad. The football? I don't care, really. It's been a long time and there's lots to talk about, I guess.'

He feels Max's eyes boring into him, as if he knows Aaron's lying and is searching for the truth. Aaron's well-practised deception doesn't waver, and after a moment he sees a softening in his father's pose.

'Okay, we can talk, but not here. Give me twenty minutes or so to finish up and we can go around the corner to the Maori Chief for a drink. You're eighteen now, right?'

Max remembers his birthday. That's something positive, thinks Aaron, and he feels a flicker of hope pass through him, a glimpse perhaps of how it was before his grandfather destroyed it all.

'I'll wait for you in one of these cars, then,' Aaron says casting an optimistic eye over the showroom.

'No, no, you can't do that,' Max replies sharply.

It's like a punch to Aaron's stomach, hurting and disappointing him. Max pulls back his cufflinked shirtsleeve to check the time on his expensive-looking watch, stainless steel with gold dial markers. Aaron instinctively estimates what he would get for it on the black market. There is no guilt attached to this thought.

'We'll go now and catch the happy hour. Wait for me outside,' Max says with a dismissive tone before walking off toward the young salesman, now in his office with the woman customer.

Fuck you, Aaron says to himself under the cloud of rejection. Why should he wait outside? Max wouldn't ask one of his suited-up customers to do that. No. They'd be drinking espresso coffee in a comfortable chair in the specially designated lounge. The hurt and disappointment have turned to anger, and it is fuelling his determination to step into the ring and take his father on. The thin soles of his runners remain defiantly attached to the polished concrete floor.

~

They walk side by side to the traffic lights on Kings Way without a word. Aaron recognises the silent treatment his father gave him as a child when he wouldn't do as he was told. It bothered him a lot then, but it doesn't now. Making Max start the conversation gives Aaron a welcome feeling of control. Pushing the round metal button to stop the flow of traffic adds another layer to that feeling. He feels good as they cross the busy road in front of the banked-up cars with headlights glowing softly into the April dusk.

Aaron can see the Maori Chief Hotel on the corner a block away, and with each step they take toward it, he can feel his anxiety creeping back. Why hasn't his father said anything yet? He's obviously got better at the silent treatment after years of practice. Aaron remembers how Max wouldn't talk to Vicky for several days after one of their big arguments, with him sleeping on the couch in the lounge room until it eventually went back to the way it was.

Just as Aaron is about to capitulate and say something, anything, to ease his rising anxiety, Max beats him to it.

'Are you heading off somewhere?'

Aaron glances at him quizzically. In the moment of unease, he has no idea what Max is talking about.

'The backpack.'

Okay, what to say, he asks himself as they continue up the street. The truth? Why not?

'Mum asked me to leave.'

'Why?'

No, this is not the way he wants it to go. Where is that feeling of control he had just moments ago? Now he feels only an urge to scream out a string of obscenities. Instead, he lies again.

'No big deal. We just weren't getting on.'

'So, this just happened, did it?'

'A few weeks ago.'

'And that's why you've come to see me. I get it now.'

No, you don't get it at all, Aaron says to himself as they reach the narrow, three-storeyed hotel dominating the corner of Moray Street.

There's a huge painting of a Maori Chief above wooden double doors, which Aaron pushes open to lead his father into the noisy front bar packed with workers of various trades and colours. Most are clustered along the L-shaped solid timber bar, with others filling the space in front of a large television screen, enthusiastically watching a rugby match between Australia and New Zealand. Over the din, he hears Max telling him to grab the small empty table in the corner while he gets the beer.

He takes the seat in the small space that separates the bar from the lounge, his chair facing the eight-ball table where a man in his fifties is playing against a much younger woman. He wears a suit, and she is dressed in tight-fitting jeans and a leather jacket, with her short-cropped spiky hair and full lips reminding Aaron of Zoe. He turns away quickly to avoid the wave of sadness the memory creates in him, and his eyes find his father attempting to grab the attention of a bartender in the midst of a collection of burly workers.

The sight of this diminutive, unfamiliar father is a sharp reminder of the difficult conversation Aaron has ahead of him, and his hand instinctively feels for the foil of heroin in his pocket. Sitting alone and anxiety-ridden on the hard wooden chair, he formulates an escape through the swinging double doors and out onto the street to find relief in a nearby laneway. As he reaches for his backpack, he hears the scraping of a chair behind him and then feels a heavy weight crushing his shoulder.

152

'Sorry, mate,' slurs a bearded man in a blue singlet before he staggers off toward the toilets, knocking the end of the young woman's pool cue as she lines up a shot. Unflustered, she smiles with a shake of her head and then casually pots the black ball. Aaron feels another wave of longing wash over him, escalating his desire to escape to comfort. But it is too late: Max is now struggling through an unyielding bunch of drinkers with two pots of beer held high and his eyes firmly on his destination.

Aaron is trapped. The encouraging, supportive voices in his head have gone silent, overwhelmed by a fearful gut telling him not to challenge his father. His panicked eyes are drawn to the wall at the end of the bar and a copper-plated hanging of a Maori warrior with intricate tattoos carved into his face and body, his muscled arms holding a broad whalebone staff weapon, his tongue extending below his chin and his eyes bulging in a stance so fearful as to frighten off even the most powerful of enemies.

Aaron's father sits down opposite, looking flustered – weak, even – in comparison to the image of the Maori warrior that is now screening in Aaron's head, willing him to be strong and fierce. As Max gulps down half of his pot of beer, Aaron squares his shoulders firmly back and imagines himself in the warrior stance ready for battle.

'You can't stay with me, Aaron,' Max blurts out. 'In case you've got any ideas,' he adds before licking beer froth from his lips. 'I just needed to say that so we don't get off on the wrong foot.'

Okay, this is it, thinks Aaron. You are the Maori warrior: attack.

'Why did you believe him and not me?'

Max's eyes are bulging now – with confusion, with surprise, and then with anger.

'You fucking little prick,' he mutters almost inaudibly before gulping down the rest of his beer and pushing his chair back to stand. 'I'm not putting up with this bullshit again.'

The bearded man in the blue singlet staggers back from the toilets to block Max's exit, and their short verbal exchange gives Aaron the seconds he needs to rethink his tactics. His Maori friend has helped him to find the courage to come this far, but now the warrior is hidden behind a wall of inebriated workers. A faint voice in his head tells him to try the softly, softly approach, just like his mother does when an argument threatens to boil out of control.

'I just need you to explain it to me again, Dad. Please?'

He watches Max looking out over the bar room as if weighing up whether to walk through the throng of masculinity and out the door, or sit back down with the son he has not seen or spoken to in eight years and give him the answer he is asking for. His eyes turn down to his empty pot on the table, and Aaron seizes the moment to push his own untouched beer across to him.

Max slowly and grudgingly sits back down to fix a dark gaze on Aaron, long enough to tip his son's emotional scales back to fear and uncertainty. Aaron curses the explosion of nerves in the pit of his stomach and the fragility that comes on him so quickly. His head swings past Max to the young woman lining up a shot along her pool cue, pointing directly at him. He wills her to lift her eyes up to his, to smile at him encouragingly, affectionately even. Instead, she slams the ball into the middle pocket and walks around the table to bump her arse flirtatiously against the older man. Aaron comes nervously back to his father opposite.

'I'm bloody angry with you, Aaron,' he says before swigging more beer. 'I wouldn't have agreed to do this if I'd known you were going to bring that up again. Jesus.'

Aaron looks at the gentleman in the top hat painted on the toilet door and for a brief moment considers finding heroin relief there, but just as quickly he dismisses that inviting option, telling himself again that there will be a reward when this is over. He has no choice but to act now or drown in a flood of anxiety. The group of inebriated workers splits open and his Maori friend is back with him: *Be brave, Aaron, be brave.*

'Why didn't you believe he did those things to me?' Even in the asking, Aaron sheds some fear.

The response is quick and still angry.

'Because he was my father and he would never do that!'

Max swigs more beer and returns with a less hostile tone.

'Aaron, you took what was a perfectly innocent thing and turned it into something that it wasn't. With a big helping hand from your mother, I might add.'

Max leans closer with a slight smile, read by Aaron as an attempt at fatherly warmth, and it scares him. He knows what's coming next.

'It is perfectly normal for a father, or a grandfather for that matter, to show a boy how to roll his foreskin back and clean it properly. Boys need to know why they get an erection and what to do with it, Aaron. It's called sex education. It was a good thing. It brought me and Dad closer together.'

Aaron sees only his father's lips moving as his peripheral vision descends into darkness, and he can no longer hear the words that tumble from those lips. He is in the lounge room watching the football with his grandfather. The front door shuts and his grandmother is on her way to the bridge club. His grandfather unzips his own fly, takes out his penis and asks Aaron to roll the foreskin back so he can show him how to take good care of it. His grandfather gets an erection and asks Aaron to rub baby oil along it while he explains the biological details.

A loud roar brings Aaron back to the bar room, and the New Zealanders in front of the television celebrating the All Blacks' narrow win over the Australian Wallabies. His father drains his glass of beer and places it down on the table with a look of self-approval.

'I'm glad we've had this talk. Should've done it sooner. But there you go. I just hope we can move on now, Aaron. Spend some time together. Go to a game. I'd like that. What do you say?'

Aaron desperately wants to challenge his father's version of that 'sex education' and tell him what his grandfather actually did to him in his own words, something he was unable to do when it was happening ten years ago, when it was left up to his mother. Max has forced him to peer through the window into the lounge room of his grandparents' house, but to walk through the door and describe it in detail would be to experience the same intense pain all over again. So, he stays silent and watches the frustration rise in Max as he fiddles with his empty glass of beer.

'Well, are you going to say something or not?'

Aaron reaches for his grandmother. It feels safer.

'Nanna knew what he did to me.'

Max bangs the glass down on the table, his face flushed red.

'That is complete bullshit! Your whole story, she didn't believe a word of it. She knew you had a vivid imagination. We all did.'

Aaron can no longer look at Max, so he turns to the eight-ball table where the young woman and her friend have gone, replaced by two men in hi-vis vests arguing loudly about the rules. Aaron's Maori friend has also disappeared, behind another wall of drinkers, so he looks reluctantly back at his father who is now staring into the bottom of his empty glass, his hand shaking, his face twisted in anguish.

'I had to ask Mum if she thought Dad was touching you up. Can you imagine how hard that was for me?'

Max seems so pathetic sitting hunched over on the other side of the table. A forty-five-year-old man making it all about him, refusing to even consider that his father was capable of doing terrible things to a young boy.

'It killed her. I'm sure of it. And Dad too, in the end.'

But he's not dead to Aaron. He is alive inside him, a weeping, aching, toxic cyst that he hoped Max would help him lance. He screams it out, but his brain doesn't connect to his mouth and the booming words reverberate through him with no pathway out.

'The old man really appreciated that I believed him, so that does give me some comfort.'

The pain is unbearable. Aaron stands and picks up his backpack in one motion, weaves through the gaps in the congested mob of workers and glasses of beer, and pushes through the swinging double doors, out onto the cold street.

14

Aaron sprints away from the Maori Chief Hotel in an attempt to distance himself from the emotional assault his father has just inflicted on him. He is crying and wanting his mother to comfort him, to tell him he was very brave, that Max is an arsehole who doesn't deserve to have a son like him, and that he can come back home to live. But as he runs instinctively into a dark and narrow side street, he knows that it is wishful thinking. Heroin is the only thing that will kill his father's words reverberating through every cell in his body. *It didn't happen, Aaron. You imagined it all. Look what you've done to us!* He stops running, sucking air into his lungs, eyes closed with a too-familiar, uncensored scene screening in his head. He is in bed at his grandparents' with the sound of heavy footsteps approaching, a door

159

creaking open then shutting, a big body on the bed, a hand sliding under the doona.

He opens his eyes to a two-metre-high metal fence through the vertical gaps of which he can see a concreted backyard of a retail business, lit by a security light fixed above a double roller door. A shipping container sits hard against the parapet wall of the neighbouring building, and in the soft light he can see the container's door latch is unlocked. A quick glance up and down the deserted street and he pulls himself up and over the fence into the yard.

The container is completely empty except for a stack of pine pallets in the corner. He props open the door enough to let in a stream of light from a nearby street lamp, drags two pallets over to protect him from the cold metal floor and sits down to do the job he so desperately needs to do. The inverted Coke can is between his knees and he wastes no time measuring out a larger-than-usual dose of the heroin he has left, the reward he promised himself before the long walk to Max Peters Mercedes-Benz. He adds the water to dissolve it and then draws the murky solution through a cigarette filter into the syringe. He flicks out the air bubbles, pumps his fist and taps impatiently on the skin of his bent arm until a vein stands out enough in the pale light. Nothing else matters in this moment of intense anticipation. The plunger descends, and the rush of the heroin through his body is like a magic trick flying him to heaven with white doves.

He sits for a long time drifting with the lightness of his being until he feels the cold biting at his face and fingers. Slowly he makes up his bed on the wooden pallets – the plastic tarpaulin, the blanket, the backpack as a pillow – and he rolls into a long, peaceful sleep.

~

He wakes to the sound of a motorbike starting with a roar then revving through the gears to the end of the street. Through the gap in the propped-open door, the sun's first rays purple the sky. He is cold, hungry and depressed. His drug paraphernalia is scattered across the metal floor, reminding him of the two doses – smaller than his usual – still left in his pocket. He feels for it. Yes, it's still there. Realising he needs to move quickly before the neighbourhood wakes, he sits up with the blanket wrapped tightly around him to formulate a plan.

Back over the metal fence, he stands in the narrow street ticking off the first item on his list. He is busting for a piss, but an elderly woman is walking toward him with a small, white dog on a leash, so he decides he'll wait until he gets to the public toilets near Coles where he can kill two birds at the same place. He walks toward the woman and her dog, and as he is about to pass them, the dog growls and lunges suddenly at his ankles. His instinct is to kick out at it, but the woman pulls it back sharply and keeps walking with no acknowledgement, no apology, nothing but a disdainful look down her powdered nose. Aaron glances back at the dog, still pulling hard on its leash and snarling at him. He wishes he had kicked it.

He turns the corner into South Melbourne's main shopping street – understandably deserted given it is so early on what he calculates is a Saturday morning. A van is delivering boxes of vegetables to an Indian restaurant where the smell of frying onions and spices wafts through the open door he walks past. He tries to remember when he last ate. Was it the souvlaki Samantha gave him? No. It must've been the dry muffin his mother bought him in the cafe when she convinced him to see Max. This immediately conjures an image of his father sitting across from him at the Maori Chief Hotel, and he tries hard to block out the soul-crushing words spewing from Max's mouth, but he can't. His stomach cramps and nausea climbs into his throat, forcing him to dry retch as he walks across the intersection against the lights. A speeding taxi swerves violently to miss him.

A further half a block and he is walking through the automatic doors into the almost empty foyer of the Clarendon Centre. A handful of shoppers are lined up at a Coles checkout; the chemist, the hairdresser, the sushi shop and the cafe are all shut. Aaron bounces up the stairs to the first floor, fearing a locked toilet door. He pushes on it and it swings open. It smells clean, and his urine flows hard and fast into the ceramic receptacle the instant he has his cock in his hand. Relief, with more relief to come.

At the basin, he fills his plastic bottle with water, his face staring back at him from the scratched mirror above it. His hair needs washing again, and for an instant he thinks about visiting his mother at the salon. No, she will make him relive the experience with his father. Just the thought of it hastens him into a cubicle to prepare a hit, knowing that he only has one dose left for later in the day and that he needs to ring the Man. Sex for money for heroin: that's the equation. As the drug surges through his bloodstream, he decides he'll make the call after he buys something to eat with the Centrelink money in his bank account. He stays sitting on the toilet, listening to the exhaust fan whirring gently overhead and thinking of Timmy's funeral. It's today, but he still needs to find out what time.

At first, he hears the distorted sound of music coming from a set of headphones. Then, through the gap under the cubicle door, he watches a pair of blue Doc Marten boots crossing to the urinal. The sound of piss streaming against ceramic mixes with the music, but Aaron recognises the jangled guitar lines of the indie-rock Melbourne band, Twerps, and one of his favourite songs, 'Dreamin'. With his eyes closed, he taps his foot and nods his head to the driving rhythm as he sings along with the chorus. When he opens his eyes, the Doc Marten boots are pointing directly toward him under the door and Aaron stops singing, barely breathing for what seems like an eternity before the boots and the music depart and there is only the whirring of the fan.

He keeps his head down as he descends the stairs and walks through the foyer of the Clarendon Centre and out onto the footpath. The plan again? The bank, something to eat, ring the Man and then the funeral. What time is it? He turns on his phone. It's 8.10. He turns it off and walks the short distance to the ATM to withdraw twenty dollars, leaving a balance of two dollars before crossing the street to the Old Paper Shop Deli. He's hoping to sit at the table by the window where he sat with his mother every Sunday morning after his father left. They would both have French toast and bacon, and when he turned twelve, she let him have a weak cappuccino. After he turned fourteen, he didn't want to get out of bed so they both stopped going.

A confident man in his early forties walks toward Aaron carrying a menu, and Aaron can feel his eyes checking him over: the grubby and slept-in clothes, the backpack, all very obvious.

'Hey, Aaron. It's been a while.'

'Hey,' Aaron says with half a smile, appreciating the welcome but not remembering his name. One of the brothers – Peter, he guesses.

'You're in luck. Your table's free,' he says indicating the small table at the window. 'And Vicky?'

'Just me.'

He remembers now. It's not Peter; it's his brother, George. Vicky flirted with him. She knew he was married but it didn't stop her. It didn't stop George either. Something might have happened between them, but he doubts it. He would have known.

'Don't tell me. French toast and bacon and a cappuccino?'

Aaron nods and heads toward the table, passing a large table of noisy men in lycra who are drinking coffee and eating muffins. He removes his backpack and sits down to look out the window and scan their expensive bikes, all locked up together. The morning sun shines through the glass, warming him nicely. He glances across at the two women behind the glass-fronted counter stacked with colourful salads, ready-made rolls and sandwiches, trays of moussaka, schnitzels and meatballs in thick tomato sauce. Maria is the mother and Thalia the daughter who Aaron thinks is even more beautiful than he remembers. Peter is at the coffee machine. The barista. It all comes back to him now, and he relaxes into the wooden chair enjoying the familiarity. Perhaps he should ring the Man now from his comfortable office with the street views. Why not? The number is on the screwed-up piece of paper still in his pocket. He dials it as George arrives with his coffee. He nods his thanks and waits for the Man to answer.

'Donald Richmond.'

'It's me.'

Silence. Aaron touches the handle of his coffee cup and taps it nervously as the seconds pass. He needs this to happen.

'I'll pick you up at eight-thirty. Southern Cross.'

Donald hangs up, leaving Aaron staring at his phone, uneasy

suddenly about the night ahead of him. George arrives with the French toast and two slices of crispy bacon.

'You okay?' George asks.

Aaron can't tell him about the Man, but he has an invitation to say something. 'I'm going to a funeral.'

'Whose?'

'A friend.'

'A good friend?'

Aaron nods. George glances around the cafe to see that everything is under control and then pulls out a chair to sit down with Aaron, who is wondering what's going on. Is he going to ask about Vicky? He hopes not.

'Don't let me interrupt your meal, please. I'd just like to share something with you. It might help.'

The bacon smells good and he's definitely hungry, so why not eat and listen? The kindness in George's eyes is as irresistible as the food. Aaron cuts into the toast and bacon and fills his mouth with the sweet, greasy combination.

'When my father died ten years ago, I needed something to comfort me. My uncle gave me a book on Greek mythology, and I read about Hades, the god of the dead who rules over the Underworld.'

Aaron eats with George's serious eyes fixed firmly on him.

'At the moment of death, the soul is separated from the corpse and it takes on the shape of the former person. Coins are placed over the eyes or in the mouth to pay for the boat that transports the souls across the River Styx that separates the worlds of the living and the dead. The gates at the entrance to the Underworld are guarded by Hades' multi-headed dog, Cerberus, who allows everyone to enter but none to leave.'

George pauses momentarily to watch the number 12 tram rattle past the cafe before he turns back to an eager Aaron.

'Once through these gates, the soul appears before a panel of three judges who pass sentence based on the person's deeds in their previous life. Some are to suffer in the afterlife because of the bad things they have done, while others – like my father, and I imagine your friend – will experience nothing but happiness for eternity.'

'George,' a female voice cuts sharply through their shared moment, suspended in another world.

Aaron barely notices George stand, but he feels his strong hand on his shoulder.

'Breakfast's on the house, Aaron. Hope it all goes well for you.'

He wants to thank him, but George has gone before the words reach his lips. He stares out through the window to a busy Saturday morning footpath where a pretty girl catches his eye momentarily before she disappears, bringing him back with melancholy to finish his French toast and cappuccino.

15

Aaron weaves his way slowly through the foot traffic, unable to shake off the blanket of sadness and indecision that has fallen over him. He turns right at the 7-Eleven on the corner and instinctively continues up the gentle eastern slope of Emerald Hill toward the Town Hall as if he was returning home after breakfast with his mother. He pauses at the op shop window displaying the very best of their second-hand items: framed paintings, dolls, cushions, a half-mannequin dressed in a woman's frilled shirt, and a pair of men's patent-leather shoes. He peers in at the *Size 9* printed on the leather insole and makes a mental note to come back when it opens. The thought of replacing his worn runners with a pair of shiny new shoes pokes a hole in his sadness, but only fleetingly. He has forgotten about them by the time he reaches the next building, Café Zappa, where Stephano the *propriétaire straordinario* treats every customer as if they are his best friend. Aaron is relieved to pass between the umbrella-covered outdoor tables and past the front door without being noticed by Stephano. As he crosses narrow Layfield Street, he glances down toward the rooming house – a reminder that Dave and Samantha have moved into a flat together. *Moray Street, two thirty-nine.* He remembers important things.

Sitting on the steps of the Town Hall and looking out at a familiar horizon helps him to regain his bearings. He starts to work on a strategy to get through the day before the night. He's going to Timmy's funeral; he knows that. He glances up at the clock in the tower directly above him. It's 9.30 and he doubts it would start before 11, but he doesn't really know that. He walks across to his mother's house and decides he could leave his backpack outside there somewhere while he's at the funeral. She'll be at work and he can get it back later. Maybe he'll see her then, maybe he won't. He'll make that choice later. He scans past the police station opposite, then further down, beyond the roundabout to Park Towers standing tall and distinctive a block away. A moment's thought and he decides he'll wait outside for Timmy's mother and sister to appear, then he'll walk with them to the church. Now he feels a little better – apprehensive still, but having a plan helps his mood. It seems to, almost always.

After depositing his backpack under the overgrown pittosporum at the side of Vicky's house, he walks the block to the grounds of Park

Towers where he chooses a patch of grass between two small eucalypts to lie down on, a vantage point from which he can keep an eye on the main entrance. The sun is warm on his face, and he relaxes with the low-key hum of the reduced dose of heroin in his system. Half a dozen pre-teenagers are kicking a football end to end nearby, and he imagines joining in. It would be fun, he thinks, but only briefly. He simply doesn't have the energy. Instead, he concentrates on the flow of people in and out of the thirty-two-storey building, some arriving home with full bags of shopping, others lingering to talk for a moment as they cross paths, a couple walking off to one side, discreetly exchanging something small from hand to hand before separating.

The minutes pass by with the sun and the drug drifting him off to sleep and into a boat, happily fishing with his father on a slow-flowing river. He gets a bite and winds in a very big fish, laughing with excitement as it flips around madly at his feet. He looks up at Max, who has a very tiny fish on the end of his line and a scowling, angry face. Dark clouds extinguish the sun, and a roar of water explodes in Aaron's ears. The river is a raging torrent speeding the boat toward a watery abyss – closer and closer, louder and louder. He grips the gunwales of the boat with bleeding hands, screaming out. *Dad! Dad! Please help me!* Max is standing on the riverbank laughing and waving goodbye.

'You okay, Aaron?'

His eyes snap open to see Timmy's twelve-year-old sister, Amee, and he immediately jumps to his feet.

'Yeah, yeah, all good,' he replies unconvincingly as he catches sight of Lita and Roger waiting on the concrete path behind her. He wasn't expecting to see Roger. Timmy told him ages ago that he had walked out on Lita and moved to Tasmania to live with another woman.

'You coming to the service?' Amee asks.

He nods and she smiles then follows her to Lita, who greets him with tears in her eyes and a big hug. He makes brief eye contact with Roger, long enough to see that he's lost weight and the skin on his face matches the grey of his ill-fitting suit. Aaron hopes he's sober.

They walk together in silence down the winding path between the ready-to-mow grass and the clusters of trees until they reach the north-west corner of the Towers. They step out onto the footpath, and Roger thumps the pedestrian button at the lights to cross a busy thoroughfare. Aaron looks across at the old grey-stone building on the corner opposite with *The Melbourne Camera Club* written in large gold letters above the door. The green pedestrian light appears, and as they cross the double lanes of traffic, Aaron's eyes drift up to the top of the building. The just-discernible grey-stone letters tell him it was once the local Freemasons' hall. A stab of anxiety accompanies the reminder of what has been and what is to come. Lita turns to him with a comforting smile as if she can see his distress. He wants to hug her, to feel her comforting arms around him again, but they are already on their way down the tree-lined street, and the longing lingers.

They walk onto the grounds of St Peter and Paul's, an imposing Gothic-style bluestone church with an elaborate traceried rose window like a giant eye above the arched entrance. Aaron is glad that he's not alone; if he was, he thinks that he would run away. Instead, he stands on the patched bitumen between the church and the gardens of the double-storeyed rectory, watching Roger and Lita rolling cigarettes and hoping to be offered one. Roger hands over his packet with a nod that seems to say, *I was a prick and I'm sorry for that.*

They stand together smoking, with the sound of passing cars and birds calling each other in a nearby tree. Aaron can sense that Lita and Roger are as nervous as he is, and he finds some comfort in them treating him as one of their own. He sees Roger reach out for Lita's hand and thinks that he must be sick because something has definitely changed him. He seems softer and nicer, and Aaron allows himself to wonder if his father would also become a nicer person if he got really sick. Amee looks up at Aaron from under her mother's comforting arm.

'Father Brian asked me to pick out some songs to play.'

'Cool.'

'I hope you like them.'

'I will,' he says, knowing it to be true.

'Do you think he did it on purpose, Aaron?' Lita asks as she lifts a shaking hand to draw hard on her cigarette.

Aaron feels three pairs of expectant eyes on him, and it gives him a boost. What he says is important to them. The dream he had in Timmy's room is still with him, and he is pleased that he can confidently tell them what they want to hear.

'It was an accident.'

'You don't really know that,' Lita says on the edge of crying.

'If anyone knows, he does,' Roger says, comforting her. 'Isn't that right, Aaron?'

'He didn't want to die, I know that for sure.'

A black hearse swings past them to stop in front of the church. Two tall, thin men in their seventies with matching comb-over haircuts and long, sharp noses emerge through the church doors to greet the two undertakers. Together, they slide the coffin from the rear of the hearse, lift it onto their shoulders and carry it up the steps into the church.

'This is it then,' says Roger, butting out his cigarette with a polished black leather shoe.

Aaron throws his into the rose garden, takes a deep breath and follows the family to the bottom of the well-worn stone steps and then up through the gaping double doorway into air so still and light no sound is left unheard. His eyes are drawn up to the steeply pitched white ceiling, framed in a network of timber beams and supported by two lines of stone pillars arched along the length of the church. Looking down between the rows and rows of the highly polished timber pews, he sees Timmy's coffin sitting high on a stand next to the altar. There Father Brian, wearing a purple cape over a long white robe, is lighting the last of a series of tall candles. The priest turns to face them with his short fingers clasped at his ample waist, and on cue one of the thin twins gets up from his seat and picks up an iPod from a table at the end of the pew. Seconds later, a scything guitar strum and the funereal beat of a bass reverberate through the church. Father Brian reaches his arms out to the congregation and they begin their long walk to the altar accompanied by the melancholic melody of Rowland S Howard's 'Autoluminescent', with lyrics imagining a return from a nightmare existence to soar as a comet through outer space.

As they reach the front pew, Aaron looks up behind the altar to the brightly coloured stained-glass window depicting Jesus Christ rising up to heaven, his outstretched hands showing the wounds of his crucifixion and rays of light pouring down on him.

Aaron slides into the pew next to the others and looks directly up into Father Brian's eyes, wondering what he thinks of the lyrics. The priest smiles gently down at him before picking up a gold holy water pot and stepping across to sprinkle its contents over Timmy's coffin.

For the first time, Aaron notices a framed photo of his friend, with his black eyes and gap-toothed smile, in front of the altar. He is overcome with sorrow as Rowland's deep and wailing voice fades to silence. Lita sobs uncontrollably and is held tight by Roger's consoling arm. Behind them feet shuffle into pews, and Aaron turns to see Dave and Samantha wearing dark glasses directly behind him. Sitting a pew further back are half a dozen of the boys from the Layfield Street rooming house. They were not Timmy's good mates, but they're all in the same boat. If you lose one, you pay your respects. A tenuous family indeed.

Father Brian faces the congregation.

'In the name of the Father, the Son and the Holy Ghost.'

'Amen,' mutter a few voices behind Aaron.

'The Lord is with you.'

'And with you.'

'May almighty God have mercy on us, forgive us our sins, and bring us to everlasting life.'

'Amen.'

Aaron only faintly hears the prayer because his focus is completely on the coffin, imagining Timmy inside, wondering what he is wearing and whether he has coins over his eyes or in his hands. The priest cuts across his musings.

'When I stand in front of human beings like yourselves, that is where I find God. We are here to put ourselves at the service of everyone in the neighbourhood. The men and women sleeping rough or in the rooming houses are as important as the people who fill these pews on Sundays ...'

Aaron drifts away from the priest's words to gaze up at the stained-glass windows along the side walls of the church, each of them depicting a biblical story in a brilliant palette of red, blue, purple and emerald green. He doesn't recognise any of the figures in the windows except for Jesus, who is standing on a cloud and reaching his hand out to a woman holding a crucifix and a box with flames coming from it. Another window shows a crowd of angels gesturing adoringly up to him, while another illustrates an old man holding a hooked staff with a snake coiled at his feet. Aaron sees a young woman in blue robes surrounded by a body halo, and then a winged man, an eagle, and even a winged ox: all alluring images bathed in soft light, telling him not to be afraid. *Rise with us, Aaron, into heaven.*

Aaron comes back to Timmy in his coffin with the words of Father Brian reaching him again.

'Timmy was a member of our neighbourhood, but he was disconnected from it in too many ways. He did not have a safe and secure home, he did not have a job, and I suspect that he felt he never really belonged among us.' Father Brian turns to the coffin. 'We were not there for you in your hour of need, Timmy, and for that I am truly sorry.'

Aaron hears Lita sobbing and feels Amee trembling beside him. Roger tries hard to contain his hacking cough. A police siren rises in volume outside then fades away into the suburb. The priest looks out over his congregation, small dots on a giant canvas.

'You feel helpless when you've lost someone you love, completely helpless. You tell yourself that you should have forgiven them before they died. Or perhaps that you should have asked for their

176

forgiveness. Well, you still can. We are not powerless. The Lord is listening to us. So, I ask you to take a moment to pray for Timmy now, to help him pass through the narrow gate into heaven.'

Aaron closes his eyes and he sees himself with Timmy walking along Emerald Hill Lane just before midnight. They are fifteen years old and it is Aaron's spontaneous idea to break into Chemist Warehouse through a rear window. Timmy is unusually reluctant. Roger has told him to be home by midnight and he knows what will happen if he's late. Aaron twists his arm, and after smashing a window into the toilets, they set off the alarm while entering the shop floor. In a panic, they abandon the drugs and climb out through the window to find a police car coming down the lane toward them. Aaron gets away, but Timmy doesn't. He pays the heavy price of twelve months among violent bullies in juvenile detention.

Aaron opens his eyes to the coffin and asks Timmy to forgive him. It was his fault, and he wishes he had told him how sorry he was before he died.

'May almighty God bless you with kindness and pour out his saving wisdom upon you.'

'Amen,' replies a chorus of voices infused with detectable relief.

Roger, Lita and Amee lean in to each other and Aaron feels isolated and alone on the hard wooden pew. Samantha's hand squeezes his shoulder from behind, and it gives him some comfort knowing that someone is aware of how he is feeling. Father Brian nods toward the twin on the end of the pew, who goes to the iPod again as the priest extends his hands out to the congregation.

'Go in peace, ladies and gentlemen, by loving and serving one another.'

~

Walking slowly down the steps of the church, Aaron sees the long wooden box being pushed into the back of the hearse and is overcome with the desire to climb in with Timmy on his passage to a better place.

Cigarettes are lit as the hearse leaves the church grounds. Lita thanks Aaron for coming, and she tells him that she hopes it goes well for him. He doesn't know what to say to her, so he just nods back with a clenched smile. Roger coughs into his handkerchief and Amee gives Aaron a sad little wave as he stands in the gloom watching them go. A voice calls his name from behind, and he turns to see Dave and Samantha in the shadows between the church and the rectory.

As Aaron reaches them, Dave lights a joint, and they pass it around in reflective silence with the cloud of smoke drifting into the branches of a nearby elm tree. Aaron gazes down at a brass plaque in the small flower garden at their feet. It reads:

This fountain is dedicated to local young people whose
dreams turned into nightmares (drug-related deaths)

'Where's the fucking fountain then?' Dave asks.

Aaron shrugs. He wondered the same thing when Father Brian let him sleep in the gardener's shed behind the elm tree. He didn't get a chance to find out before the gardener dobbed him in to the parishioners, who subsequently passed it on to the Archbishop. Samantha offers Aaron the joint again, but he turns it down. He doesn't want the anxiety that too much marijuana invites. He's contented to just drift along with the low buzz and change of perspective the drug has given him, until he gets to the heroin waiting for him in his backpack at his mother's.

They watch Father Brian crossing from the church to the front door of the rectory with the twins walking on either side of him.

'Something about being in a church makes you think that everything's going to be alright in the end. Heaven is there for us,' Samantha muses.

'Bullshit. There's nothing there. Just like there was nothing there before you were born,' Dave says, tossing the butt of the joint in among the dying marigolds. 'Just like there's no fountain. Big fucking promises and no delivery.'

Dave isn't one to argue with, so Aaron doesn't. But he doesn't agree with him. He knows there's a better place waiting for them because he has seen it, almost. He has certainly felt its attraction. A place where there is no pain.

They walk together away from the church with Samantha talking non-stop. She believes in angels. They look after her, and if she wants something she only has to ask for it. Aaron laughs spontaneously, a welcome release helped by the joint.

'It's true, Aaron. Like, I asked them to find me a nice husband. And here he is.'

'Yeah, someone to look after all your pharmacological needs,' Dave replies dryly.

'I'm going to ask them to take good care of you, Aaron,' she says, before throwing her arms theatrically into the air and shouting, 'to guide you on the path to love and everlasting happiness!'

Aaron and Dave smile with the madness. They reach the top of Emerald Hill, where a wary young couple pushing a pram with a toddler in tow give them a wide berth. Aaron and Dave follow Samantha up the steps to stand with her between two stone pillars looking out over the police station and the nineteenth-century buildings lining the busy streets in front of them. Samantha maintains her exuberance with a big voice.

'This is our kingdom. Or, I should say, queendom. Behold you, our loyal subjects going about your daily chores. Take heed, my friends. Beware those bearing you ill will.'

Passers-by turn their heads toward them, some muttering to each other. Two policemen getting into their car pause to look across the street at them. Aaron decides quickly to move to the bottom of the steps, where he glances up at the clock in the tower. It is almost one o'clock. He has just enough time to retrieve his backpack before Vicky gets home from work. Anxiety is back with him now, and his brain switches automatically to scoring again. Thanks to George, he still has twenty dollars left – enough, he hopes, to do a deal with Dave this afternoon.

'See you later on, then,' Aaron says.

Dave doesn't respond; he is too intent on leading Samantha away from the attention she is drawing to them. Aaron crosses the street to his mother's front gate with its familiar noisy squeak. He turns the corner of the house expecting to see the blue of his backpack under the pittosporum, but there is only the green of the tiny leaves. He panics, scratching his face as he forces the thin, brittle branches apart to expose the bare black soil. His heart and head are racing. It's definitely not there. Has someone seen it from the street? No, not possible. He walks a few agitated steps down the path and then swings back again to the same spot. It's still not there. He catches movement in the corner of his eye and turns his head to find his mother looking at him through her bedroom window. Now he knows where it is.

He is angry as he walks up the path to the backyard, imagining Vicky has found the heroin and got rid of it. Through the glass doors, he sees the silhouette of a man sitting on the couch and immediately thinks it's his father, come back to join Vicky in a conspiracy against him. He slides open the door telling himself to calm down. He doesn't want a scene, he just wants the heroin.

It's not Max. It's a younger, fitter-looking gym-junkie type in a T-shirt and tight Carlton Football Club shorts. Vicky appears at the entrance to the hallway, carrying the backpack and looking like she has just got out of bed. Aaron crosses the room to take it off her.

'Why didn't you leave it where it was?'

'How was I to know it was yours?'

'Don't lie,' he says as he unzips in a hurry.

'I didn't touch anything, Aaron.'

He wants to believe her, but he needs proof before he leaves and he's relieved to discover she is telling him the truth. Now he feels some embarrassment at his desperation being revealed to a stranger.

'Who's he?' he asks as he shoulders the backpack.

'Greg, this's Aaron. Aaron, Greg.'

'G'day, buddy.'

Aaron almost tells him he's not his fucking buddy but ignores him instead.

'I'm going,' he says to Vicky without looking at her.

'I'll see you out.'

Aaron reads this as code, knowing she'll ask him if he's seen his father.

'Hang on,' she says before going to the kitchen bench to pick up an envelope to hand to him. 'This came for you. Centrelink.'

He folds it in half and puts it in his back pocket, and they go down the hallway to the front door, where the anticipated question arrives right on cue.

'Did you see him?'

He nods.

'Well?'

'He's a prick and I don't care if he dies.'

'Tell me what happened.'

'Nah,' he says with his hand on the doorknob, feeling for the first time in his life that he doesn't like his mother very much. She asked him to leave and he understood her reasons – it was a relief, in a way, to get away from the constant bickering and conflict between. But now, with the new man sitting on the couch in his jocks, he feels betrayed.

'Oh, Aaron. What are you going to do?'

'About what?' he asks, knowing exactly what she means.

'With your life.'

'Yours is all good, I see.'

She smiles, a little embarrassed, and then reaches out to touch his face. He pulls back and instantly regrets it. He can see he has hurt her. Her face before the tears.

'I love you, Mum,' he says.

She says nothing and turns her head away from him. He walks outside into the cold air, feeling utterly miserable. Charlie Doyle is coming down the footpath in his wheelchair, his clothes and hands spotted with different-coloured paints, reminding Aaron of his gig at the market.

'I didn't make it for that portrait, sorry.'

'That's okay, Aaron,' he says in his slurred speech. 'I understand.'

'Timmy's funeral.'

'Hope it went well.'

'I suppose, yeah.' What else can he say? Then on impulse he asks, 'Is it real, Charlie? Where you go after you die?'

'Heaven and Hell, you mean?'

'No, that other place, where Hades lives. The Underworld.'

Charlie lifts his long, twisted fingers from the controls of his wheelchair and turns them skyward with a shrug of his big shoulders.

'All I know is that some people choose death over living. That's a shame, don't you think?'

Aaron looks back at him thinking it's not a shame if there's a better place waiting for you after you die. But he can't say that, not to a paralysed man in a wheelchair.

'I have to go,' Charlie says. 'Anthea's got lunch waiting for me. If you change your mind about a portrait, I'll be there again next week. You take good care of yourself. I mean it.'

He whirs away down the footpath with Aaron wishing they could continue their conversation. Charlie has a way of making him feel unusually hopeful. After his accident Charlie said he wanted to get married, but no one thought it would ever happen. Anthea lived in the country somewhere and had read an article in the paper about him taking up painting as part of his rehab. She wrote to him, and they exchanged letters for a long time before he asked her to marry him. She said yes. Everyone in the salon said it wouldn't last. Goes to show what they know.

Aaron turns and walks away from his mother's house, longing to return one day to show her that he has made something of his life, to give her something that she can talk to her clients about with real pride.

16

He stands in front of the op shop staring through the window at the patent-leather shoes, imagining them on his own feet and the sound they would make on a timber floor. He hears laughter and turns to see a group of young men approaching. Recognising them, he turns quickly away. They pass behind him, and he glances sideways as they file into Café Zappa. Envy eats into him. Why isn't he with them, wearing the same jeans and jackets, studying law at university, drinking beer after a game of football, going out with girls and playing in a band? He walks off down the slope, shifting the weight of the pack on his back and cursing the hard bitumen he can feel through the soles of his runners.

The number 112 tram rattles along the street, and he crosses the tracks behind it unable to stop thinking about the Café Zappa boys.

He would like to have a life like theirs; he can admit that, if only to himself. He continues down the street beside the long line of brush boxes shading the diagonally parked cars with one question hammering away at him. What does he have to do to make it happen? Ideas pass through his head like clouds collapsing on a windy day. He could go back to school. No, not when he's living on the streets. Where would he study? He couldn't afford to buy the books. He could look for a job, but who would employ a homeless eighteen-year-old with no qualifications or experience? He could give up heroin. No.

Large white letters on the tinted window – *Your Creative Future Starts Today.* The word *Music* catches his eye and he stops at the bottom of the steps leading up to the front door of the JMC Academy. It's in one of the concrete office buildings dotted among the double-storey Victorian terraces. He reads *Contemporary Music Performance* on a list of courses. He thinks about going in but it makes him feel nervous just like he would get on the way to a North Melbourne game with his father: wanting the excitement and joy of a win, but fearing the opposite.

Fuck it, he thinks, and goes up the half a dozen steps and through the door into the reception area. A low-lying counter is on the left with several computers and no staff behind it. Two glass doors at the far end lead somewhere further into the building. On his right is a wall covered in posters of successful, happy students. A bike leans against the wall, fixed-gear, red with whitewalled tyres and a leather seat. He listens carefully, hearing only a low, distorted and bass-heavy guitar rhythm coming from somewhere beyond the glass doors. He thinks it might be the Scientists, a post-punk band from Perth, but he's not sure. His full attention has been drawn back to the bike and an opportunity. He scans the room once, then twice, and takes several quick steps to wrap his hands around the handlebars. A squeaky door opens with the music lifting in volume at the final line of the chorus. Aaron turns to look directly into the eyes of a middle-aged woman standing at the open glass doors with a violin case strapped across her shoulders and a helmet in her hand. He knows she knows, and there's nothing he can say or do but swiftly exit the building onto the grey-black footpath with one negative emotion after another coursing through him. More than anything, he is angry with himself.

~

Number 239 Moray Street is a 1960s yellow brick-veneer cottage sharing a boundary wall with a two-storey Victorian building that once operated as a milk bar, its doors now closed with a *For Sale* sign on the large side window. Light rain is falling, and he pushes open the rickety gate hoping that he remembered the number correctly. It could've been 339. Or even 329. He dodges water dripping from a hole in the guttering above the front step to knock firmly on the door. He waits in the dark space shadowed by the adjoining parapet wall and an overgrown lemon tree, his anxiety dialled up to the maximum. The door opens to Dave, and Aaron follows him up the dank-smelling hallway, past a closed door on the right and into a lounge room lit by a single light bulb hanging from a broken ceiling rose. A black vinyl couch, a card table and two plastic chairs are the only pieces of furniture. Dave's paintings are stacked against a wall that's covered in psychedelic-patterned paper with images of doves and peace signs and love hearts against purple, blue and yellow swirls.

'She's in bed. Asleep, I hope,' Dave says before Aaron has a chance to ask. 'She went fucking troppo, so I dosed her up on rohies. Had to, mate. Jesus, you saw her. It got worse, I can tell you.'

It's all no surprise to Aaron, and he doesn't understand how it could be to Dave either. What did he expect?

'Can I use your bathroom, Dave?'

'Through there,' he says, indicating an open door behind him.

Aaron walks into a galley-style kitchen to find the bathroom at one end. Dave's voice follows him in.

'I can't get hold of any antipsychotics, that's the fucking problem.'

Aaron shuts the door behind him with a blinkered focus on his own drug need. He removes his pencil case from the backpack, lays its contents out on the ledge next to the pink handbasin and begins the ritual: the heroin, the water, the mix, the spoon, the filter, the syringe, the vein, the blood. The plunger descends and a wave of pleasure rushes through him, leaving cotton-wool comfort in its wake.

A slow walk back to the lounge room, where Dave is sitting on the black vinyl couch– a peace sign on the wallpaper directly above his head – and looking lost in thought as he rolls a cigarette. Aaron anticipates the conversation going back to Samantha, so he decides to get in first. Dave's a hard person to interrupt. He takes his last twenty dollars from his pocket and puts it down on the card table.

'That's all I've got till tomorrow.'

Dave pats the couch next to him. He's in control, so Aaron sits.

'I've made a big mistake,' Dave says as he passes over the packet of tobacco.

Aaron floats gently back into the vinyl, welcoming the idea of a cigarette.

'I can't marry her,' Dave says, blowing a plume of smoke toward the ceiling. 'I love her but ... fucking hell, she has to go.' He coughs a few times then turns to look directly at Aaron. 'So, what do you think about that, then?'

Aaron watches his own fingers trying to roll the paper around the slug line of tobacco while he searches for the right answer. Dave prefers people who agree with him. So, does he do that? Or does he tell him that Samantha would be heaps better if she got back on the depot? Maybe he doesn't have to choose.

'I don't know what to say, Dave.'

'Yes, you do.'

Okay, he does have to choose. The words fall slowly from his lips.

'I couldn't live with her either, Dave.'

He can feel Dave relax back into the couch beside him, and he allows his heavy eyelids to have their own way. Rain hits the kitchen window. Dave talks to someone on his phone. Other sounds come and go in the fog. Aaron hears doors opening and closing, the whistle of a boiling kettle, heavy footsteps, and earnest conversations. He smells oil paint in the dark. He sees his eight-year-old self. His mother's hand is leading him through a wall of long legs and showbags to the laughing clowns with their different-coloured hats and big, red, open lips turning side to side. A man without a face is spruiking to the crowd. He looks down at Aaron and passes him a ball. Aaron's mother smiles down at him encouragingly, and as his little hand reaches up to place the ball in the clown's mouth, it morphs into the laughing head of his grandfather.

Aaron's eyes spring open and he sits up straight, with an elevated heart rate and a hazy image of Dave sitting in front of his easel, brush poised over a thin sheet of plywood. Through the open door, the kitchen window tells Aaron that the day has turned to night.

'What's the time?'

'Dunno. Seven? Have a look on my phone,' Dave says, indicating the card table.

It's eight o'clock and he's only got thirty minutes to get to Southern Cross Station. The twenty dollars he left on the card table has disappeared into Dave's pocket, and he regrets not having already negotiated a deal with him. He wills himself to stay calm with the stress of the moment working against the effects of the heroin he has left in his system. He thinks of Samantha, wanting her to be in the room with him. She must still be asleep. Or she has gone already. He doesn't want to ask. Dave dips his brush into the purple on his palette to add to his replica of the psychedelic swirls and love hearts and peace signs on the room's wallpaper. Aaron doesn't want to ask why. He hasn't got time.

'Dave, what d'ya reckon? I can fix you up with the other eighty bucks tomorrow. Guaranteed.'

'There's only one thing in life that's guaranteed, Aaron.'

Aaron doesn't want a philosophical discussion. He wants two points of heroin. Now. Dave wipes his brush clean and then very slowly wanders across to his drug drawers to make a selection, returning just as slowly to hold out two foils in an open hand. Aaron reaches for them, but Dave's hand closes tightly.

'Where's the money coming from?'

Aaron has to be quick, and it helps knowing that he's a well-practised, confident liar. But nothing comes straight to mind that will hold water with Dave. It's the pressure. Fuck it, he decides. He wants the drugs, and he's pretty sure Dave has guessed anyway. He's positive Samantha has.

'A bloke.'

Dave nods knowingly with one corner of his mouth hinting at a smile. He hands over the heroin and Aaron goes straight to his backpack.

'I got her some olanzapine.'

'Sweet, I hope it works,' Aaron says, meaning it. 'Gotta go, Dave.'

~

He runs in a straight line down Moray Street with his backpack bouncing on his shoulders. Directly ahead, the lights of the city promise uncertainty. He has already dismissed the idea of catching a tram. It would eat up too much time. A taxi pulls up outside the Maori Chief, and he slows to a walk with his stomach knotting hard at the reminder of the night before. Three young women in very high heels and short dresses get out of the taxi, and without a second thought, he jumps into the back seat. He needs to go, quickly, away from the lingering imprint of his father. The spruiker has a face.

'Southern Cross,' he says to the driver, whose eyes appear in the rear-view mirror, dark and suspicious.

'I'm catching the eight-thirty train to Sydney,' Aaron says as he adjusts his pack on the seat next him. 'Back at work next week.'

His lie seems to reassure the driver, who turns up the volume on his radio before U-turning back toward the city, where cars and people and buildings merge in the night with an upbeat rhythm and an exotic melody coming from instruments Aaron cannot name. The clock on the dashboard tells him he has fifteen minutes to get there, and it calms him a little. So too does the thought of the two points of heroin in the backpack beside him. He relaxes back into the seat with the music transporting him to places he has never been. There are shiny new buildings, tall and elegant, like the women on the crowded streets where tourists bargain for souvenirs and food is cooked on mobile stoves. He meets the driver's smiling eyes in the rear-view mirror and he wishes for a moment that he could pay the fare.

The traffic slows as they approach the Spencer Street Bridge and then stops completely at the lights, allowing a horde of pedestrians to continue along the southern bank of the Yarra River. Many are in search of a restaurant or a bar, while others are just walking or riding their bikes. Some, he knows, are avoiding the lure of the dark river after having had their wallets emptied at the Crown Casino again.

Aaron's thoughts drift with the slow and hypnotic rhythm of another track on the taxi's stereo. He recognises the beat of a hand drum and he's sure the stringed instrument is the one with no frets and a body shaped like a pear. Maybe he knows it from SBS. Above the taxi, huge curved-steel girders supporting the Flinders Street Viaduct carry trains east and west on the city loop. The lights change from green to amber, and as the driver accelerates across the intersection, the music increases dramatically in tempo, jolting Aaron back to the moment. He has to make a move soon; the station's undulating roof is bathed in blue light at the top of the rise. A number 112 tram rattles to a stop just ahead of them, and a young man desperate to catch it sprints into the path of the taxi. The driver slams on his brakes, and in an instant,

Aaron flings open the door and is dodging through the foot traffic away from the sound of an angry car horn.

He stands among the usual mix of commuters and opportunists at the entrance to Southern Cross Station, checking the cars on the street. He watches a Silver Top taxi turning right at the nearby intersection and feels no guilt. He would have done once, but he knows that his life is easier without it. Now he thinks of Zoe. He wants her to walk through the swarm of people, her beautiful smile saying how happy she is to see him and that he should visit her again. But she is nowhere. A group of noisy young men and women brush past him in their football scarfs and beanies, telling him that North are playing Essendon. Momentarily, he imagines himself with his father. Longing collides with anger before something attracts his attention through the strobe-like gaps in the foot traffic. It's the Man in his black car.

Aaron slides into the passenger seat. The Man, in his dinner suit and bow tie, waits impatiently for the click of the seatbelt before he merges with the traffic. Once again, classical music is at a low volume on the radio, and as they travel with the congestion through the traffic lights toward the West Gate Bridge, Aaron feels increasingly like he's trapped in a bottle of Old Spice with a shark. He's thankful there is no conversation, but is aware of the Man's hungry eyes on him. Something is coming.

The railings on the bridge are silhouetted against the lights of the warehouses and factories and houses sprawling west from the banks of the Maribyrnong River. Headlights from oncoming cars dance with the night. A set of tail-lights swerves sharply in front of them in a last-second manoeuvre to exit to Williamstown. Aaron keeps his head cocked to the left as they continue along the West Gate Freeway, where powerlines are strung between multi-armed metal giants standing guard over the industrial landscape.

'Stop looking out that fucking window.'

The words bite hard, and Aaron knows exactly what it means. Pay him attention. Be his boy. Earn the money. He forces himself to turn and look at the smile shaping on the Man's lips.

'You are looking at the newly elected Grand Master of Victoria's Grand Lodge.'

'Congratulations,' Aaron says softly. They accelerate past a semitrailer as the violins and cellos duel in what seems to be to him a never-ending composition.

The truck's headlights fade in his rear-view mirror. He wouldn't mind becoming a truck driver. Stopping at a roadside cafe, ordering a hamburger and chips, flirting with the girl behind the counter.

'There are two hundred and fifty Master Masons in Victoria, but there is only one Grand Master,' the Man says, holding up a finger. 'One!' He lets the number hang in the air for a long moment. 'Isn't that a glorious thing?' he asks rhetorically.

Aaron is thankful he doesn't need to answer him. He can only wonder at the Man's belief in his own importance. Who is he really?

Does he have a family? Do they know he fucks boys? There are fewer cars on the road now, and with a cloud-covered moon it all seems so much darker. He feels a hand on his arm.

'I am now your Most Worshipful Grand Master. And you, my boy? You are my little Timmy.'

The incessant music, the rush of a passing car, the smell, the pain. Aaron turns to look directly at him.

'Timmy's dead,' he says, feeling it deeply to be true.

The Man says nothing before turning his dismissive eyes back to the highway, and the concrete overpasses, and the exit signs siphoning traffic to the brick-veneered houses spreading across the flat plains. The violins and cellos fade to silence, and a soothing voice tells them they have been listening to String Quartet Number Seven in A minor by Czech composer Antonín Dvořák. The original version was composed in 1873, the presenter says. It was an audacious attempt by Dvořák to create an uninterrupted stream of music. Aaron drifts away from her words and the solo piano piece that follows them.

He feels the vibration first, then the sound of tyres rolling slowly over gravel. His eyes open from sleep expecting to see the Man's house at the end of his long driveway, but it's a truck stop. The Man parks close to a thinly spaced border of eucalypts and turns off the motor and lights. Dread and pain are in lockstep, assaulting Aaron's whole being. He has no control. It is an illusion. He knows well to pretend that his body below his waist is not his and to take his head to another place. Through the windscreen, he can see the dark peaks of the You Yangs, still inexplicably familiar. It gives him something to concentrate on, something to block the images of his grandfather that are invading his head. The peaks? Did he see them in a dream? Maybe, but he doesn't think so. Then where? A flash of light and he is on the rooftop of Park Towers with Timmy, wagging school and eating the fried banana rolls Lita packed in Timmy's lunch box. The still-crunchy spring roll wrappers are dusted in brown sugar, and the boys bite into them looking west to avoid the glare of the morning summer sun. The distinctive peaks of the You Yangs are there on the distant horizon, but Aaron and Timmy don't pay them any attention; they are just shapes in a world far beyond their own.

Aaron ejaculates, the unwanted pleasure instantly replaced with the guilt he knows too well. The Man sits back in his seat to wipe his mouth with a perfectly ironed handkerchief. Aaron zips his jeans back up, longing for the heroin in his backpack to take him into its comforting arms. The Man starts the car and turns on the headlights. A wallaby is frozen in the glare, its eyes startled red. He blows the car horn and it bounds away between the eucalypts with Aaron wanting to fling open the car door and follow it into the night. Instead, he is back on the narrow road, thinking about how he can escape from the constant struggle his life has become. There has to be another way. He turns to look at the Man behind the wheel, not knowing what that way might be but certain he will find it. Anger is telling him that now. It has grown in him, stronger and more demanding.

'I'll cook something up,' the Man says. 'We'll drink some nice wine and watch a movie on the couch together,' he adds, as if issuing instructions. Aaron knows he has no choice in the matter.

17

He stands naked in the mist-filled bathroom, almost smiling with heroin-induced contentment. His skin is flushed pink from the hot shower, and he picks through his backpack for his last clean pair of jocks. A light flicks on outside in the backyard, and he peers through the blinds to see the Man walking to the woodpile in his light-blue Adidas tracksuit pants and jacket. On his feet are large black moccasins. Aaron watches him pick up the axe with the red-taped handle and begin splitting a block of wood into smaller pieces. He admires the Man's skill for a moment before wiping clear the fogged-up mirror and running his fingers through his damp hair. He thinks of his mother holding her scissors with the sweet smell of her favourite moisturiser on her hands. Then he sees her new bloke sitting on the couch in his football shorts, acting like he owns the place, so he steers his thoughts back to the task of dressing himself and to the letter from Centrelink poking out from a back pocket of his jeans. He knows what it will tell him, but he tears it open anyway to read that he has not met his mutual obligation requirements and his payment has been suspended. It goes on to say that he has fourteen days from the date of the letter to request a review, otherwise ... he stops reading and screws the letter up in his fist. Fuck them. And fuck their one hundred and fifty dollars a week.

He walks out to the smell of onions cooking in butter and the sound of dry wood crackling in the open fireplace. The Man is breaking eggs into a bowl.

'The wine's on the table. Help yourself.'

'No, thanks. I'm good.'

'Pick out a film then,' he says with noticeable irritation.

The tone in his voice puts Aaron on edge with memories of an irritated and impatient father.

Get me the wire-cutters.

Where are they?

In the shed.

Where in the shed?

In the fucking toolbox.

I don't know what they look like, Dad.

Jesus!

Always ending in tears.

He walks across the room to throw the Centrelink letter into the flames before scanning the room for the DVDs. Where the fuck are they? The Man turns around to sip from his wineglass, saying nothing. Aaron feels his eyes on him and he gives up his search. Fatigue is weighing heavily on him now and he simply can't be bothered. He shrugs.

'In the drawer under the television,' the Man says with a much lighter touch.

What's he playing at? Aaron wonders as he goes to the big drawer under the very big television. He slides it open to more than one hundred home-recorded VHS tapes.

'Your choice,' the Man says.

Aaron didn't want to hear that. What if he picks the wrong one? No, that's just being paranoid. The Man must like them. They wouldn't be in the drawer otherwise. His eyes roll across the selection and sees the name *John Wayne* handwritten next to the title on almost every VHS. *How the West Was Won*. Then, *True Grit*, *The Undefeated* and *The Green Berets* – all John Wayne. A limited choice, so he's on safe ground at least. He randomly picks one out.

'What've you got there?'

Aaron glances up at the Man tending to an omelette in a non-stick frying pan on the stovetop.

'*The Shootist*.'

'A notorious gunslinger with cancer rides into Carson City wanting to die a quiet death. A great performance from a wonderful actor and a great man. Good choice. Put it on and I'll be with you in a moment. You must be hungry.'

Aaron slides the disc into the VHS player, almost on autopilot now. He'll do what is asked of him but with a desperate eye for an escape route.

'By the way, you look very nice down there. Beautiful.'

~

Aaron is hungry and enjoying the omelette, but sitting on the couch next to the Man is teetering on the unbearable. If it weren't for the heroin, he would run into the night like the wallaby and out of harm's way. Instead, he stays put with the drug suppressing the pain his vivid memory wants to impose on him. The movie is a helpful distraction. The opening credit sequence tells Aaron that the John Wayne character, JB Books, is a former lawman who has killed thirty men. He rides into Carson City and goes to see the town doctor, who confirms his fear that he has cancer and will die a very painful death in a matter of one or two months.

'The Duke died of cancer himself a few years after they finished filming,' the Man says, scraping the last of the omelette from his plate. 'In fact, he was in remission from lung cancer while they were making it. He only had one lung.'

Aaron tries hard to stay focused on the film, avoiding the Man's eyes as they rest on him.

'Are you enjoying it?'

Aaron nods as he watches the doctor give Books a bottle of laudanum, telling him it's the most potent painkiller doctors have at their disposal.

'That's not true,' Aaron blurts out spontaneously.

'What's not true?'

'What he just said. Heroin's stronger than laudanum.'

'They didn't have heroin in those days, obviously,' the Man says dismissively.

'It said this's 1901, so they must've,' Aaron says, his confidence gained from reading a pamphlet his mother handed him in one of her many attempts to get him to stop using. His self-esteem gets a little boost knowing something the Man doesn't, so he goes on.

'Heroin was made from morphine in some London hospital in the 1890s to treat morphine addicts,' he says as the Man takes his plate, 'and now they hand out methadone for heroin addicts.'

'Well, I know one thing for sure, the Duke would not have used heroin for pain relief in any of his films,' he says as he stacks the dishwasher. 'He was a Freemason, you know. A law-abiding man of high moral standing.'

Just like yourself, Aaron thinks as he watches Books swig from his bottle of laudanum in front of his landlady. A love interest maybe, although she doesn't seem very keen to have a notorious gunslinger in her boarding house, even if he is dying.

The Man is back on the couch talking over the dialogue.

'He wasn't just a Freemason either. A Master Mason. Not a Grand Master like myself, I might add,' he says, letting it hang in the air as if savouring it. 'The Marion McDaniel Lodge number fifty-six in Tucson, Arizona. A big lodge, as I understand it.'

Aaron stays focused on the screen and the son of the landlady, a young man his own age named Gillom, establishing a relationship with Books. Gillom obviously looks up to the gunslinger, who seems to be enjoying the role of father figure. The story is really intriguing Aaron now, and the Man's voice is becoming more and more annoying.

'He was a vocal Republican in Hollywood and a prominent anti-communist,' he says before attempting his John Wayne impersonation. '"I don't believe that a fella should be able to sit on his backside and receive welfare."'

Aaron hears him laughing in a self-congratulatory way, then the sound of his hand patting the couch next to him.

'Come closer.'

No, not now. Can't he wait until the end of the film? He slides across to the Man with his eyes still fixed to the screen. Books and the landlady are riding through the countryside together in a horse-drawn buggy. Books tells her that he doesn't believe he ever killed a man who didn't deserve it. Surely only the Lord can judge that, she replies. Aaron feels the Man's hand on his thigh. A moment later, a phone rings.

'Someone ringing to congratulate me. Don't you go anywhere, my boy.'

The light-blue tracksuit and oversized black moccasins cross the floor to the wall-mounted phone in the kitchen. Aaron hopes that it's a very long conversation – or, even better, that the Man has a massive heart attack and dies right there on the black-and-white tiles. Aaron can take his credit card and max it out.

He doesn't have a heart attack. His loud voice is testament to that.

'Thanks, Trevor, that's very kind of you. To be honest, it is an honour I wasn't expecting so soon.'

Aaron reaches for the remote and turns up the volume on the television. Books is in bed and in pain, swigging laudanum, when he hears a noise at the window. He stacks a pillow under the blankets and hides behind the curtains, his gun cocked as an appropriately loud and dramatic score plays.

'Turn that bloody thing down,' the Man spits out with his hand cupped firmly over the phone.

Aaron does as he's told and watches Books shoot the two would-be assassins dead. Young Gillom rushes excitedly to tell his mother that JB Books has been involved in a shoot-out and that their house is now part of history. That is nothing to be proud of, she retorts. He hugs her and tells her he loves that old man. She tells him that Books is dying. Gillom is devastated.

The Man's voice is muzak, only noticeable to Aaron in a lull of action on the screen. Books is teaching Gillom how to shoot and is impressed by his skill. They walk away from the bullet holes in the tree trunk and the young man asks Books how he ever killed so many men. The gunslinger tells him that he has lived most of his life in the wild country and has survived by a set of important rules: he won't be wronged, he won't be insulted and he won't be laid hands on. He doesn't do those things to other people, and he requires the same from them.

The light-blue tracksuit appears in Aaron's peripheral vision. The Man is searching for something. A drawer in the desk opens and closes. The Man looks in his briefcase and then tosses it to one side. He scans the room in frustration. Where the bloody hell is it? His eyes fall on the glass-topped coffee table beside the couch and he crosses quickly to pick up a red notebook from the floor beneath it before quickly returning to the telephone. Aaron shifts his focus back to the story and the landlady telling Books that he is in fine fettle this morning. Books says he should be, he's full of laudanum. Over breakfast they argue about her plan to invite the town preacher over to absolve Books of his sins. He refuses. For him, a man's death is about the most private thing in his life and no one else's concern. She curses him for the pain he has brought into her house, and he walks out without another word. Aaron hears the Man winding up his telephone conversation far too soon.

'Yes, I know he's a very busy man, Trevor, but if you ring him on that number he'll answer it. Only his friends have it ... Of course, mention my name. And you can tell him my good news ...'

No, no, keep talking, please; *The Shootist* is reaching the final act. Aaron focuses as hard as he can on the screen, where Books is ordering a headstone from the undertaker to be inscribed with the year 1901 but with no day or month. The gunslinger then asks Gillom to go to the three most violent men in the town and tell them to be at the saloon at eleven o'clock the next day, his birthday. The Man walks into the frame, glass of wine in one hand and hunger in both eyes.

'Take your clothes off.'

A poison flows through Aaron, leaving any possibility of contentment in its wake.

'I want to watch the end of this first,' he says, sounding like he's eight years old again. The tone is so familiar.

'Take off your clothes and I'll tell you how it ends,' the Man says, turning off the television and ejecting the DVD.

Aaron stands and starts to undress.

'Good boy. It's been an exhausting day for me. Very exciting, but I'm tired now. We'll go to bed and you can tell me all about what you did at school today.'

Immediately, Aaron is forced into a battle against the memories and emotions bombarding him from the dark side. First, he pretends that the words were not directed at him, but to a boy sitting next to him. Then, he robotically takes off his jeans, staring hard at the blank television screen and wondering why Books has asked the three most violent men in the town to meet him at the saloon. If this is his way of avoiding a painful death from cancer, as the doctor advised he do, then how?

'Pack your clothes up neatly, please,' the Man says, running his long fingers through his dyed black hair.

Aaron does as he is told again while imagining Books walking through the doors of the Metropole saloon, the famous gunslinger that has never lost a fight. He must be planning to lose this one deliberately, but that doesn't make any sense to Aaron. What if he wins it? Then what? Does he kill himself? He feels a hand smack him gently on the bum and it brings him back to the room and the Man. Holding his clothes against his naked body, Aaron follows obediently behind the Man, who is switching off the lights on the path to his bedroom.

Anger kicks hard. *Feel me now, Aaron, I'm getting way stronger. Soon you won't be able to control me.*

⁓

He wakes in the dark, shivering and aching through to the bone. The digital clock says it is five o'clock. The Man is snoring peacefully beside him, his face a mask. Aaron slides carefully out from under the doona, picks up his neat pile of clothes and steps quietly out to the lounge room. A soft light bleeds through the curtains from the outside courtyard, showing him the way to the bathroom and a face in the mirror he barely knows. Who are you? You don't look well. Your eyes are bloodshot and you're very pale. That's right, you're a heroin addict. He opens his pencil case and sets out its contents on the ledge of the washbasin, his heart racing. His mother jumps into his thoughts, lingering there with sadness and guilt until the drug rushes through his veins, bearing bliss.

The television screen is sitting up in the almost dark. He goes to it across the thick carpet, pulling on his jeans. The couch is softer than he remembers and it's all so quiet and peaceful. He reaches for the remote control and returns to *The Shootist*, where an anxious Gillom is watching Books enter the saloon from the other side of the street. The doors swing open to reveal the three invited gunmen seated at different tables across the saloon. Books walks up to the barman declaring that it is his birthday and he would like to drink the best in the house. He sizes up the gunmen he can see behind him in the mirror, raising his glass to each of them as the barman retreats to safety. The first gunman draws his gun, and Books dives over the bar for cover before shooting him dead. The gunman at the next table shoots Books in the shoulder before he too is shot dead. The third and final gunman fires and wounds Books, again in the shoulder, before a cat-and-mouse game sees all three attackers dead.

Aaron presses the pause button and turns his head toward the Man's bedroom to check that he hasn't been disturbed by the gunfire. He hears only the rhythmic rumble of the Man's snores, so he returns to Gillom running across the street and into the saloon to find Books holding himself up at the bar, three dead men on the floor. The barman appears, pointing a double-barrelled shotgun at Books's back. Gillom yells out a warning but it is too late; Books is shot and collapses on the floor. The young man rushes to Books and takes his gun, turning to the barman, who is reloading his shotgun. Dramatic music plays as Gillom looks at the gun in his hand then hurls it in disgust across the full width of the saloon. Books looks up at him with a nod and a smile, then he dies. With tears in his eyes, the young man lays his coat over the old gunslinger and the credits roll.

The screen fades to black, and Aaron tries to make sense of the final scene. It's obvious Books didn't want to lose the gunfight – he fought too hard. And he couldn't have known that the barman would shoot him in the back. So, what was the point of picking the fight in the first place? Aaron gives up thinking about it and leaves the couch to look out across the backyard to the You Yangs, emerging like a sleeping giant in the dawn light. The urge to walk across the flat plains and climb the highest ridge is still with him. He will do it, one day.

Closer to him, a pair of spotted doves are perched on the roof of the woodshed, fluffing and preening. Below them, a dozen or so sparrows peck for food under the woodchips and squabble for position

211

on the chopping block where the head of the red-taped axe is wedged firmly at its centre. His mind wanders back to the film and Gillom. What will happen to him? Aaron really liked him. Loved his hat – a flat cap, soft and brown. The young man won't follow in Books's footsteps and become a shootist, Aaron is sure of that. Not the way he threw that gun away and got approval from the dying gunslinger for doing it. Maybe he'll become a sheriff, upholding law and order? Whatever he does, he'll make his mother proud.

Aaron is thirsty now, so he wanders across to the kitchen and opens the fridge. A beer will do nicely, and he stands in the banded light falling through the partially opened venetian blinds, sipping Corona and gazing at the photos on the lounge and dining-room walls. They are all of the Man being a Freemason, a very important man. There are no family photos anywhere. No wife. No children. No parents. Who will he leave all his money to? The house? The car? Does he have a will? He must have. He's old. But it doesn't matter anyway. Aaron could easily type a new one out on his computer and forge the Man's signature. People change their minds about who to leave their money to all the time, like to a carer or a lover who the family and friends have never heard of. He's seen it on *A Current Affair*. He could smother the Man with a pillow now. But he doesn't. Instead he thinks about returning to the bed before he wakes. He needs to be there beside him to avoid him discounting the nightly rate again. He puts the stubby down on the bench and closes his eyes to feel the full pleasure of the heroin. There is hope in comfort, there is none in pain.

He opens his eyes to the small red notebook the Man was so keen to find the night before. It is there on the *Melway*, under the wall-mounted phone. Treasure or trash? He flicks through the pages. Names and phone numbers with titles scribbled beside them. Important people, just like the Man himself – a politician, a judge, a QC, a detective, a priest – all members of a Masonic Lodge somewhere in Victoria. An opportunity presents itself. Money, certainly: enough to set off on a different course, just like Gillom walking out of the saloon leaving mayhem behind him. The Man will say it's blackmail; Aaron will say it's payback.

The snoring stops and the house is filled with the sound of birds enthusiastically greeting the day. The bed creaks and then the snoring starts up again but in a slower rhythm. Aaron treads softly into the lounge room to a small desk upon which is a laptop, a printer and a jar of pens. Taking out a sheet of paper from the printer, he hurriedly copies down names and numbers from the red notebook. Six is enough, he thinks.

He slides into bed next to the snoring man with the heroin and the promise of his escape plan shielding him from the ugliness of it all. It is peaceful in the soft morning light, and he closes his eyes imagining buying the patent-leather shoes from the op shop in Bank Street and then catching a tram to the city to buy a guitar. He knows exactly which one. A second-hand Martin D-28. It has a deep scratch in its solid spruce top, but it doesn't affect the sound. He will busk every day, all day, get back on to Youth Allowance, find somewhere to live, give up the heroin (try, anyway) and he will make his mother proud.

Sleep descends on him and he is soon running with Timmy through the yellow-flowered canola on the wide flat plain below the You Yangs. They are laughing as they race each other up the smooth granite surface to the top of the highest ridge. They sit together looking east to Park Towers where they are five years younger, wrestling playfully on the rooftop until Timmy gets angry. Then they are fighting, and there are punches and blood. Aaron turns away from the fight to see Timmy chasing a wedge-tailed eagle soaring into the air above them. Aaron screams out, but his words are carried away in the wind. Timmy plunges off the ridge and then there is only the sky and the eagle.

A hand is on his thigh, long fingers and a body spooning him. The hand finds his penis. It stays limp. Warm and stale breath in his ear.

'It's either now or later. Your choice.'

No, that's not a choice. His penis responds to the oil on the Man's fingers and he switches into survival mode, separating his mind from his body with the dawn chorus outside in the garden telling him that it is a new day and he *will* have a choice soon. He comes with empty pleasure and then feels the Man's lips on his back.

'You're a good boy. Pancakes for breakfast now.'

~

He sits opposite the Man at the dining-room table, soaking up a pool of maple syrup with his last piece of pancake. The list in his back pocket is at the centre of his thoughts. He considers making his move now, but being alone in a country house with an unpredictable man makes it a silly idea. Especially when you tell him you're going to tell the most important people in his life that he pays young men for sex and pretends they are schoolboys.

'What are you looking at me like that for?'

Aaron shrugs. No reason. The Man stands and carries the plates to the dishwasher.

'I'll take you to the train,' he says, taking off his apron and going to the mahogany wall stand just inside the front door. He puts a light-blue jacket on over his black polo shirt and fawn trousers. Not the usual suit and tie but no less ugly.

The sun is shining warmly onto the courtyard. There is not a breath of wind, and the roses are in late bloom. Reds and yellows and whites, all in their own sections. Neat and tidy like everything else in the Man's life. For the moment, anyway.

'I'll be deadheading soon,' he says, gesturing at the roses as they walk the few steps to the car.

'You said you'd teach me how to drive.'

'Not now.'

'Just down the driveway?' he says, hating the pleading tone to his voice.

'No, I said.'

The Man gets in behind the wheel and Aaron gets in beside him.

'I've got fifteen minutes to get to church,' he says, starting the engine. 'Next time.'

They drive in silence down the tree-lined driveway with Aaron aware that there won't be a next time, not with what he has planned. There is no conversation, only the sound of the tyres rolling over the gravel and an occasional stone hitting the undercarriage of the car. He gazes through the uniform gaps in the pine trees lining the driveway. Dry brown paddocks and an occasional homestead flash by until they cross the cattle grid and the Man brakes to a stop at the junction with the road. A dust-covered twin cab ute passes by with the bearded driver casually lifting his index finger from the steering wheel. The Man acknowledges him with the same gesture, then they accelerate west on the narrow, unsealed road. Directly ahead of them is a water tower perched high on a steel frame next to a cluster of houses and sheds. In the far distance, the dark shape of the peaks is visible through a fence line of eucalypts. Aaron thinks about the eagle in his dream.

'Are there eagles around here?'

'Wedge-tails,' the Man says as a car passes with another casual exchange of a raised finger. 'They're supposed to be a local Dreamtime thing. Who would know? They can make up as many stories as they like, as far as I'm concerned. As long as it brings in the tourists.'

The Man stops at the intersection where the gravel meets the bitumen on the main road into town. While he waits for a semitrailer to pass, Aaron looks across at the small red-brick church on the opposite corner. The dark granite of the mountain range in the background frames the large cross on the steeply pitched tiled roof.

'Is that your church?' Aaron asks while thinking about the name and number of the priest he has on his list.

'It's Catholic. A no-go zone for Freemasons since the eighteenth century,' the Man says as they follow the semitrailer the short distance to the edge of town. 'We're all heretics, according to the Pope.'

'What's a heretic?'

'A heretic, my boy, is someone whose beliefs and actions are not compatible with the religion they claim to belong to.'

'What religion are you?'

The Man's eyes turn on him with a flash of contempt. 'I'm an Anglican.'

He turns right at the big red sign advertising the Little River Hotel and all it has to offer. A hundred metres of silence later, they pull up in the almost empty car park of the train station. The Man takes out his wallet and hands Aaron six fifty-dollar notes.

'By the way, I don't pay you to ask questions.'

Aaron listens to the black Toyota Lexus accelerating away as he walks across the car park toward the station underpass. Feeling rough bitumen through the thin soles of his runners has him thinking again about the patent-leather shoes in the op shop. The sun is warm on his back, and there is still heroin lingering in his bloodstream. He has three hundred dollars in one pocket, and in the other, a list promising opportunity. It's enough to make him smile, almost.

18

Aaron stands in the shade of the op shop's awning looking through the large timber-framed window at the patent-leather shoes on display. If the shop was open he'd buy them now, but he will be the first through the door tomorrow morning. He glances up at the clock in the Town Hall tower telling him it is half past ten. It's been almost five hours since he last used, and the effects are wearing off. He pictures his mother at home drinking her second coffee while flicking through the newspaper with a CD on in the background. He guesses Paul Kelly. She has all his music. He would love to join her but knows he can't. Nothing has changed in his life that would see her welcome him inside.

Crossing the street to where the sun is shining onto the footpath opposite, he imagines having the power to go back ten years in time.

He would be that little boy again, tucked up in bed at his grandparents' house reading the Phantom comic his father let him take with him for that weekend stopover. The door would creak open, and his grandfather would appear under the guise of saying goodnight. But this time, when his big hand slid under the doona, Aaron would have no doubt it was wrong and he would scream at the top of his voice and his grandmother would come running to rescue him and it would never happen again because he would always say no you can't do that to me because that would completely destroy my life.

He is not returning home; he is walking in the opposite direction, toward Dave and Samantha's place, where he will pay his debt and satisfy his desire to be friends – or at least the closest thing he has to friends.

The streets are not busy. Fewer cars, going slower. Pedestrians searching for coffee or brunch or salvation. Passing the music academy, he hopes he doesn't see the woman whose bicycle he wanted to steal. What could he possibly say to her that would change her opinion of him? He reaches the intersection and glances left toward the Maori Chief Hotel and an image of his father propped up at the bar with his mates, talking and laughing. The sun is shining but there is no comfort for him on these streets.

Dave answers the door in his jocks. His thighs are the same width as his calves, his shoulders square and his ribs bold on his chest.

'Weren't you told to ring first?' His tone reminds Aaron that Dave's not really his friend. He's his drug dealer.

'I've got that eighty bucks for you,' Aaron says, touching his pocket, 'and enough for more.'

Dave quickly scans the street and beckons him inside before shutting the door. They stand in the dark hallway with the strong smell of mildew.

'What do you want?'

Aaron peels off two hundred dollars and hands it to him. Dave takes the money and sets off toward the thin shaft of light sliding under the door to the lounge room at the end of the hallway. Okay, Aaron thinks, I'm being told to stay here.

'We're making a baby, Aaron.' Samantha's voice.

Aaron takes two steps along the hallway to the open door, through which she is propped up in bed under the doona.

'Everything's sweet then?' he asks, hoping it to be true.

'I'm a very happy girl. And I want you to be happy too.' She throws out her arms exposing her large breasts to the world. 'So come here and give me a big, big hug!'

He does as he is told because he wants to. She is warm and soft and kind.

'There you go,' she says as she releases him and covers up her breasts to the sound of bare feet coming back down the hallway.

Dave comes in with two points of heroin and twenty dollars change. Aaron wants to stay, have a shower and wash away the smell of the Man, hit up, maybe have something to eat and then sleep over on the couch. The perfect preparation for the big phone call tomorrow. But Dave turns to the door with his arm out, making it very clear that he should leave now. Aaron turns instinctively toward Samantha with a silent plea for her support. She bounces out of bed with the doona wrapped around her.

'Tea or coffee, Aaron?'

'Coffee.'

'How many sugars?'

'Four please.'

~

Aaron is sitting on the couch having ticked off two items on his wish list. He's had a long, hot shower and is nicely stoned, watching Dave hang his psychedelic painting on the wall covered in the same psychedelic wallpaper. The colours don't match exactly, but the patterns are a direct replica. Dave's always liked to dress well, but now he's gone up a notch with the RM Williams boots, the Wrangler jeans and the checked Levi's shirt. His business is obviously paying dividends, just like Samantha said. Dave steps back from his painting to check that it's level.

'What do you reckon?'

Aaron's brain is too slow. Dave makes a slight adjustment and now he's happy. Samantha comes in from the kitchen, towel-drying her hair and wearing green Adidas shorts and a black mohair jumper. Her black eyes are sparkling and she is wanting to talk.

'Don't you love his new painting? It's a concept. He explained it to me. What did you say, Dave? A dance of two realities. Isn't that clever? Do you like my shorts, Aaron? From Smith Street. I love that street. And look at him dressed like a cowboy. Handsome as. And we bought a slow cooker, didn't we, Dave? Splashed out, we did.'

Dave's phone rings and he goes out into the hallway to do his business, looking like he's relieved to escape. Aaron stares up at a bubbling Samantha.

'Do you like our place, Aaron? Nice, eh?'

'Yeah, it is,' he says. Bugger Dave. 'Do you reckon I can stay here tonight?' He is about to add that he has a big day tomorrow and he needs a good night's sleep, but it isn't necessary.

'Of course you can. Music! I want to dance, Aaron!'

She goes straight to the ghetto blaster on the floor under Dave's painting, hits the play button and stands stock-still as the ghostly sound of wind, a howling animal, heavy breathing and footsteps open the track. She starts moving to a fast-tempo electro-pop beat and singing along with a voice Aaron thinks he recognises as Shakira. Not his preferred style of music, but it is obviously Samantha's. She knows all the lyrics and has the disco rhythm and Shakira's moves down pat. Aaron can't help but smile and sing the chorus along with her. Dave comes back in to the lounge room as the music fades out with a clap of thunder.

'Encore, encore!' Samantha says, going to the ghetto blaster.

'No more!'

Dave's jaw is set square with his thumbs in his silver buckled belt. Aaron can't help but think Dave needs a horse, or a guitar. Certainly a stetson.

'No, Dave. We're having fun. Please don't spoil it.'

Dave takes a pill from the press-studded pocket of his shirt and holds it out to her.

'I don't want it now. I'll have it later, I promise.'

His hand and the pill don't move. She glances across at Aaron, but there is nothing he can say or do to stop Dave getting what he wants. She takes the pill, swallows it and then sticks out her tongue crudely, as if to say, 'up yours'. Dave turns to Aaron.

'You can go now.'

'No, Dave. He wants to stay tonight and I said he can.'

'Did you just?' he says with a bitter edge. 'So you didn't think it'd be a good idea to consult Dave first?'

Aaron watches Samantha's brave posture collapse in a flash.

'I'm sorry, Dave.'

Aaron feels sadness rolling through him. Sadness for himself and for Samantha. They both know she has to play his game or she'll be back on the streets. He picks up his backpack and heads to the door with a quick smile for Samantha and Dave as they follow him out.

A cold wind bites at him as he walks up the street to the top of Emerald Hill where the clock tower above the Town Hall is telling him it's four. The top ten or so levels of Park Towers reach above the trees lining the opposite side of the street, and he thinks of Timmy in his coffin, never to be seen again except in a dream. He imagines Vicky at home in the warmth of the house he once called home too, but quickly shuts it down. It only invites pain. Instead, he reminds himself of the one hundred and twenty dollars and five hits of heroin he has in his pocket and finds some comfort. He is hungry now; perhaps it is the cold, but he remembers he hasn't eaten since the pancakes the Man cooked him for breakfast. The fish and chip shop will be open on Clarendon Street, so he decides he'll buy a chicken burger and chips, eat on the seat outside and think about his plan.

He hopes he doesn't run into his mother. What would he say to her?

Hi, Mum, you won't have to worry about me soon.

Why's that, Aaron?

Well, I'm going to extort money from a man who pays me for sex and then I'm going to buy a guitar and go busking and give up the heroin.

Give up heroin? Just the thought of doing it fills him with dread. And he can't tell her about the Man either. No, if he sees her he'll just say he's working on a plan that will make them both happier.

That's not a lie.

Jacko is at the deep-fryer when Aaron comes through the door of the South Melbourne Fish and Chip Shop. He's a big bearded man with red hair who has run the shop for as long as Aaron can remember. Jacko lifts the basket of golden-brown chips from the oil, sits it on the draining rack and turns his head to Aaron.

'G'day, mate.'

Aaron steps up to the counter and puts down twenty dollars.

'Jacko. Chicken burger and chips.'

'You don't look the best, mate. Everything alright?'

'Yeah, yeah good,' he says softly, acutely aware of the only other customers in the small shop: a little boy about four years old and a grey-haired woman who could be the boy's grandmother.

'And Vicky?' Jacko asks as he gives Aaron his change.

Jesus, Jacko, too many questions. Just cook my burger and chips and leave me alone. 'She's good.'

He steps back from the counter feeling the little boy's eyes on him. He looks down at him and smiles instinctively. The little boy smiles back while gripping the woman's leg tightly. She smiles at Aaron too, and for a fleeting moment he feels its warmth before she turns away to collect the parcel of chips Jacko has placed on the counter and takes the little boy's hand to exit the shop.

'Watch the game last night?' Jacko asks as he flips the chicken burger on the grill.

'No. Was it good?' Aaron asks, hoping to get a drawn-out description so he can tune out without being noticed. He is not disappointed. Jacko delves immediately into the details of the game between his team, Hawthorn, and the team he hates the most, Collingwood. With his monologue successfully muffled, Aaron turns his head to look out at the little boy and the woman crossing Clarendon Street at the lights. He is holding her hand and skipping beside her, all innocence and joy. They reach a parked car where a grey-haired man is behind the wheel, waiting for them. As the woman buckles the boy into the child's seat, the man turns to look directly at Aaron, who sees only the lustful face of his grandfather. His stomach knots, and the fear sweeping through him forces his attention back to Jacko's monologue.

'Worst bloody umpiring display I've ever seen,' Jacko says, putting the burger and chips down on the counter. 'Twenty-seven frees to thirteen. A fucking disgrace.'

Aaron is eating his chips from the top of the bag as he walks the few steps along the footpath to sit at the bench seat. The wind is colder now than it was twenty minutes ago, so he pulls his hoodie over his head and disappears into the world of his thoughts to eat and make a plan. When will he make the phone call? How much will he ask for? He feels for the list in his pocket. It's still there. Mayonnaise from the burger runs down his chin, and he wipes it off with the sleeve of his dirty and well-worn hoodie. He will buy another tomorrow morning from the op shop when he buys the shoes. That's if they have one. He decides he'll tell the Man he wants one thousand dollars. He could ask for more, but he calculates that's all he needs. Besides he doesn't want him to get too angry. Who knows what other friends he has in that red book of his? Someone might owe him a favour. Paranoia? Probably, but Aaron knows he's an unpredictable man. He picks at the last of the chips, cold and soggy now. He won't ring him tonight though. He'll do it first thing in the morning, after he's had his breakfast heroin.

The sun is setting as he turns a corner with the intention of camping in the container he slept in two nights before. It is more a lane than a street: very narrow, with one-way traffic only and just the one surviving house amongst the back walls and roller doors of various warehouses and industrial offices. The house is a double-fronted red-brick old cottage with a large gold-plated plaque at the front door. In the fading light, he can just make out *Custom Brokers* written in black lettering. Aaron hadn't noticed it before, and he wonders what Custom Brokers do. Do they find drugs hidden in cans of Italian tomatoes and barrels of Columbian olives? Or do they make sure the drugs get through customs without being found? Probably a bit of both, he thinks. He reaches the metal fence to the adjacent property and quickly checks that the street is clear of cars and pedestrians before peering in at the still-unlocked container. The time is now. He needs shelter and he needs heroin. The backpack goes over and he follows right behind it.

Inside the container, everything is just as he left it. Hopefully he can keep using it until he finds somewhere decent to live, the third item in his grand plan. He sits down on the two pallets he uses for a bed and wastes no time preparing the hit. A shaft of light from the nearby street lamp falls through the propped-open container door directly onto his arm, and he guides the needle into a vein and pushes down on the plunger.

The sound of a siren. A police siren somewhere inside his head. His eyes open. No, it's on a street close by. The squeal of tyres. He sits up, aching everywhere. The light from the street lamp is fading in the dawn, and he remembers the Man and the phone call he has to make. The thought amplifies his anxiety, and he considers not going ahead with it, but only for the moment it takes him to reach for his drug kit. He will shoot up and ring the man while he's still in bed, still drowsy. It will put him on the back foot.

Very stoned, he turns on his phone. The anxiety has been soothed away and replaced with a cloudy determination underpinned by subterranean anger. The small Nokia screen comes to life and he dials the number embedded in his memory. He closes his eyes as he decides on a time and place. Pick up, you bastard.

'Yes?'

'I've got a list.'

'What are you talking about?'

'Names and numbers out of your little red book.'

Silence. Aaron can feel him squirming.

'One thousand dollars cash or I ring everyone on it.'

'You fucking little prick.'

'Twelve o'clock today. The bottom of La Trobe Street. There's a park on the corner near the water.'

He hangs up and flops back on to the blanket- and tarp-covered pallet with a smile creasing his cheeks. One thousand dollars. The first step in his grand plan, done. Well, almost done. He hasn't got the money in his hand yet, but it doesn't stop him imagining busking and the money piling up in the cap on the footpath in front of him. What will he play? He'll need at least twenty songs, he thinks, so there's definitely some he'll need to practise first. Some he knows well enough already. Nick Cave's 'Into My Arms' is the first to form in his clouded brain and he drifts subconsciously from there to the French guy at the backpackers, then the watch he stole from him, then to his haircut, then to his mother and the sound of her scissors and the smell of her skin.

A loud voice outside brings him back to the daylight and the sounds of a city fully awake. A man is talking loudly on his phone next to the container. What to do? Stay quiet and hope he doesn't see the propped-open door? What if he sees it and closes it without looking inside? Trapped. The voice moves slowly and inexorably toward the rear of the container. Aaron could pack up all his things and make a run for it. No, it's too late now. A hand reaches through the gap. The door swings open and Aaron is staring into the startled eyes of a skinny middle-aged man wearing a suit at odds with the large gold earring in one ear and the tattoo-covered hands.

'I'll ring you back,' he says, before putting his phone into his pocket.

Aaron starts to pack up his gear. What else can he do? He's been caught red-handed. His drug paraphernalia is collected up first.

'How long have you been sleeping in here?'

'Just last night.'

Aaron rolls up his blanket and tarp thinking it's not going to end well.

'Did you piss or shit in there?'

'No way,' he says, pulling his pack onto his back wishing he didn't feel so wasted. He can barely feel his feet and his brain is mush. Not the ideal condition for any form of conflict. He wants to say, please let me go, I won't do it again, but his mouth refuses to move.

The man steps back from the door.

'Off you go then.'

Aaron hesitates, thinking he's being set up. But he has no choice. He steps out expecting a clip around the ears, or worse.

'Better straighten yourself up, mate. You won't like gaol, believe me.'

19

Aaron walks back and forth in front of the op shop, eating a doughnut and brushing sugar from his lips. Each time he turns he glances up at the Town Hall clock ticking closer to ten. Next door, Café Zappa is humming with customers either ordering takeaway coffees or sitting at an outdoor table attempting to grab the attention of the flustered waitress. Aaron's eyes are drawn to the exposed briefcases and handbags, but only fleetingly. It's a habit he's happy to avoid. Stealing has only ever been a means to an end, and it never makes him feel good. The heroin does that. He swallows the last of the doughnut thinking about the thousand dollars he will soon have in his pocket. Will it be in fifty-dollar notes or in hundreds? He'd prefer fifties because the wad will be thicker, but he's not fussed. The clock chimes once, and he fixes his eyes keenly on the glass door of the shop. On the tenth chime, a woman walks through the array of second-hand goods to open it.

Aaron goes straight to the patent-leather shoes.

'How much?' he asks of the woman, who reminds him of the queen. She is very old and very well dressed with blue wavy hair stiff with product.

'The price is on the tag. Thirty dollars, I believe.'

He reaches into his pocket without a second thought.

'Do you think you should try them on first?'

Yes, he should. He sits down on the nearest chair and slips off his runners, sensing the woman taking a step back from him. Even he can smell them now. Or is it his socks? He ties up the laces on the shoes and stands. They fit perfectly, and he can see his face in the patent leather.

'Do you have any hoodies?'

~

It's a purple hoodie two sizes too big, but he loves the authoritative sound his leather-soled new shoes make on the bluestone laneway. It makes him feel taller, and he wants to show them to his mother so she can see he is trying to be a better person. Maybe she can love him again like she used to. But standing on the footpath opposite the salon, second thoughts stop him from crossing the street. The shoes won't be enough to impress her. Much better to wait until he can show her something solid, like the cash he will have after a day of busking. Even then, it won't be enough for her. The heroin will still be the problem. He can feel it leaving his system now and he is already thinking about his next hit. It is reassuringly in his pocket, but if it wasn't? The pain and the panic are very easily imagined.

He keeps walking to the end of the street and gets on a half-empty number 112 tram to the sound of his shoes on the metal steps. Passengers look up and then turn away as he walks down the aisle to find a free double seat at the rear. He looks west, thinking of the Man driving toward the city from Little River, and it makes him nervous. Maybe more toey than nervous, like he would get before a game of football when he would be totally focused and utterly determined to win every contest ahead of him.

The tram rattles into the expanse of shade under the concrete overpass carrying ten lanes of traffic to and from the West Gate Bridge. His head turns toward Kings Way with the memory of waiting for his father amongst the Mercedes-Benz cars a few nights ago. It's a memory that only stirs his anger. He forces his thoughts back to what's waiting for him and the opportunity he has to show his father he can do something positive with his life despite his complete lack of support. Up yours, Dad!

He stares out through the window reflecting on his decision to meet the Man at the small park near the water in Docklands. It's an open space and not very populated, just like the places where characters in films meet when exchanging information or something illegal. He won't get in the car, that's for sure. The Man will want the list and Aaron is happy to give it to him. He wants him out of his life completely. Looking at the office and apartment towers mushrooming along the banks of the Yarra as the tram crosses over the Spencer Street Bridge, he wishes he had asked for more than a thousand dollars. It's too late for that now.

The tram continues slowly down Spencer Street, between large advertising billboards above supermarkets and takeaway shops on one side, and modern glass towers swallowing the city's heritage on the other. He gets off at the next intersection, where he is confronted with the red bricks and narrow barred windows of the Melbourne Assessment Prison on the opposite corner. Razor wire runs along the wall at the rear of the main five-storey building, enclosing what he imagines is an exercise yard. The words of the thin man who busted him at the container return to him – *You won't like gaol, believe me.* No, it wouldn't be nice being locked up in there, but he's not going to gaol, he's going in the opposite direction.

He crosses over the concrete-and-steel bridge that spans the confluence of rail lines servicing the suburban, regional and interstate networks. Peering down at the crisscrossing iron tracks and the trains converging under the undulating, dune-like roof of Southern Cross Station, he can almost feel his father's hand holding his. It's a warm memory this time, in part anyway, and he goes with it willingly. It is 2002 and he is eight years old, going to a North Melbourne game at the brand-new stadium at the western end of the bridge. The Kangaroos won all but two of the games they played at the Dome that year. Those wins gave him a few hours' joy and some respite from the turmoil in his young head about what was happening on the stopovers at his grandparents'.

Coming off the bridge, he can see the blue water of Victoria Harbour beyond the T-junction at the bottom of the gently sloping street. This is it, his big moment. He hopes he's early. A young woman in activewear and wearing designer sunglasses is pushing a pram with a toddler past him.

'Have you got the time?'

She hesitates briefly. 'Almost twelve.'

'Thanks.'

He reaches the small park across from the waterfront. On the opposite corner, the facade of a tall building is panelled with black-and-white squares like a chessboard. White yachts and large motorboats are moored around the edge of the U-shaped harbour where cranes sit atop partially constructed apartment towers. There is no sign of the Man's black Lexus, so Aaron takes off his backpack and sits down in the shade of one of the small eucalypts bordering the footpath and two empty car spaces. It feels deserted. Not many cars or pedestrians, and only an occasional bicycle and tram – all just as he planned.

There he is at the lights. The green arrow appears, and the black Lexus turns the corner and stops in one of the empty car spaces in front of Aaron. He gets up with his heart thumping in his chest and walks to the car. The tinted passenger window slides down, revealing the Man behind the wheel in his suit. Aaron leans in with his elbows on the window frame, trying hard to appear nerveless. The heroin will go down well when this is over. The Man doesn't look at him.

'I want the list.'

Aaron relaxes slightly. It's a sign that the exchange is about to happen. The Man turns to look at him, his face flushed red and ugly.

'And you'd better not have a fucking copy.'

Aaron pulls the list from his pocket and holds it up.

'No copy.'

The Man reaches into the inside pocket of his suit jacket and pulls out a wad of fifty-dollar notes held together with a rubber band. Aaron leans further into the car, holding the list tightly in one hand, the other ready to take the money. The Man grips the list and Aaron grips the money: coupled by competing needs.

'I've got other boys, you know. You're not the only one,' the Man says spitefully.

Fuck off, Aaron wants to say. Do whatever your twisted mind wants as long as it's not with me. He pulls hard on the money and lets go of the list at the same time. The Man releases the money, and Aaron stands back from the car with a thousand dollars in his hand and the patent-leather shoes on his feet. The tinted window slides smoothly back up, and the black Lexus accelerates away.

Aaron finds a secluded spot against the two-metre-high fence dividing the park from the Docklands stadium precinct. The black-panelled fence is covered in torn remnants of posters, the words *Bill Posters Will be Prosecuted* stencilled in white letters at regular intervals along it. He sits in the shade of a lone eucalypt feeling as excited as he can remember, a half-point of heroin primed to go into his arm. Buying the guitar is next on his list, and he can almost feel it in his hands. Yes, his grand plan is coming together and he deserves a reward. The drug enters his bloodstream, and the surge of pleasure obliterates all in its path. In too short a moment, the best part is over and he feels the heavy weight of his eyes and body before lying back on the grass and falling happily to sleep.

He wakes to voices and laughing and three young friends walking through the park. Indian students he thinks, all so happy. A familiar ache gnaws at him, forcing him to turn away to the glistening blue water on the harbour and to rekindle his determination to get a life like theirs.

20

He stands in front of Coleman's Guitars, a stone's throw from Flinders Street Station. It's Phil Coleman's shop – Shotgun Phil, they call him, because he loves to put the burning end of a joint in his mouth and blow a thick stream of smoke into other people's open mouths. Aaron walks in and moves through the array of cheaper guitars on the ground floor. The man himself is with a customer on the mezzanine floor above where the more expensive guitars are on display.

'I hope you're here to buy it this time,' Phil says, leaning over the metal railing.

Aaron looks up at a short man in his mid-forties with dreadlocked blond hair and a high-pitched voice. Aaron smiles and nods. The Martin D-28 is still for sale on a stand near the shop window, and

Aaron sits down on a wooden stool to tune it. It feels great in his arms, and he starts to play 'Everybody Moves' by Died Pretty, an Australian alternative rock band he first heard on Triple R. The song made him feel better. It has an uplifting rhythm with lyrics about moving from darkness and despair to the light and the sounds of all we yearn for. It is definitely on his busking list.

'You play that well, mate,' Shotgun Phil says as he approaches.

'Six hundred. Cash.'

Phil shakes his head. 'The tag says seven, mate.'

'Six fifty. And a case.'

Phil turns his head to acknowledge another customer coming through the door.

'Fuck, mate, I can do a soft case, that's it.'

Another win. Aaron follows Phil to the counter where he hands over the cash and fits the guitar into a padded nylon case.

'Sweet,' Aaron says, unable to hide the excitement. Time to declare it. 'Bourke Street Mall, here I come.'

'Got your permit then?' Phil's high-pitched voice is a siren sounding trouble.

Aaron barely shakes his head. 'You have to have one?'

'Bloody oath. The council have cracked down on it. You need to fill out an application then wait 'til you get an audition. And it'll cost ya.'

'Fuck that, then.'

'They'll fine you, mate. Big time. Gotta go. Customers.'

Aaron walks a crowded footpath to the steps at the entrance to Flinders Street Station, where he sits down to rethink his grand plan in the wake of Shotgun Phil's unexpected news. He has three hundred and fifty dollars in his pocket, a guitar he just paid six hundred and fifty dollars for, and no heroin. He certainly can't wait the weeks or months or whatever it takes to get a fucking permit. He has no choice. He'll busk without one. He'll play two songs in one place before moving to another. He'll be a moving target, one step ahead of trouble. He hears the *click, click, click* of the crossing signal and pedestrians stream across the intersection in front of him, half coming toward the station and the other half leaving it. He looks down the street, where more commuters are swarming to and from the entrance to the underground station. It's a no-brainer. He'll start in there, in the thick of it. Doubt, uncertainty and anxiety hold him to the granite steps where more and more students with heavy bags are gathering to smoke or flirt or show each other something funny on their phones.

He forces himself to stand and walk, but he doesn't go far before his eyes are drawn to the shopfront immediately adjacent to the station steps. He sees a brown flat cap just like Gillom's amongst a dozen different styles of hats displayed in the ornately framed window of City Hatters. He needs a hat for busking. He has the money in his pocket, and he feels faintly excited as he walks down the granite stone steps to the shop entrance in the recess below the footpath. Everything about the hat shop speaks of old-world style: the black iron railings, the polished stone pillars, the gold trim on the window, even the man who greets him when he pushes through the heavy timber-framed double doors into the sweet-smelling shop lined floor to ceiling with shelves of hats. There are akubras, pork pies, trilbies, fedoras, stetsons and Panamas, to name only some.

'What can we do for you today?'

The salesman is in his early forties with dark, short-cropped curly hair and a large handlebar moustache. He's wearing a checked three-piece suit with a tailor's tape measure around his neck in the manner of a doctor with a stethoscope. Aaron feels intimidated and is thankful for the shoes on his feet tipping the scales at least slightly in his favour.

'The brown cap you've got in the window there.'

'You mean this one?'

'Yeah, that one.'

'A very nice cap indeed. Genuine Harris Tweed with quilted lining for comfort and warmth,' he says with a cock of his unusually long head. 'This one is priced at ninety-eight dollars. However, we do have cheaper options.'

'I'll have that one,' Aaron says quickly, even though it's a lot more than he planned to spend. He wants to put this man back in his place, and he wants the cap, badly.

'What size are we?' he asks with barely disguised surprise.

'Can't I just try it on?'

'No, no, no,' he says pulling the tape from his neck. 'That's not the way we do things here. You're not shopping at Dimmeys today.'

Aaron walks out of City Hatters with the flat cap on his head. Size M/57 and a perfect fit; not too tight and not too loose. Pity about the oversized purple hoodie (a rash purchase) and the worn, out-of-shape jeans between the cap and the shoes, but he'll deal with them later. After he's filled the cap with money.

He descends into the station underpass providing access to all of the thirteen platforms and weaves his way through the rush-hour commuters feeling good about himself, confident even. The cap and the shoes and the guitar are telling him he's getting closer to pulling off his grand plan. He'll soon be ready to say, 'Look at me now, Mum. Look what I've done.' There is still the heroin, but strangely it is not on his mind as he continues along the underpass. Normally he would be thinking about the drug five hours after his last hit, but now he is completely distracted by the anticipation of the moment.

He picks a spot opposite the gate leading to the steps up to platforms six and seven. It's roughly at the midway point, he thinks, so it should maximise the number of people passing him. He sits down on his backpack as tight as he can against the water-stained ceramic-tiled wall as a train clatters slowly across the tracks directly above him. He takes out his guitar to check the tuning and play a few chords. There is no need for an amplifier in this tunnelled space, or a microphone. He takes off his cap, places it in front of his crossed legs and strums the opening chords of his up-tempo version of Nick Cave's 'Into My Arms'. His voice is soft and hesitant at first, but when the coins start to drop into the cap from knee-height hands, the caution evaporates as if by magic, releasing him to perform with optimism and enthusiasm for more.

The song ends and he quickly calculates that he has about ten dollars in his cap. So, if he plays ten songs, he makes a hundred dollars. If he plays twenty songs, he makes two hundred. He cradles the Martin D-28 lovingly in his arms and plays on without a thought for anything but the joy of the moment. Nirvana's 'Come as You Are' this time, one of his favourite songs, with lyrics Cobain described as being about accepting people for who they are. Aaron has always found it comforting, and he belts out the chorus line over and over having already made up his mind to abandon his two-songs-move-on strategy. He wants to hold on to how he is feeling for as long as he can. But then he spots the distinctive blue-and-white checked bands around two caps descending the steps at the entrance to the underpass. Dread smothers joy in an instant. He needs to move very quickly, and he does. The money goes into the large pockets of his hoodie, the cap goes on his head, the pack onto his back, the guitar into one hand and the soft case into the other, and then he is dodging through the oncoming foot traffic toward the Yarra River exit.

Outside the station, he doesn't hesitate to turn up the short and gentle incline to the footbridge crossing the murky, green water to the restaurants and bars lining the promenade on the south bank of the river. He jogs over the arched steel footbridge with his arms tight against his side, stopping the coins from bouncing out of his hoodie pockets. When he reaches the promenade's bluestone paving, he stops to put his guitar safely back in its case, peak-hour pedestrians and cyclists streaming around him. He's desperate to return to the sense of fulfilment busking gave him. It was everything he had hoped for and more. It was proof that his grand plan is not a dream. But where he stands in the midst of the buffeting foot traffic, his anxiety peaking, a familiar voice in his head is growing louder and more insistent. You need to score, Aaron! Don't go thinking about anything else until you do!

Stepping into clearer space closer to the edge of the promenade, he hears the sharp ding of metal on metal, and a split-second later a bicycle glances the base of his guitar case.

'Fuck you too, mate!' he shouts after the rider disappearing into the congestion. His desire for heroin jumps up another notch.

Then he sees them. Four this time: two men and two women strolling in their black boots and blue uniforms twenty metres from him. One is talking earnestly on her mobile phone. It's about him. It has to be. He turns and walks briskly away toward the Princes Bridge, the battle in his head yet to be won.

245

Walking close to the black wrought-iron railing on the river side of the promenade, Aaron is barely aware of the four young women pulling on the sweep oars of their racing shell and gliding across the surface of the rippled water. Nor does he notice the long line of tourists waiting to board their riverboat cruise, or the lovers kissing under a wilting plane tree. His focus is completely on the small crowd gathered around a busker singing Bob Dylan's 'Like a Rolling Stone' and playing his guitar. He has a microphone and harmonica cradled at his mouth and a drum kit harnessed on his back, its beat driven by strings attached to the heels of his shoes. Aaron takes an instant dislike to him. He's not impressed with his music or the way he is bantering with the crowd between lines of the song. But the crowd loves it, cheering him on and filling his guitar case with money. The bastard has a permit. If only. The music fades into the chatter along the promenade, and when Aaron reaches the squat granite columns supporting the southern end of the Princes Bridge, he takes a sharp turn right and climbs up the steep bluestone steps to the traffic crossing over it.

The pedestrian-clogged footpath runs alongside the bumper-to-bumper cars inching their way across the bridge to the city centre. A tram travels faster on its designated line, but not as fast as the cyclists in their laneway immediately beside Aaron. He keeps his head down, watching every step his patent-leather shoes take with a white-knuckled grip on the handle of his guitar case. Both are physical connections to the way forward. The shoes leading him away from the call of the heroin, and the guitar case carrying his hope for another way of being. That hope is real – he knows that because he felt it so profoundly in the underpass. He also knows that he is facing a critical test of his grand plan. If he can't busk without hitting up first, then what hope has he?

21

At Flinders Street Station, he forces himself to turn away from his usual sources of heroin to walk east instead, toward what is referred to as the 'Paris end' of town. He calculates that he's not as likely to be caught busking without a permit because there'll be fewer police patrolling. His aching leg muscles resist every step he takes up the slope to the intersection where Louis Vuitton and Gucci sell their luxury items from heritage-listed buildings, and where two nineteenth-century churches with tall bell towers and elaborate stonework dominate the hilltop. He crosses at the lights and continues down the incline in the shade of London plane trees until he sees a steady stream of people going into the Greater Union cinema complex. Immediately, he makes the decision to set up close by. If they like movies, then they'll appreciate music: that's his theory.

He sits down on his backpack a few metres up from the entrance, places his cap on the ground and unzips his guitar case, intending to return to his two-songs-move-on strategy, no matter what. The hard bargain made with his addicted self demands it. The reassuring feel of the guitar in his hands releases some of the agitation swarming through him, and without thinking, he finds his fingers going straight to a G chord to play Bill Fay's 'Be Not So Fearful'. The English folk singer released two albums in the seventies that didn't sell and his label dropped him. Nick Cave and other prominent musicians covered some of his songs, and twenty years later the albums were reissued. Vicky listened to 'Be Not So Fearful' every day for weeks, and Aaron played the pared-back, melancholic song often, drawn to its narrative about being brave and freeing yourself from the past in order to live a better life.

The coins are not dropping into the cap like they were in the underpass. There are fewer people, and most of them are passing as if he isn't there, too caught up in conversation – perhaps about the film they have just seen or are about to see. He nods an acknowledgement to those who do reach into their pockets. As he plays and sings, his eyes meet those of a young woman standing on the footpath opposite, under the awning of the Theosophical Society building. She smiles at him, or at least he thinks that she does. The light is fading and the street is busy with passing cars. When he glances again, she is walking directly toward him: tall, with long brown hair, large eyes and a beautiful face. For a second, he struggles to remember where he is in the song before recovering quickly.

She steps onto the footpath in front of him. Probably twenty years old, he guesses as she drops a dollar coin into his cap. He strums the last chords of the song, his eyes following her as she takes up a position against the wall, close to him. Now his heart is beating faster and his brain scrambles to find what to play next. He wants it to be something he knows and plays well so he doesn't stuff it up in front of her. It really is just her now; few others are paying him any attention. They all have plans he's not a part of. He imagines being back home playing 'Drunken Angel' with his mother. The words and the chords flow freely, and he stays in the lounge room with her until the last lines of Lucinda Williams's song to her alcoholic friend. She is asking him why he gave up his guitar and let his life get so bad.

He leans his guitar against the wall without looking at the young woman, but her presence is palpable, and not only because of her sweet perfume wafting over him on the evening breeze. She's in his head, and he's annoyed with himself for allowing thoughts of a future with her to form so quickly. It is the call of a beautiful woman again, and he doesn't want to answer it like he did with Zoe. He wants to run away and get completely wasted and fade the fantasy to black.

'No, don't pack up. Play some more.'

He has to answer her now. He would feel silly if he didn't.

'I've got enough. It's been a good day,' he says, picking up his cap and emptying another ten dollars into a pocket of his jeans.

'Sweet. Maybe I'll catch you tomorrow then.'

The cap goes back on his head and the guitar back into its case with him expecting her to leave. She doesn't.

'I'm Rebecca, by the way.'

Shit. Be not so fearful. He glances at her briefly.

'Aaron,' he says, intending it to sound confident and final. It is neither.

'Love your shoes.'

Bloody hell. She's coming on to him. It's all too much. His need for comfort is intense.

'You okay?' she asks.

Fuck it. 'I'm hangin'.'

'I can help you with that.'

Please. That would be perfect. The backpack is on his shoulders. Ready to go. She flicks her head toward the laneway alongside the cinema, then he is following her across the white-pointed bluestone paving. They reach the alcove of a garage roller door opposite three storeys of faux-Parisian apartments with tiny balconies and curved-iron balustrades. They sit down together in the concrete recess of the garage with the light from the shuttered windows falling softly over them. He has walked willingly into a dream with Rebecca now and is unable to take his eyes off her. She smiles at him as she takes a drug kit from her khaki shoulder bag, and for the first time he sees her chipped front tooth and the picked scabs on her very thin arms. She is still beautiful, but it tips the fantasy reassuringly toward reality and the possibility of them walking hand in hand into a better future together.

~

Aaron is floating in a bath of warm velvet water, peering through heavy eyelids at the vision beside him. Her heroin is good and strong, and he doesn't want to speak, not yet. In their soporific silence, he slides his hand toward her and their fingertips touch lightly. He tries to stretch out further, but her hand retreats and then she is moving.

'We need to go.'

Aaron sees him now too: a grey-haired man on his second-storey balcony, with a phone to his ear and his eyes fixed down on them. Aaron doesn't need to be told twice. He moves as quickly as he can to follow her back up the laneway. The balcony man yells something at them as they go, his exact words blurred by the roar of a large motorbike accelerating away from outside the cinema.

It's a short quick walk down to the edge of Chinatown. Rebecca doesn't obey traffic lights, so neither does he. Cars blast their horns and flash their lights. A tram bell dings through the night air. He follows her, turning right up an incline, dodging people staring at menus in restaurant windows or waiting for a spare table outside a busy cafe. A mass of knotted hair and a bearded red face juts out from under a pile of dirty blankets at the entrance to a closed barbershop. Aaron briefly considers the irony of the man's choice of shelter before he feels Rebecca taking his hand. His heart swells and she leads him across four lanes of traffic to the steps of Parliament House.

'Let's stop here for a bit,' she says.

He sits down eagerly with her on the sandstone steps with the grand colonnades of the neoclassical building behind them.

'You sleeping rough, or what?'

He nods. She's going to offer him something. He feels it. Adjusting his plan to accommodate her will not be a problem.

'I'm in a squat. Clifton Hill. All boarded up, with heaps of rooms.'

He's in a boat drifting toward paradise. No rapids in sight. What can he offer her?

'Where'd you score the gear?' he asks. 'It's good.'

'A friend. Sort of a friend, anyway.'

He knows exactly what she means. They have parallel lives. He opens his legs slightly, enough for their knees to touch. So nice.

'I've got cash.'

'From busking?'

'Yeah,' he says, meaning the future.

He feels her knee push against his and he leans back in the boat, drifting on with the hum of traffic, an occasional voice and the rattle of a passing tram.

'What've you got on you now?'

'Two fifty.'

She could ask him anything. She is an angel.

'You make that every day?'

'More,' he says with growing confidence.

She smiles, a long pensive smile that makes him wonder what she is thinking.

'Come on,' she says, standing. 'Let's walk and talk.'

They set off together along the path through the small, triangular-shaped Parliament Gardens, with its manicured lawns, palm trees and a fountain cascading water into a pool below its stainless-steel tubing. He waits for her to talk, but she says nothing and it makes him nervous. He needs to fill the silence.

'Where're we going?'

She glances at him but says nothing, and his anxiety jumps. His pace slows and she stops to hold her hand out to him. He accepts it readily. She is still his angel.

They walk out of the gardens, and there it is at the top of the rise: St Patrick's Cathedral, bathed in yellow light with its main spire reaching toward heaven. It is more elaborate and much bigger than St Peter and Paul's but still a Gothic bluestone reminder of Timmy in his coffin. Dead. They turn the corner away from the cathedral with

Aaron wondering what happened to his friend after he passed through the gates into the Underworld. Is he suffering in the afterlife? Or is his soul in a state of eternal happiness, like George the Greek predicted?

He feels Rebecca let go of his hand, and he quickly comes back to her and the multiple lanes of fast-moving headlights in front of them. She pushes the big silver button, and he watches her impatiently shifting her weight from one foot to the other. Why isn't she talking? Walk and talk she said. Or did he imagine that? She smiles her broken-tooth smile and then they are on the move again, down the main street into Fitzroy, once a working-class suburb surrounded by factories and industrial sites, now gentrified with renovated cottages, converted warehouses and heritage-listed Victorian terraces alongside Atherton Gardens, a high-rise public housing estate.

'We're going there first,' she says, indicating the top levels of the four estate tower blocks reaching into the night sky.

'That's where my friend is.'

'I guessed that,' Aaron says, looking up at the lights shining in the square windows of the concrete buildings, replicas of Park Towers. All so familiar. Just as in South Melbourne, these were built after the Housing Commission demolished the dilapidated and overcrowded houses the poor had been living in for decades.

'You good?' she asks him as they cross the street. There's a view down the gentle incline to the bustling nightlife of Fitzroy.

'I'm good,' he says. Why wouldn't he be? He's nicely stoned, has money in his pocket, a beautiful guitar in his hand and her by his side. Aaron and Rebecca. Rebecca and Aaron.

They navigate the next intersection and walk through an open gate onto the expansive grounds of the housing estate. A concrete path leads them between the lawns below the eucalypts and street lamps to where they sit down together on a bench seat. There's the hum of slow-moving traffic, a man shouting somewhere out of sight and a dozen mostly African teenagers playing a noisy game of basketball at the base of the nearest tower block. He feels the twinge of excitement that comes when he knows he is about to score. It's even stronger now he is with her.

'So, two fifty then,' she says, putting her hand on his knee.

Two fifty? No. Why two fifty? It's all he has except for the twenty dollars he got from busking. He feels her hand move up to his thigh.

'I get my money tomorrow, babe.'

Babe? What is that? A declaration of some sort? It must be. What else?

'Okay,' he says, standing, ready to go.

Her hand pulls him back down next to her.

'Just me, babe. That's the way he likes it. I'll be super quick and then we're off.'

Where to? The Promised Land? He is looking up at her now, wanting her to hold him.

'We'll be in Clifton Hill before you know it.'

That's right, Clifton Hill. The squat. She'll hold him then, when they're tucked up in bed together. He hands her two hundred and fifty dollars and she kisses him lightly on the top of his head just like his mother kissing him before rushing off to work.

His eyes focus on the door she disappeared through what feels like twenty minutes ago. There is still no sign of her, so he scans the lighted square windows on each of the thirty floors once again, having already calculated that if the dealer lived on the top floor it would take her ten minutes max to get to his door. Adding another ten minutes to do the deal and she should be walking back toward him very soon. He scratches at his forearm, doubt and anxiety arriving to annoy but not torment him – yet. She did say she'd be real quick, didn't she?

'Hey bro. Play us a song.'

Aaron turns to look at two Aboriginal men in their forties standing in front of him. One is carrying a cask of red wine and has a big smile under his cowboy hat. The other is wearing a West Coast Eagles football guernsey.

'Do you know any Jimmy Little?' asks the Cowboy.

'I'm waiting for someone,' Aaron says, turning his attention back to the tower block, wishing they'd leave him alone.

'Be his sweetheart, ya reckon?' the Cowboy asks the Eagle.

'Reckon, yeah.'

'Do ya reckon she'll show up, bro?'

The Eagle follows Aaron's gaze to the tower, and after summing it up with a knowing eye, he shakes his head gently and looks directly back at him.

'If ya wanna join us,' he says with a head flick to the right, 'we'll be over yonder, under that big old tree.'

'It ain't that old, bro,' the Cowboy says to the Eagle as they wander off down the path.

Aaron watches them go, momentarily missing the distraction of their little performance before he is drawn back hard to the pool of fluorescent light at the entrance to the tower block and his aching desire to see Rebecca walk toward him through the glass double doors, smiling. But there are only the basketball-playing teenagers wandering slowly back home with laughing faces and repeated high-fives.

The minutes grind slowly by. People come and go through the glass doors: a tall woman in a hijab with three small children clinging to her long, flowing dress; two spiky-haired young women in tartan skirts, sleeveless denim jackets and big boots; an old man in a heavy overcoat and bare feet; but no Rebecca with long brown hair, big eyes and two hundred and fifty dollars worth of heroin.

Doubt and anxiety rise closer to torment now, forcing him to stand and pace about in front of the bench seat in search of a logical explanation for her no-show. She's been robbed on her way back down in the lift. Or she's been given a taste on the house and has nodded off. Maybe her dealer's run out of stock and she's waiting for the promised, soon-to-be-delivered supply. All are possible, but none calm the dread. Fuck! He'll go in. No. What would be the point? He doesn't know what floor she'd be on let alone what flat. Fuck again! She's done the dirty on him, big time. Sucked him right in. How did he let it happen? Why was he so fucking stupid? His thoughts are firing in all directions. He needs to make a plan. That will help. It always does. But what? He'll wait until she comes out. She has to come out sooner or later.

He moves into a dark patch beside the thick hedge bordering the footpath where he has a clear view to the tower's entrance – better than before, a wider angle. Lying back on the soft grass, he props his head up on his backpack, pulls his guitar closer to him and locks his eyes on the glass doors. When she comes out, he'll sneak up on her. Give her no chance to run. He's pretty sure he won't get his money back, but he'll make sure he gets the heroin she has bought with it. He will shout at her, he knows that. He is so fucking angry with her, with himself and with the world.

A woman laughs on the footpath and car tyres squeal somewhere further down Brunswick Street. Aaron glances across at the Cowboy and the Eagle under the big old tree fifty metres from him, where they are now in a loose circle of eight, drinking and yarning to the strumming of a ukulele. He would love to join them but knows he can't. He has a plan and he has to stick to it. With only twenty dollars in his pocket and no heroin, there is no alternative, except ... he holds the guitar tighter in a gesture of reassurance. He would never hock it, ever. He loves it, and not only because it's a vital step in his grand plan, every one of which is getting harder. But the determination to keep going sits like a hard pebble in the pit of his stomach. He won't let her deception defeat him. And he will get a permit to busk, one way or another. A half-moon appears from behind a drifting cloud directly above the tower block. 'Everything's going to be okay,' he says in a whisper to his guitar. 'I promise.'

His hopeful thoughts and the heroin still in his system combine to sooth him a little, and his heavy eyelids begin to open and shut in a slow rhythm with the hum of traffic and the sweet, soft sound of the ukulele. He falls into a fitful sleep disturbed frequently by dark figures passing through the pool of fluorescent light outside the doors to the tower block like actors walking onto a stage. When will Rebecca make her big entrance? The question repeats itself over and over until he finally sees her, a silhouette walking toward him, holding up a small package in her right hand. She hasn't betrayed him and all is forgiven. He rises effortlessly to hold her tightly in his arms. Her hair and skin smell like fresh grass. He is in heaven. Then he feels her being pulled away from him and he clings on harder until something hard smashes into the side of his face, forcing him to release her.

His eyes snap open and he is looking up at a tall, thin man with a goatee beard and hollow cheeks, holding his precious guitar in its soft vinyl case. Instinctively, Aaron jumps to his feet ready to lunge at the thief and wrestle it back, but it is already flying through the air into the arms of his accomplice positioned five metres away, and all Aaron can do is watch his prized possession disappear through the gates onto Brunswick Street. The thief's triumphant smile exposes a row of decayed teeth, and Aaron feels a wave of uncontrollable anger surging through him. If he had a gun in his hand, he would kill him without hesitating.

22

He watches the sun come up over the grounds of the housing estate, considering staying where he is until he dies of hunger and withdrawal symptoms, but the urgent need to piss forces him to get up. As he relieves himself against the hedge, he knows that if he does want to kill himself one day, it will be by overdose. But he's not ready to join his friend in the Underworld just yet. That tiny pebble of determination is still sitting deep inside his badly cramping gut, helping him to put one foot in front of the other as he shoulders his backpack and walks away from the heartache of Atherton Gardens toward the main spire of St Patrick's Cathedral, dominating the top of the gentle incline like a beacon offering hope to lost souls.

He doesn't see or hear the packed tram rattling past him, or the cyclists with reflective pants straps and panniers, or the steady stream of slow-moving cars. His world is entirely inside his misery-filled head, where his desire for heroin is dialled up to the maximum. How can he score? Where can he score? He thinks about Dave and Samantha, but the thought of going back to South Melbourne right now fills him with dread. He is an eight-year-old boy again, with his grandfather's imposing frame beside him, taking his hand as they wave goodbye to his grandmother and then taking him down the long, dark hallway to his bedroom.

St Peter's Eastern Hill Anglican Church is on the opposite corner to St Patrick's Cathedral and, just like its Catholic neighbour, was built of bluestone in the mid-nineteenth century, though not in the same grandiose Gothic style. Without spires above its high-pitched slate roof, it's more like a village church. Immediately next to it is the more modern red-brick St Peter's Hall where they serve breakfast every morning to the homeless and the poor, half a dozen of whom are waiting in the morning sunlight falling across the footpath. Aaron crosses the road toward them thinking of the twenty dollars he has left in his pocket. It will get him a pill or two, an opiate of some description – anything to relieve the pain so he can think about how to readjust his grand plan.

'Got a smoke for me, mate?' asks a wrinkle-faced man wearing a bright-orange and black bomber jacket.

'Sorry, mate.'

The green metal gates are unlocked, and Aaron joins the quickly growing line filing into the outside space between the church and the hall, where three volunteers are at the barbecues, flipping piles of bacon and sausages and hamburgers and onions. Aaron recognises hunger pangs somewhere in amongst the nausea, so he grabs a plate and casts his eye over the gathering while the line inches forward. There are a lot of older men with grey beards and downcast eyes under baseball caps, and only two women he can see. One is Pacific Islander, with a mass of frizzy black hair and dark sunglasses; the other is a young woman about his own age with short-cropped blonde hair and a confident, don't-mess-with-me walk.

He carries his plate of food to the dining room where he needs to choose the right chair next to the right person. It's not an easy decision to make. He could guarantee that everyone in there will be on something mood-altering, legal or not. There is virtually no conversation or eye contact around the two long tables, except for the social worker and the Aboriginal man she is sitting next to. They are both smiling and chatting as if they are old friends. A man with big round eyes looks up at Aaron, who quickly decides to take the seat next to him, for no logical reason other than that he looks different from all the others, with his fisherman's beanie and his wispy hair in a ponytail. Thirty-something, Aaron thinks, with an interesting style – sort of city hippy. Aaron cuts into a sausage, wondering how to start the conversation.

'You come here much?'

'Every day except Wednesdays when I visit my mother,' the man answers with a slight stutter. 'She's in a nursing home. In Shepparton.'

Aaron chews on the sausage but it's slow work. His stomach is resisting it and his new friend sees him struggling.

'I came for the food first-up. Then I got introduced to medical access. Got my teeth done, then what else do we need? I'm blind as a bat, so glasses, and then that was like wow! 'Cause I'm a reader, you know. Bachelor of Arts in literature, and once my eyes went, it was, like, the worst.'

Aaron looks at the assortment of characters chewing in silence around the table. His new friend is his best bet.

'Got any pills?' he asks, leaning closer to him.

'Painkillers, I'm guessing,' he says without hesitating.

Aaron makes brief eye contact with the smiling social worker at the end of the table, then turns away anticipating that she'll be making her way toward him soon. He's wired and needs to get out of here.

'I've only got twenty bucks,' he says without attempting to conceal his desperation.

'Two tramadol?'

'Sweet.'

Aaron changes his mind about taking the second tramadol as he walks through the cast-iron bollards into Edinburgh Gardens, a block from St Peter's Church. A hundred milligrams is not enough to kill all the pain, but it will help ease the anxiety and give him a chance to think. He can take the second one when he's worked out his next move. He chooses one of the many paths crisscrossing the twenty-four-hectare park where the autumn sun shines through the bare branches of an avenue of mature elms. He continues on past a group of young Indian men throwing a frisbee, three mothers watching their toddlers playing and a busload of meandering Chinese tourists. Eventually he reaches a small patch of sunlit green grass and claims it as his own.

Laying his head down on his backpack, he very quickly concludes that one pill is not going to be enough to calm him. And he feels sick, like he's rotting inside. So he pops the second pill into his mouth, chews it into powder and swallows it before running his tongue around his teeth like a vacuum cleaner sucking up the residue. While he waits impatiently for the drug to kick in, his restless gaze falls on the light towers of the Melbourne Cricket Ground. The familiar white shapes are poking through the leaves of the tall eucalypts bordering the southern side of the park. He lowers his eyes to Wellington Parade, where his eight-year-old self is walking from Flinders Street Station to the game with his father and grandfather. He forces himself to turn away, but the anger stays with him. Since Atherton Gardens, it feels like it's trying to take up permanent residency. It's certainly harder to shift.

He closes his eyes and starts counting back slowly from twenty-eight to zero. It's a technique his mother suggested once when he woke her with his screaming after another night terror. She told him that if his thoughts interrupted the counting not to be cross with himself but to go calmly back to twenty-eight and start again. It rarely worked, and now on the first attempt he only gets to twenty-five, then to eighteen, then to fifteen before he starts to relax a little, helped by a softening at the edges of his brain. The tramadol is kicking in, and he welcomes it with a heavy sigh. It's time to readjust his not-so-grand plan.

The shoes are still on his feet and the cap still on his head, so it's not like he's going back to square one completely. He needs to buy another guitar. Ah, his beautiful guitar. Laughter nearby brings him back to a young man in a suit flirting with an older woman on a bench seat next to the path. Now he is angry. Angry with Rebecca, and angry for allowing her to do it to him. He needs to walk to stop his head exploding.

He reaches one of the many exits from the park but immediately turns back, telling himself he can't leave until he works out how to go back to that feeling he had playing in the underpass with money dropping into his cap. He walks on beneath the trees, his eyes fixed on the bitumen path, jumbled thoughts with snippets of possibilities filtering through. Of course he needs money, much more than stealing a handbag, or a bicycle, or a watch will bring him. A break-and-enter might be enough, but it depends on what he finds. Televisions, computers and cameras won't do it. Jewellery would, but more than likely it would be locked up in a safe. Five thousand tucked under someone's mattress would be perfect, but that's a dream.

Another possible exit appears in front of him and he stops. He could re-engage with the Man – the tramadol is helping. Four or five overnighters would do it. Four or five nights of pain. But. The exit beckons him. He'll make it work this time. No fuck-ups. He'll up his price and stop as soon as he has the money he needs. A magpie lands on the branch of a tree above him, cocking its head inquisitively at him, as if asking the same question Aaron is asking of himself. How can he entice the Man to take him back after what he did to him? The magpie continues to interrogate him with its gold-brown eyes. *Well, come on, what can you possibly say to him?* Aaron reaches for some woodchip mulch at the edge of the grass and hurls it at the bird. It flies up to the nearest branch with its eyes still fixed on him.

'It's me and I'm sorry for taking those phone numbers.'

The Man says nothing, but he doesn't hang up. Encouraging enough for Aaron to go on.

'It was stupid and I'll never do anything like it ever again. I promise.'

Still, the Man says nothing. Aaron can feel him exerting his power in the silence.

'I'll do everything you want. I'll be your best little boy.'

23

Aaron looks up at the clock inside the entrance to Southern Cross Station. It is 6.15pm. He walks back out onto the crowded footpath cursing the Man for being fifteen minutes late. The effects of the tramadol have long since worn off and it's been twenty-four hours since his last hit of heroin, in the laneway with Rebecca. Then it was beautiful. Now it's torture. A set of headlights swings in beside him and he gets into the aftershave-filled space next to the Man.

'I need to score first,' he says with his hands tapping rapidly on his thighs.

The Man pulls a U-turn at the lights, and Aaron hears the click of the doors locking.

'Not this time. You've been a naughty boy and you need to be punished.'

Panic attacks Aaron with such force he struggles to breathe. He unclips his seatbelt and stabs at the locked window button, but there is no escape. At the intersection with Flinders Street, he looks back toward the train station: at the lights and the people and the loss of what he desperately needs to soothe and protect him. Instead they are heading west past Wurundjeri Way and a statue of Bunjil, a wedge-tailed eagle and spirit creator of the Kulin Nation. The twenty-five-metre-high statue makes Aaron think about the dream he had of Timmy trying to fly from the top of the You Yangs with the eagle. Right now, trapped in the Man's car with hot flushes, scattered thoughts, trembling hands and legs, and a crushing sense of foreboding, that's exactly what he would like to do too.

They merge with a continual stream of trucks and cars on the West Gate Bridge with a solo violin playing rapid arpeggios on the radio and colliding head-on with Aaron's anxiety. They follow the unbroken line of tail-lights off the bridge as the orchestra's brass section comes in with dramatic broken chords before the piece plunges into an intense question-and-answer pattern. Aaron is about to explode and his hand reaches out for the buttons on the radio, but the Man slaps it away.

'Do you want to change the music?'

'Yes.'

'Then you ask me first.'

Aaron recognises this game and does what he's told.

'Can I change the music?'

The Man curses the refrigerated truck braking in front of them but as he attempts to overtake it, a car horn blows hard in the passing lane, forcing him to retreat quickly back behind the truck. With the violin concerto playing on relentlessly, the Man tries again. Successfully this time.

'The music?' Aaron asks, submissively. 'Can I change it, please?'

The Man glances across with a face of authority matching his black suit and his cufflinks.

'You may.'

Aaron quickly finds 102.7FM on the dial, where he hears the driving drum and bass beat of Dick Diver's 'Head Back'. It's a song about taking a break from a chaotic existence, and he lip-syncs the first chorus as they flash past the concrete bollards and hoardings lining both sides of the night-lit freeway,

You take a week
From doing all the things you usually do
You start doing
All the things you want to.

He tries to imagine himself on stage with the band playing a red guitar, the sparse melody lines, the playful solos, but the thought of what lies ahead in the Man's house at the end of the dark road refuses to budge. Listen to the music, Aaron. It's only four nights, maybe only three, and you can start doing all the things you want to.

'What's wrong with you?' the Man asks.

As if he doesn't know what's wrong. It's his grandfather again, pleasure without remorse.

'Nothing,' he says habitually.

'Open the glove box,' the Man says as they pass another exit sign to another new suburb sprawling across the flat land.

Aaron opens the glove box instinctively; it's a distraction from the conflict in his head. He is looking at a tarnished pewter hipflask.

'Whisky. Single malt.'

Aaron takes the flask out and unscrews the top, feeling like he is being cajoled with an ice cream or a hot chocolate. *It's all going to be very pleasant, Aaron, so you just need to calm down. It will be better that way.*

Scattered house lights fade to rows of eucalypts and post-and-wire fences in the car headlights. The music shifts to a band Aaron recognises as LCD Soundsystem, but he doesn't know this track: 'I Can Change'. He swigs again from the flask of whisky, which helps him to stay with the electronic rock beat. The singer says he can change, over and over and over.

Aaron thinks about his mother and the words she stopped listening to a long time ago. A blanket of melancholia descends on him and he yearns to be with her at home, to touch her, to smell her, to hear her laugh.

The *tick, tick, tick* of the car indicator brings him back hard to the Man taking the exit to Little River. They swing back over the freeway and onto the narrow country road with the Triple R announcer chatting enthusiastically about the bracket she has just played. The Man reaches across and kills the radio.

'That's enough of that.'

Aaron doesn't object; his eyes are fixed on the familiar shape of the You Yangs lying dark and alluring across the distant horizon. Through the hum of the tyres on the bitumen he thinks he hears a voice – faintly at first, then, as they continue down the narrow road, the words become clearer. *Timmy is here waiting for you, Aaron. He has an answer to all your pain.* Is it real or is it the whisky? He doesn't care; just the thought of Timmy being with him comforts him, and he holds on to it tightly. The road changes direction a kilometre further on, and the granite peaks disappear completely behind a thick stand of trees. Anxiety bites at him until they come out of the sweeping bend and he can feel his dead friend's presence again in the ancient ridge dominating the night skyline.

He swigs from the flask wanting more of the calmness the whisky induces in him. As more alcohol is absorbed into his bloodstream, he does feel braver and ready to face whatever is in front of him. 'Dutch courage' springs to mind, a term that his father often used, and he allows himself to wonder where it comes from. Are the Dutch famous for their courage? A wombat appears suddenly in the headlights with its stocky body on short legs moving slowly into the path of the car. The Man makes no effort to avoid it, and Aaron feels it thump against the floor under his feet. He looks across at the Man, who glances briefly in the rear-view mirror before driving on as if nothing happened.

~

The car vibrates over the cattle grid, and Aaron can see the house softly lit at the end of the tree-lined gravel driveway. He swallows the last of the whisky as they enter the stately courtyard and drive around the fountain at its centre. The Man parks the car in front of the house and turns off the motor and the headlights. He doesn't move, and Aaron can hear him breathing, slowly and deliberately. He glances across to see that the Man's eyes are closed. Fuck, what's he doing? Then he hears him.

'You've had a long day at school, my boy. All those sports you play. You must be very sweaty.'

'Can we go in?' Aaron asks softly with his hand poised to open the door.

'Of course. You have a nice warm shower to freshen up while I heat up our dinner. Sausages and chips. How does that sound?'

Play the game, Aaron. Just play the game and get it over with.

'Sounds good.'

He hears the click of the central door lock and then he is standing on the gravel with the smell of blood and bone rising from the flowerbed under the bay window.

24

The shower is soft and warm on his skin, but inside his head the battle rages on. The coach's pep talk. You can do this, you can! Be strong, Aaron. He turns off the water and steps out onto the shaggy lime-green mat. The house is quiet except for the random cracks of dry wood burning in the living-room fireplace. He pulls a towel from the rack and starts to dry himself. He's in no hurry. His clothes are in a crumpled heap on the floor next to his backpack, his flat cap and his dust-covered patent-leather shoes. He conjures an image of himself coming off the escalator onto the menswear floor at Myer and wandering from one brand name to another with a pocket full of money, choosing exactly what he wants. The bathroom door opens and the Man steps in wearing a satin dressing gown, burgundy with silver edging, his hairless chest and long, thin legs exposed.

'Here, let me do that.'

The Man takes the towel, and Aaron closes his eyes. The Myer image has vanished, so he tries hard to find something else to focus on, anything to distract him from the Man rubbing the towel over his body. There is only the dark and the overlapping sounds of the cricket on the television, heavy footsteps on floorboards, and a creaking door. The towel drops to the floor, and Aaron feels two hands turning him to face the vanity basin. He opens his eyes to the reflection of the Man in the mirror pressing against him, his smile thin and his eyes eager. Aaron watches him spit into his right hand and then reach around for Aaron's cock. He braces himself against the white ceramic basin and lowers his gaze to the gold-plated plug lying at its base. He searches for Timmy and finds him walking through the field of yellow-flowered canola toward the You Yangs. Aaron attempts to catch up with him but is held back by the arms wrapped around him. The more he tries to escape, the tighter the grip becomes. The breath on his neck is hot, the pain deep and unrelenting. Timmy stops in his tracks and looks back at Aaron. His lips move but he is too far away to be heard. Timmy summons the eagle and it flies across the yellow carpet to deliver two words: *Kill him.*

Aaron looks up into the mirror and the Man cupping his hand to his mouth and swallowing his semen. He wipes his lips and smiles.

'You won't need any clothes. I've got the fire going and it's lovely and warm in there.'

A gentle classical piano piece is playing, and Aaron is sitting naked at the table across from the Man. He can see through the sliding glass doors behind the Man to a dim outside light falling across the banana lounge, the woodpile and the axe in the chopping block. Beyond the backyard, he feels Timmy's presence in the dark and he hears again the two words the eagle delivered to him. He lathers more sauce on to his crinkle-cut chips while trying hard to block them. They scare him to his core.

'Do you like the sausages? I get them from the local butcher. Italian. Nice fellow, he is.'

Aaron chews on a mouthful and nods without looking up. He manages to swallow the food despite the nerves and the nausea and the relentless craving for heroin.

'Now, my boy, tell me what you did in school today. I want to hear everything.'

The vice tightens on Aaron's sweating body and his stomach lurches violently. He forces himself to lift his eyes from his plate to the Man, Timmy's two words reverberating in his head. He starts talking as a way of stopping them.

'We kicked a football on the oval, end to end ...'

'How old are you?'

'Eighteen,' he says automatically.

'No. You're eleven and so are the other boys. Yes?'

'Yes.'

'Go on then.'

'I took a mark,' he says, picturing it exactly how it happened as if through a window in a dark room. 'It was a pack mark, and I kneed another kid in the head. Then he wanted to fight me.'

'Did you?'

'Yes.'

'Good boy. Now stand up and let me look at you while you're talking.'

Aaron stands with his eyes sliding outside to the axe, spotlighted with its red-taped handle and its head buried in the chopping block. A wave of panic propels him back to his story and the piano solo playing on, broken left-hand chords against a haunting high-note melody.

'He threw a punch at me and then I got him in a headlock on the ground.'

'You wrestled him?'

He nods, describing a teacher breaking up the fight and the other kid and all his mates blaming him for starting it. He got suspended from school and his mother went straight to the principal to argue his case, but it fell on deaf ears.

'Poor boy,' the Man says softly.

Aaron looks at him sitting opposite, an omnipotent king on his throne. Dyed black hair as a crown and a burgundy silk dressing gown as his robe. *Kill him.* No, Timmy. Aaron can't do that; he has a plan, a grand plan! Three nights, that's all it will take. Then he'll buy another guitar, get a busking permit and have money in his flat cap when he returns to knock on his mother's front door. She'll answer it and he will say, 'I've come back home, Mum, you don't have to worry about me anymore.'

'Come. Let me comfort you.'

Aaron does as he is told, walking around the table to the Man as the music shifts gear from the gentle solo piano to the opening movement of an orchestral symphony. The string section announces a distinct sense of foreboding. Brass and timpani respond, punctuating the movement as if leading Aaron into battle. He is a little boy again, running onto the oval to play against boys twice his size, determined to see the night through no matter the pain.

The Man stands and undoes the tie on his dressing gown, exposing his loose-skinned paunch above his flaccid penis. Aaron shuts his eyes tightly as the Man's hands pull him into an embrace. He feels his warm, slightly clammy skin and smells his fading aftershave.

'You're my little boy now. And I'm going to take very good care of you.'

The Man's lips descend from the top of Aaron's head to his neck with the orchestra now playing the slower more lyrical second movement of the symphony. The music draws Aaron back into the dark room where he is looking out through the window at a swimming pool on a hot summer day. He is in the shallow end, with his grandfather groping him under the water before tossing him into the air, over and over. He is crying, but nobody sees the tears washing away in the chlorinated water. The door of the shower cubicle is locked. His grandfather has an erection.

Aaron's eyes snap open to the Man kneeling in front of him, reaching out to run his long fingers down over his hips and thighs. A tidal wave of anger hits and he shoves the Man away. Gasping for air, he stares out through the glass doors at the light on the woodshed shining down on the axe. He feels the Man grabbing a fistful of his hair before he is dragged to the couch and slammed down onto his stomach, his neck gripped by long fingers, his legs spread wide by a bony knee, his bare skin draped in the smooth silk of the Man's dressing gown. Through the terror and the struggle to breathe, he hears his words.

'You're my little boy, Timmy. You know that, don't you?'

Aaron grunts under the force of the fingers pushing him down into the fabric of the couch.

'Sorry, I can't hear you.'

'Yes,' Aaron says, knowing that he can no longer allow it to be true.

'And that means if I want to suck your cock or stick my finger up your arse, I will.'

No, you won't. Not anymore.

The Man releases his grip and the silk dressing gown slides away.

Aaron turns over as he is tying it back up. *Kill him.* Yes, Timmy. The axe is in the chopping block.

He is thinking like a hunter again.

'I'll chop some more wood for the fire, will I?'

'Yes, you will. That's a good boy,' he says. 'You'll find some already done. Grab an armful and I'll wait for you on the couch.'

The couch. His grandfather. The cricket on the television. An unzipped fly. Aaron walks to the sliding glass doors, a dam wall straining against a raging torrent. He steps into the stage-lit backyard and peers out into the darkness beyond, wanting to hear Timmy's voice. There is nothing but a silent black wall. He's on his own now. He's been shown the path forward. Now do it. He picks up an armful of firewood, prises the axe from the chopping block with the other hand and walks back to his naked image reflected in the glass doors. A monster? No. The monster is inside, sitting on the couch in front of the blank television screen.

Aaron slides the door open. The symphony is still playing, with the horns and trumpets building to a climax against the sharp chords of the strings. He places the axe softly down against the side of the fireplace and lays the firewood piece by piece onto the fire. It crackles to life.

'Waiting,' the Man says impatiently. 'Hungry for your cute little arse.'

The axe is in both hands. The Man is still talking but the words are not heard. Aaron walks up behind him seeing only his grandfather's silver hair, set like waves rolling onto a beach. The first blow with the blunt side of the axe glances off the top of his head and he tries to push back up. Aaron brings the axe down again, then again and again, every blow in harmony with the single notes of the French horns triumphantly ending the symphony. A moment of absolute silence and stillness descends on him. He is cradling his eight-year-old self, telling him everything is going to be alright now and how sorry he is that it has taken so long. The blood-covered axe slips from his fingers and crashes to the floor. He feels the warm blood dripping from his face onto his naked chest. He sees the Man's head, smashed in a pool of blood on the couch. He hears the smooth voice of the radio announcer floating across the room:

You've been listening to Symphony Number Nine in E Minor, popularly known as the 'New World Symphony', by the Czech composer Antonín Dvořák. It premiered in New York City in 1893 and has been described as one of the most popular of all symphonies. So popular, in fact, that Neil Armstrong took a tape recording of it to the first moon landing.

Aaron switches the radio off with a blood-smattered finger and turns slowly back to the scene of his crime. A dead body, a half-eaten sausage and sauce-covered chips on the table, the sound of a tree branch scratching against a window in the wind. So, what about your grand plan now, Aaron? The anger has drained from him. He needs to go to sleep.

He walks into the Man's bedroom, gagging at his lingering smell. The clock radio on the chest of drawers beside his bed clicks over to ten-thirty. He doesn't open the top drawer, knowing it contains only bottles of lubricant and porn magazines. He slides open the drawer under it to find the Man's medications. He rifles through them, tossing packets onto the floor, all names he doesn't recognise until the Endone and then the temazepam. He chews four of each on his way to the bathroom, where he swallows them with a mouthful of water from the basin tap. A quick glance at his blood-spattered body in the mirror and he steps under the shower to watch the water swirling around his feet change colour from red to pink to soap-streaked clear.

He shuts his eyes under the hot, fast-flowing water, willing the pills to do their job. He needs to block out what he has just done and make a new plan. But does he? Nothing really has to change, does it? He'll find the Man's wallet and credit card in there somewhere. *What about the Man dead on the couch, Aaron? His head is caved in with an axe.* No one knows he has been in the house. *What about the exchange in the driveway with Geoff the builder?* What about it? No names were mentioned. Only some story about helping the wayward son of a former colleague to get back on his feet.

The sudden loss of heat in the shower water brings him back to the now. He turns off the taps and steps out onto the cold tiles to dry himself before the fogged-up mirror. Instinctively, he reaches out to wipe it clear with the towel. Under his wet hair, he sees a face that is challenging him. *Do you really think you can hide from what you've just done, Aaron? Do you?* He turns away from it, pulls his oversized purple hoodie over his head, his dirty jeans up over his skinny legs and walks down the hallway to a single bed in an otherwise furniture-free room. He climbs under the musty-smelling pink chenille bedspread, lies down on the bare mattress and drifts off to sleep with the help of the pills and an image of himself looking good in his flat cap behind the wheel of the Man's black Lexus.

25

He wakes in the dark with a leaden head, nausea and a sweating body under the thin bedspread. His first thought is of the Man lying dead in the living room. Heroin, please. If he had some he would use it. Just once more, that's all. He slides his feet out onto the flower-patterned carpet and walks across the hallway into the Man's bedroom. The temazepam goes into his back pocket and he swallows one hundred milligrams of Endone on his way to the bathroom. He sits down on the plastic stool to put on his patent-leather shoes, thinking only about the Man's wallet and car keys and the road ahead of him. The flat cap goes on his head, the backpack over his shoulders and he turns to the mirror where he finds the same questioning reflection. *Who are you, Aaron? You know the answer to that. You're an addict.* Yes, but that's no big secret. *A thief too.* Yes, but only when it's necessary. *And now a murderer.* Piss off.

He turns the light on in the living room. The clock on the wall tells him it is 6.45. The bloodied axe lies on the floor where he dropped it behind the couch. The Man's body is hidden from view. He finds the car keys in a small metal bowl on the Man's desk. He'll practise changing gears around the courtyard before he hits the road. It won't be too hard. He practised enough in his father's showroom cars. The wallet? It's in the pocket of the Man's jacket hanging on the hallstand near the front door. Three hundred dollars in cash and two different credit cards. He'll buy the Maton first, then the clothes, then the permit. And heroin? Though his body is craving it intensely, he can feel a determination to resist it. But it's fragile. His head turns enough to glimpse the Man's body. He carries the suit jacket to him and places it over his head. *Still pretending, Aaron?* He looks up at the eye at the centre of a Freemason's apron, gazing down on him from the wall of the Man's photographs. What did he call it? The Eye of Providence watching over everything we do? He needs to escape, so he does, out through the sliding glass doors, into the backyard and the biting dawn air.

He sits down on the chopping block to watch the first rays of the sun touching the You Yangs like an artist's brush painting them into existence. Below the blue dawn sky, the black granite ridges take on a familiar outline before the steep slopes appear flashed with grey. A wedged-tailed eagle circles high above the field of gold-tipped canola, flight feathers stretched like fingers, its head cocked to the ground, hunting. It dives like an arrow into the canola and then out again, soaring into the sky with a rabbit hanging from its talons. Aaron follows its journey toward the You Yangs, imagining it to be returning to its nest high in a rocky crevice, a mother with food for its chicks. It makes him think about his own mother, and he is hit with an urge to return home to her too, now, today. No. Not until he can show her he's changed. *But you've just murdered someone. You can't change that, can you, Aaron?*

The Endone is helping to calm him slightly, but it does nothing to loosen the grip of the persuasive voice in his head. He stands and walks to the cyclone wire fence dividing the Man's backyard from the field of canola. What's happening to me, Timmy? Nothing comes back, only the sound of a truck changing gears on the main road behind him. He turns back to face the house. He can't deny it. The evidence is there on the couch. He feels a twinge of excitement at the thought of going home to his mother and owning up to what he has done. *You'll go to gaol, Aaron.* Yes, but the courts will understand and they'll be lenient. Maybe even a suspended sentence. *You're being very optimistic.* He doesn't care. It all seems so clear now. It's the price he has to pay to be free.

The thought of his mother's embrace carries him back into the house. The Man is still dead on the couch and the bloodied axe is still on the polished floorboards. He allows himself to wonder what his father will think about having a murderer for a son. What will he say

289

to his friends? What will he say to himself knowing in his heart how it has come to this? Fuck you, Dad.

He puts the car keys back in the metal bowl and holds the wallet in his hand. *Take the cash, Aaron, buy that guitar on your way home.* He resists. Everything has changed. It's all very clear now. He puts the wallet down on the desk, picks up his backpack and goes out through the front door to the gravelled courtyard with the tiered water fountain at its centre and the perfectly pruned rose bushes circling it. He glances at the Man's black Lexus then continues on up the narrow driveway between the rows of dark pine trees.

The gravel crunches under the soles of his patent-leather shoes as he strides toward the main road, a black strip on a wide plain. He readjusts his flat cap and imagines he is walking up Layfield Street, past the rooming house. Dave and Samantha are in his thoughts. He hopes they are happy but he doesn't want to see them. He'll give methadone a go and see what happens. Did you hear that, Timmy? He'll give methadone a go. Coffee drinkers file out of Café Zappa deep in conversation. He glances up at the clock in the tower above the Town Hall. It's nearly eight o'clock. His mother will be getting ready for work. He crosses the road past the police station on the corner. That's to come of course. Later. Well, soon. He reaches his mother's house and pushes open the squeaky front gate, walks down the cracked concrete path and knocks on the front door. When she opens it, he will give her back the boy she lost, that they both lost.

ACKNOWLEDGEMENTS

This book began more than ten years ago as an outline for a feature film. Despite failing to attract any solid interest in the project, the story idea refused to leave me. COVID-19 arrived, and my partner, Shayne Barns suggested I write it as a novel. I am indebted to her for this and for her support and encouragement of my writing over many years.

A big thank you to my son, Sam Cummins, for his help in selecting the most appropriate songs for the various stages of the narrative and for his valuable feedback on the first draft. Thanks also to the other early readers for their equally valuable thoughts and encouragement: Chris Gallagher, Eric Howard, Kerri Barns, Amanda Cummins, Amy Cummins, Liz Cummins, Susan Hoult,

Danny Glasby, Sue Hearn, Peter Worland and Hugh Morris-Dalton.

A special thank you to my good friend Peter McDonald for our long conversations during the writing process. Diagnosed with a terminal illness, Peter asked me to send him what I'd written because he thought he might not be around when I finished it. His positive response gave me a huge boost at a point when I needed it the most. He did get to read the completed manuscript before passing away with great dignity a few months later.

Thank you, Francesca Tarquinio for your insightful comments on the first draft and particularly for urging me to enter the Victorian Premier's Literary Award for an Unpublished Manuscript. (I wouldn't have done it had I not received your email a day before the closing date.) I did win the award administered by the fabulous staff at the Wheeler Centre, so a huge thanks to everyone involved there: it opened doors to the publishing world that may not have otherwise opened.

Thank you to my agent, Jane Novak, for shepherding me through the early stages of the publisher negotiations, and to Gary McCaffrey for putting me in touch with Martin Hughes at Affirm Press. Martin's belief in the book has been unwavering from the start. His contribution to the final product – with his fellow editors Laura Franks and Ruby Ashby-Orr – has been significant. To Laura McNicol Smith, Alistair Trapnell, Keiran Rogers and everyone else at Affirm Press, thank you.

Finally, thank you to the State Government of Victoria for their continuing support of the Premier's Literary Awards and to the Culture team at RMIT for making my two-week residency at McCraith House such a fruitful and enjoyable experience.